Apple of My Eye

Claire Kershaw is the author of *Head First*, a Great Barrier Reef-inspired romance. *Apple of My Eye* is her second novel. Since graduating from Emory University with a degree in English Literature, Claire has moved to the Pacific Northwest, where you can find her hiking, tending to her many houseplants, cooking her sister's (@bunsinthekitchen) recipes, scribbling half-baked plot ideas on scraps of paper, or attempting to influence strangers into buying her books (@clairekershawauthor).

Apple of My Eye

CLAIRE KERSHAW

ZAFFRE

First published in the UK in 2025 by
ZAFFRE
An imprint of Bonnier Books UK
5th Floor, HYLO, 105 Bunhill Row,
London, EC1Y 8LZ

Copyright © Claire Fuscoe, 2025

All rights reserved.
No part of this publication may be reproduced,
stored or transmitted in any form by any means, electronic,
mechanical, photocopying or otherwise, without the
prior written permission of the publisher.

The right of Claire Fuscoe to be identified as Author of this
work has been asserted by her in accordance with the
Copyright, Designs and Patents Act, 1988.

This is a work of fiction. References to real people, events,
establishments, organizations, or locales are intended only to
provide a sense of authenticity and are used fictitiously. All other
characters, and all incidents and dialogue, are drawn from the
author's imagination and are not to be construed as real.

A CIP catalogue record for this book is
available from the British Library.

ISBN: 9-781-78512-822-6

Also available as an ebook and an audiobook

1 3 5 7 9 10 8 6 4 2

Typeset by IDSUK (Data Connection) Ltd
Printed and bound in Great Britain by Clays Ltd, Elcograf S.p.A.

MIX
Paper | Supporting
responsible forestry
FSC
www.fsc.org   FSC® C018072

The authorised representative in the EEA is Bonnier Books
UK (Ireland) Limited.
Registered office address: Floor 3, Block 3, Miesian Plaza,
Dublin 2, D02 Y754, Ireland
compliance@bonnierbooks.ie
www.bonnierbooks.co.uk

To the Pacific Northwest, to my grandparents, to the people and the places that shaped me with gentle persistence.

Chapter One

Eloise

The Best Things About Coming Home

- Iced tea (preferably brewed in the sun by Mom)
- Listening to thunder from the front porch
- Sleeping underneath a quilt
- Fresh air (this is totally underrated)
- Walking down the hill to get the newspaper
- Nightly games of gin rummy with Dad
- Getting woken up by the rooster (I've never understood why people hate this)
- Watching the bees
- JJ, obviously

The country unfurls like a flower as I wind my way towards home. It's the end of July, the last crest of summer before we turn the corner into fall. Boxes are piled high in the back seat. There's an almost-full bag of bagels next to me, the one thing Dad requests from the city. Carnation is small enough that we don't have a good bagel place nearby, and I'd bet my life savings he'll pretend to be shocked there's only ten instead of the twelve that he ordered.

I'm whizzing by rolling hills of fertile green farmland, putting the city in my rear-view mirror so fast that I'm unprepared when I cruise right past the WELCOME TO CARNATION sign, a gust of fresh air carrying the smell of apple blossoms and hay into my car. I take a breath so deep I press on the brakes out of reflex.

The WELCOME TO CARNATION sign is the highest point in the hills that circle around the town's borders, and you can see all the way into the slight dip of land that makes something akin to a valley, where the rolling farmland evens out in a low spot, right where Main Street sits. Houses are sprinkled in the surrounding area, mine included, and I roll down the windows all the way, letting the farm breeze settle over me, calming my nerves.

I haven't been home since Christmas, haven't seen my parents since they were in Seattle briefly for my graduation a couple months ago. I spent the summer with my two best friends, Evan and Shari, working in an agriculture lab and volunteering at a kids' summer camp, where we spent our days washing sticky hands and mulching baby pine trees under the tagline of 'teaching the next generation how to farm'. Usually, I'm practically salivating at the promise of a freshly baked blackberry cobbler when I return home, but this time I feel a pit of dread in my stomach instead of the familiar sense of comfort. But then again, I've never lied to my parents like this before.

I turn onto our gravel drive and pass through a break in the wooden fence that surrounds our property, rolling underneath the ANDERSON FAMILY APPLE FARM archway. I come to a stop at the top of the driveway, right in front of the garage. As I get out, my gaze falls on the hill that looms behind our 1900s farmhouse, the hill that marks the start of the Parker's property. I've known our next-door neighbors, the Parkers, since I was little. Their daughters, both older than me, have moved away, leaving their parents to run the apple farm on their own. After a bad harvest last year, they are one season away from going bankrupt, the whole town knows it.

I've spent all year trying to figure out how to save my family's farm from the same fate and buying out the Parkers might just be the solution. We could use the extra land to switch to regenerative agriculture, which is better for the planet and our wallets. It's a feasible plan, but it requires a little sacrifice. I had to turn down a job offer for an up-and-coming agricultural research lab and spend my summer working on the loan application to buy the Parkers out—the last thing I have left to do is tell my parents.

As if on cue, Mom steps out onto the front porch, waving frantically. 'I thought I heard the car.' She beams. Our front door swings closed behind her, the lion door knocker that's older than the house itself clanging. She hurries down the front porch steps towards me, her arms outstretched for a hug. I do my best to ignore the guilt tugging at my conscience from keeping something so big from her. But I can't tell her about the plan until the Parkers declare bankruptcy. Mom and Dad live by small-town ethics and going behind your neighbor's back to buy their land before they're trying to sell is definitely *not* in the code of conduct.

I take in a deep breath, smelling grassy meadows with just a hint of sweetness from Mom's signature honeysuckle perfume. 'I missed you, Mom,' I murmur into her shoulder.

'I missed you too, sweetie,' she replies.

A swallow swoops overhead, the perfect accent to the dusky evening sky as I lug my first round of stuff out of the car. In sync, like usual, Mom and I unload, falling back into an easy rhythm. For a moment I feel how I always feel when I get back to Carnation—like I've stepped back in time.

In my room, everything is exactly as I left it. Evening light spills through the tulip motif on the stained-glass window, dancing across the old wood floor. Dust motes puff up into the air, shifting in the rays, as I plunk my box of books onto the floor. The first thing I unpack is a picture of Evan, Shari and me on our last day of class. Evan had just gotten frosted tips, reminiscent of '90s boy bands, and they're sticking out from beneath his graduation cap. Shari is laughing, her arms spread wide around the two of us. I miss them already. I put the picture next to the one I have of JJ, mid-stride, prancing across our back pasture.

I hear heavy footsteps on the stairs and smile. Dad's home. He bursts into my room smelling like hay and dust, and he wraps me into a gruff hug. I squeeze a little tighter than usual. He isn't a big talker, Mom tends to communicate for the both of them, but he communicates his love in other ways—taking care of JJ when I'm not home, never letting me win when we play gin rummy, and the *best* hugs.

He beelines to the bag of bagels sitting on the floor, rummaging through them with gusto before picking up the bag and inspecting the bottom. 'Hmm,' he muses, 'the bottom is intact but . . . there seems to be some bagels missing.'

I roll my eyes, but I can't hide my smile. It's good to be home.

'I'll get the rest of your boxes,' he tells me. 'You go say hi to JJ. I swear he has a second sense for when you're coming home—he was agitated all day.'

Happily, I accept his offer and run down the stairs, taking them two at a time, bursting through the back door as Dad's voice grunts behind me, 'What on earth have you got in these boxes? Gold bars?!'

JJ nickers as soon as I let myself into the northernmost barn. I tap the worn wooden plank that hangs low over the door—'North Barn', it reads. All the barns on our property are named like that—Central, East and West. East is the smallest, and used to be my favorite, home to an infamous rope swing that broke my childhood best friend Lily's nose in the fifth grade, and also to my favorite reading nook, an elevated loft of hay bales, with old, cracked windows, that are perfect for filtering out the harshest of the sun. Central and West are our working barns, where we park our machinery in the off season and store supplies. North Barn was built when I was ten, when I got the thing I dreamed of most in the world—a chestnut-colored standardbred horse, and in my throes of ten-year-old boy-band excitement, I named him JJ after Joe Jonas, something Lily has never let me live down.

'Hi, buddy.' I hand him an unripe apple I pulled from a tree on my way inside. He lets out a soft whinny of happiness and nudges his muzzle against my cheek in thanks and greeting. As he chomps away, I use my free hand to pet his downy neck, leaning in to press my cheek against his coat. 'I sure am glad I don't have to lie to you,' I whisper, looking into his big brown eyes. But he has no time for my existential crisis—as soon as he's done with his snack, he paws at the door.

'And to think, besides my parents you're the only reason I really wanted to come home,' I scold him, clipping him into a lead and letting him out of his stall. I walk him outside to the pen behind the barn, monitoring his steps as we go. 'You look good,' I encourage him, feeling overwhelming gratitude for Dad, who's been tending to JJ ever since he injured his hoof two years ago while he was riding with one of the kids in town. He was lonely while I was in college so when I left for graduate school, I arranged for some neighborhood kids to ride him while I was away. It was great for everybody—I didn't have to let JJ go and he was able to get some exercise. That is, until he got injured.

'Now we just gotta get someone riding you again,' I say aloud, 'someone a little smaller than me.'

JJ neighs, like he can understand me, and he also agrees he is only big enough to be ridden by an adolescent and begins to prance around the paddock. His chestnut mane catches the last dregs of sunlight. I snap a picture of him and send it to Lily.

Views are better in the city I'm sure 😞 I text, referencing our constant sarcasm, thinly veiled attempts to get the other one to move. There is a zero percent chance views in New York City rival a sunset in the farmlands of Washington. The last text she sent me was a picture of pizza, a giant New York slice, grease pooling in the little pepperonis:

UGH I miss Carnation pizza, this is nothing compared to the local Domino's :/

Catch up soon? I tack onto my message.

Being home usually makes me miss Lily, but I feel her absence even more acutely today. Last time she was home we did exactly what I'm doing now, watched JJ stretch his legs as we drank a beer and the sun sank behind the hills, gossiping about people we went to high school with, dreaming about our futures, Lily getting promoted at the fashion magazine she works for in New York and me as a farmer in Carnation, something Lily claimed she didn't understand. 'It's just so *early*,' she told me. 'Don't you want to do a little more exploring before you tie yourself down?'

I didn't know if this was just another attempt to get me to move or if she was tapping into something I had been worried about—was I ready to settle into such a small town, such a demanding job, *forever*?

'I did the lists,' I confessed.

Lily levelled me with a serious gaze. 'And your pro/con list told you to move home?'

I shrugged. Technically it wasn't a pro/con list, but I didn't need to bore her with semantics. I make lists for everything, so making a 'What Do I Do After College' list was par for the course. There is nothing better than pulling thoughts from my head and rearranging them into order. Once I see them on a page, I can stop holding onto them. I can *feel* the space it leaves behind in my brain for other things. I have lists on my phone for everything under the sun. Reasons I hate biking, recipes I want to learn from my mom, gas stations between the farm and school that don't stock expired potato chips.

'But how will you meet a man?' Lily whined. 'The only ones left in Carnation are like . . . Josh and Burt. Ew, what if you end up with Burt.'

I laughed out loud. 'Lily, I am not going to end up with Burt. Also, you're one to talk—you haven't met a man and you live in the busiest city in the world. I am not wasting my time on that right now. I'm in save-my-family-farm mode, remember?'

Lily rolled her eyes, grumbling that I was being a hermit, and changed tack. 'But there's so much out in the world you haven't done.'

'You're acting like I don't live within driving distance of an airport.'

'But you can't explore in Carnation!'

'Oh right, because you moved to New York suddenly you're the explorer expert?'

'Just call me Dora,' she deadpanned.

I wish she was here to celebrate with me now that I've finally done it—I've committed to saving my family farm. Now everything just needs to go according to plan.

Chapter Two

Nick

I shake my head at my computer screen in disbelief.

'This can't be happening,' I mutter under my breath.

I'm not quiet enough, because Isaac perks up from his seat across from me. 'What is it?' he asks, making no effort to hide his excitement.

Isaac is one of my closest friends, and apart from Julian the only reason I've survived business school, but for as long as I've known him, he's had an uncanny ability to be able to tell when I'm not getting my way. It makes him shamelessly gleeful.

'You get your way a lot,' he likes to point out, whenever I comment on this unbecoming trait of his. I defend myself, explaining that I work for my 'luck', that I don't accept no for an answer, that out of the three of us I try the hardest, but my rebuttals always go in one ear and out the other. 'So, it's only fair that I get to relish in the very few instances where you do not,' he always says.

Today is no exception.

'Did the capstones come in?' Isaac asks, leaning forward excitedly, running a hand through his mop of curly black hair. 'That's it, isn't it. You have to go to the farm!'

He bursts out laughing before I even have the chance to respond, reading my expression accurately as the confirmation it is.

'Congratulations!' the email reads. 'Your application to the Parker Family Farm Capstone Project has been accepted.'

'Julian!' Isaac manages to call out in between wheezes of laughter. 'Nick actually got it.' He hits the table with his palm, sending shockwaves through our coffees.

Julian slides into his chair next to mine. 'No way,' he says in a low voice, his eyes meeting mine. 'You're not serious.'

I grimace.

'Damn. I don't know if I would have gone through with it.'

'Yes, you would have,' I argue. 'You can't wimp out on a fantasy football bet—that renders the whole thing pointless. We never would have let you back in the game,' I say, referencing our annual league. It's full of my closest friends in the city, six of us from Stanford's MBA program, the other three are old friends of ours. We've made a pact to get together every year to do the draft, an excuse for a boys' weekend, a way to make sure we stay in touch. The bets are taken very seriously. This year, my punishment for losing has to do with our MBA Graduate Capstone—a two-month program in our fall semester where we apply our business knowledge to real life.

Julian shrugs. 'I don't know . . . spending the capstone period on a farm instead of in an office with unlimited snacks and an in-house barista doesn't sound worth it.'

'You *have* to do it,' Isaac jumps in, having none of Julian's attitude. 'Brett had to pretend to be a fitness influencer for six months last year. He didn't wimp out. This is only like two months. And it's not like you're missing class time, all of us will be at our capstones anyway.'

'I know,' I say, trying to seem unruffled but fighting a rising feeling of frustration. Now that August is right around the corner, two months feels like a long time. I ignore the tightness in my chest, shifting my expression into one of feigned disinterest instead. 'You guys will spend all fall wasting away inside while I'm hanging out with hot country girls eating farm-to-table food from an actual farm, not a new-age restaurant with dim lighting.'

'You say that like that's not exactly what you'll be doing come November,' Julian says, raising his eyebrows. He may seem quiet or reserved at first, but his bullshit detector doesn't miss.

Isaac doesn't look as convinced. He scratches his chin. 'Maybe you *will* have fun,' he says thoughtfully.

For the first time since I got the email, I feel my spirits start to lift. *Take that!* I think. *You thought you screwed me over when I lost that bet, but really you did me a favor.*

But then Isaac bursts out laughing. 'Just kidding, man. I'll stick to my fine dining with women who don't have dirt under their fingernails.'

'Says the guy who hasn't been on a date in weeks,' Julian says under his breath.

I feel pinpricks of disappointment in my chest, the same way I did when Christian McCaffrey got injured in week one after I locked him in as my first-round draft pick, but despite the sensation, I can't help but laugh, quipping back to Julian, 'Remember when Isaac got rejected from that application-only dating app?'

Isaac glares at me.

Julian snorts. 'Maybe you two should trade places. His game will go further without us to compete with.'

'I'm getting more coffee,' Isaac grumbles.

Julian raises his eyebrows, both of us dissolving into laughter.

Hours later and I'm forced to laugh about my situation again, this time with my mother, who is doubled over, clutching the kitchen counter so hard I can see the whites of her knuckles.

'Mamma,' I say sternly, 'it is *not* that funny.'

'You boys are so dumb,' she says, shaking her head. She fills a pot with water and puts it on the stove. The sound of the gas igniting and the hiss of the flame underneath the pot are so familiar that I feel my shoulders relax.

'Chop this,' she says, handing me a yellow onion, 'while you tell me about it.'

I stand behind the cutting board, dicing the onion while we talk. She putters about behind me, getting out ingredients for spaghetti. I'm more at home in her small kitchen than I am anywhere else. There's barely room for both of us to move around, but we've been cooking together for so long that we know how to stay out of each other's way. Although, it's mainly me staying out of her way. One thing about my mamma—she can cook on a budget and in a small space and it will always be delicious.

'It starts next week,' I tell her, 'and lasts through September.'

'Two months is a long time,' she muses. 'You live with a host family?'

I nod. The onions are diced. They hit the pan with a sizzle and the smell of olive oil wafts into the air. I open a can of tomatoes, tear up some basil and butter some bread while I explain to my mother how the process works. The host family applies, Stanford either accepts them into the program or rejects them. The stipend is only granted to a small subset of applicants and the interview process can be grueling. Whoever the Parkers are, they had to jump through a lot of hoops to get a student assigned to them—students are one of Stanford's most valuable commodities, they don't give them away easily.

Stanford sets me up with a place to stay and pays my way to get to my capstone. Some of the family business placements are international, and even though I was hoping that my application would get flat out rejected, I'm relieved that I was placed domestically, only a two-hour plane ride away.

'And you're sure this is what you should be doing?' my mom asks, arching her eyebrows at me. She is always trying to make sure that I'm doing the absolute best that I can. She worked her whole life to give me the chance at success, and she will *not* let me squander it.

'I'll be just fine,' I tell her. The sauce is ready by the time I'm finished explaining, and we sit down at the small kitchen table with heaping plates of spaghetti. 'I already have my job lined up, remember?'

She smiles, muttering, 'Nicky, Nicky,' under her breath, the closest she gets to straight up saying she's proud of me. 'What about Anna?' she asks.

I almost choke on my mouthful. 'What about Anna?' I reply once I've swallowed.

There it is again—arched eyebrows.

'Nothing's going on with Anna.'

'She's a cute girl. Successful too.'

'You've met her once. And it wasn't even on purpose.'

She sighs. 'Nicky, I just don't want you to focus so much on work you forget to focus on . . . you know . . . other things.'

'I'm dating, Mamma. Not Anna, but I am dating,' I lie. Technically I did go on a date with Anna, but the connection we'd built in class didn't exactly translate to a candlelit dinner. I haven't opened up Hinge in months. It's depressing. My last girlfriend, Mariah, was great. But she moved to New York when I started business school and it just didn't work. Not a lot of drama, no messy break-up, it was the wrong place and the wrong time.

Mamma hated that. She liked Mariah. 'Such a nice girl. Ambitious too,' she lamented when I told her we broke up, tsk-tsk-ing at me over lasagna.

She tsk-tsks at me again, but this time she seems satisfied, ready to believe that I am, in fact, dating, because she switches the topic to my aunt Martha, who's coming over for dinner next week. It will be my last dinner before I head to Carnation, Washington.

Aunt Martha is my favorite aunt, a wise-ass and a know-it-all, but one with a heart of gold. She has a couple kids, and before I know it my mom is laying into Ronnie, my cousin, for getting fired from his job at a hardware store.

'Can you believe it?' she asks, exasperation exuding from her in waves. 'The heartache he puts your poor aunt Martha through.'

'I know, Mamma, but he'll pull through,' I tell her, not entirely convinced myself.

She grumbles, making the sign of the cross dramatically across her chest, her way of saying, *Let go and let God.*

I chuckle as I dry the last plate. My mom is nothing if not dramatic.

When I kiss her on the cheek and promise to be back next weekend at 7 p.m. for dinner, I feel a swell of affection for her in my chest. I can't wait until I'm done with my MBA and making a real salary, wearing suits to work, really making her proud. I will finally be able to take care of her. Finally start to repay her for everything she's done for me. Maybe I'll even start dating again.

Anna is hovering near my desk when I arrive at class on Tuesday morning, her curtain of shiny black hair hanging in front of her face. We're both concentrating in marketing, we're both graduating early (in January instead of May). We have one class before we break for our capstone semester, our preparation and send-off class, one where our teacher will inevitably lecture us on how we are supposed to show up to our various projects, how we can make the university proud.

'Julian told me you're actually going to the *farm*,' she says, her voice dropping like she's confiding in me that she heard I got Covid. She leans towards me, her tiny diamond hoop earrings catching the light. She smells like an expensive department store candle, sandalwood and vanilla. I thought things would be awkward after our failed date, but Anna acted like nothing ever happened and we've remained friends.

'Yep,' I say. I slide into my seat. She stays put.

'You guys do the dumbest things for fantasy football.'

'Why does it matter? I have my job lined up after we graduate anyway.'

'I guess—' she shrugs her shoulders '—you could be actually learning something on the capstone though, building connections.'

I try not to grimace. As much as I want to be successful, I *hate* networking. I'm good with people, but as soon as I feel like I need something from them, the whole interaction feels off-putting. It's one of the many things that make me feel like I'm not exactly cut out for a future in business.

'I'll leave the networking to you, Anna,' I tell her. 'You'll have more than enough for the both of us,' I say, referring to the project she's taking with a huge social media company, where networking connections abound.

She shrugs. 'I'll at least be able to leverage the plan we made in this class.' She makes her way to her seat just as our professor walks in the room.

'Shit,' I swear under my breath. *The plan we made in this class*. As in, the plan I was supposed to have made so I can submit it to my professor to sign off on before I head to Carnation. The plan I now have three days to do.

Comprehensive Marketing Plan for Failing Farm, I scribble across the top of my page.

Here goes nothing.

Chapter Three

Eloise

Reasons my Parents Will Be Proud of My Loan Application*

*Written by Evan and Shari

- I am saving them from the same fate as the Parkers (bankruptcy!)
- They love me and will be grateful to spend more time with me
- Regenerative agriculture will improve the health of the soil, better for all generations to come (like their grandchildren!)**
- I will be around to take care of them as they get older instead of stuffing them into a retirement home like Linden, my older brother, would***
- It was so much hard work!

**It is worth pointing out that I made it very clear grandchildren are *not* on the horizon, seeing as I'm single as a pringle and quite literally haven't thought a man was hot in a year.

***It is also worth pointing out that, although I have beef with my older brother, Linden, I do not think he *wants* to stuff my parents into a retirement home. But I do agree with Shari and Evan that he *would*.

Even though I had been working on the loan application for months, when I finally cross off 'submit loan application', I don't feel any sort of relief or celebration.

I try modifying my ongoing to-do list, adding 'send in loan application' and scratching a clean line right through it, hoping a double cross-off will shake the feeling, but . . . nothing—no butterflies in my stomach, no sense of accomplishment or pride. I squint at the message on the computer.

THANK YOU FOR YOUR LOAN APPLICATION TO THE US FARM SERVICES AGENCY.

Why is it so . . . anticlimactic? They couldn't even animate some sort of 'CONGRATULATIONS!' banner? I think, before remembering how notoriously underfunded the Farm Services Agency is and deciding it is probably for the best that they are not wasting taxpayers' dollars on animatronic word art.

I thought it would be like the movies. I imagined myself going to the bank in person and waiting nervously for someone to meet with me. The day I started the loan application I also started online shopping for a blazer.

I planned to sit back and cross one leg over the other while a man in a suit scanned Excel sheet after Excel sheet. I was going to let a smile bloom across my face as they looked up to tell me, 'Yes, Miss Anderson, your numbers do look correct. How refreshing to have someone come in here with a well-thought-out plan to pay us back *and* save the world while doing it. Forget the firstborn son, *you* are the prodigal daughter every parent dreams of.'

In reality, the loan application was late nights after weekdays in the lab, weekends sharing pizza with Evan and Shari after volunteering at the kids' camp, ceaselessly double-checking my numbers, and almost ruining the surprise to my parents every time they asked me how my summer was going. Shari wrote up a business plan to finish her Master's degree too, but hers was to secure a loan to farm hydroponic strawberries, and mine was to save my family's apple farm.

I text my group chat with Evan and Shari.

Me: I just pressed submit. *Scream emoji*

Shari: ME TOO ME TOO ME TOO!!!

My phone vibrates loudly on my desk.

Shari: So . . . how did telling your parents go?

I grimace at my phone. I start to type out an honest response, that I haven't told them yet. But I hesitate.

Shari is leaving for Italy tomorrow, her 'Lizzie McGuire' moment before she settles down to farm strawberries, and I don't want her to feel like she has to pump me up to tell my parents all over again. Lord knows she and Evan have done that enough times already. Instead, I avoid the question, opting to ask Evan if he's lonely in Seattle yet now that Shari and I have left.

Evan: Ha! It is still *summer* in Seattle. So . . .

People who rave about Seattle summers clearly haven't spent time on a farm. Wide open spaces, clean air, and fresh eggs in the morning. Tangible work for the apple harvest—the sweet smell of dandelions and the thick smell of old roots, the feel of a gnarled branch and the bud of an apple blossom, the sight of a perfectly pruned, symmetrical orchard.

Evan: JK. I really miss you guys *Sent with invisible ink*

Shari sends a selfie in response, posing next to a half-packed suitcase.

You'll miss me even more after tomorrow!!

Shari's tall, with dark brown hair that is either cascading down her back in soft waves or pulled back tightly into a braid. Her eyebrows are dark and arch perfectly above her piercing brown eyes. She has a square chin that lends her a permanent look of defiance. In short, she's nothing like the strawberry shortcake you would expect to be running a strawberry farm. She doesn't act like one either.

The next picture she sends is a screenshot of her Hinge with her location changed to Rome. Her inbox is filled with messages asking when she's free.

Shari: *Purple devil emoji*

Shari: Emphasized 'so how did telling your parents go?'

Evan: LOU – don't tell me you didn't tell them yet?! You said you would when you got home.

Me: I will. I PROMISE. But last night was so nice. Mom made lasagna.

Me: I couldn't ruin it. *Sent with invisible ink*

Evan: Ruin shmuin. I want to be eating lasagna. When can I come.

Shari: Evan, don't visit without me. Lou—it's OK to apply to buy out the neighbor's farm. It's not like *you* are the one making them bankrupt.

Evan: Well . . . my regular person inside job doesn't start until September so . . . maybe I should just pop up to the farm and make sure Lou tells her parents.

Shari: OMG DON'T GO WITHOUT ME.

Evan: Lou, you know that fall festival thing you always talk about. CAN I COME. Plz I miss you. *Kiss emoji*

Shari: You can't be serious.

Evan: Sorry I'm not that sorry. *Sent with invisible ink*

Evan: You're on your *Eat Pray Love* journey anyways.

Shari: Emphasis on the eat and love.

Evan: Eloise, we can make little seed pods for the kids at the festival like we did over the summer.

Shari: You are horrible. You know she can't resist showing little kids how to farm.

Evan: YOU'RE THE ONE GOING TO EUROPE, BITCH. *Sent with invisible ink*

Shari: You could have come with me if you weren't such a coward.

Evan: Speaking of cowards. *Sent with invisible ink*

I gasp at my phone. 'He did not!'

> **Evan: On that note, I need to tell the man in my bed to get out of my bed. *Sent with invisible ink***
>
> **Shari: OMG have you been texting in front of him this whole time? That's rude.**
>
> **Evan: He's ASLEEP.**
>
> **Shari: Good luck with that.**
>
> **Evan: *Peace sign emoji***
>
> **Me: A COWARD????**
>
> **Me: I rly love the seed pod idea though.**

'Lou!' Mom shouts up the stairs. 'Dad wanted to know if you could help him in West. Are you done with that school thing you had to do?'

'Yes! Coming!' I heave myself up and shut my laptop.

'I still don't understand how you have more schoolwork,' she says, as I pull on my dusty farm boots. She follows me outside, a bright afternoon sky, the breeze ruffling our hair. A chickadee squawks from its perch on a nearby cherry blossom tree.

'I'm done now,' I tell her. Despite all my reservations, I feel a swell of pride as I say it. I *am* done. Whatever happens now is out of my hands. *Now I just need to tell them.*

She squeezes my forearm as I straighten to a stand. 'I'm proud of you for getting all of that finally done,' she says, her eyes wrinkling at the corners. 'We're happy you're home.'

'I'm happy I'm home too.'

She stills, her grip lightening. 'Are you?' she asks, her hazel eyes piercing. The chickadee cheeps, like it's also waiting for my answer.

I avert my gaze. 'Mom, I gotta go. Dad will be looking for me.'

She releases her hand, but when our gazes lock again I can tell she's seen right through my carefree expression.

I manage to time my day perfectly, heading to meet JJ at golden hour once again. He nickers, happy to see me, and I feed him another unripe apple, stroking the bridge of his muzzle. 'I got all my stuff done today,' I tell him as I walk him to the back paddock. He neighs. 'I know, I know. Almost all my stuff. I'll tell them tonight. I swear.' He blinks a giant brown eye at me.

Half an hour later, Mom is doling out servings of her famous gnocchi tomato soup.

'So,' she asks, sitting down and smoothing her napkin onto her lap. 'How was your day?'

Dad glances at me. 'Good.' He shrugs.

I can't help but grin. 'Good' is dad-speak for 'Eloise did well today.' Even though my parents are proud of me for going to graduate school, I never felt like they were as proud of me as they are after a hard day's work in the fields. Thankfully, Linden understood why continued education was so important to me and co-signed on my student loans, the only helpful thing he's done in years if you ask me.

'Day was fine,' I manage to say before I start spearing gnocchi and shoveling them into my mouth.

Mom laughs. 'Clearly someone worked up an appetite.'

'You have no idea,' I tell her.

We chat about what we need to get done for the remainder of the week and I wait until the end of dinner to ask, 'Are you planning to help with the Fall Festival this year?' My parents help with it most years, either volunteering at booths or baking apple pies to raffle off or helping to plan the fireworks show. Fall Festival is always the first weekend in September. The whole town comes together to celebrate the arrival of fall.

'Why do you ask?' Mom sits up a little straighter like she's already preparing to guilt me into helping too.

I sigh. 'Mom, I'm not trying to get out of it. You're confusing me with your other kid.' She raises an eyebrow at this and purses her lips together, but says nothing, waiting for me to continue. Dad stifles a laugh. 'I was thinking about throwing something together for the kids that are there. At the kids' camp I volunteered for this summer we gave out seed pods and seedlings and they loved them.'

Mom's face breaks out into a wide grin. 'That's a really cute idea, Lou.'

'Technically, it was Evan's,' I admit. 'I was thinking of asking him to come help out. Would that be OK? If he was here for the . . .' I trail off mid-sentence. There's a strangeness in the air, it's too quiet suddenly.

Dad looks across the table at Mom, who shifts in her seat. 'We love Evan, but . . . are you sure? It's a busy weekend. Especially if you tack on something child-friendly.' Her eyes are a bit wider than usual.

'I just thought it would be nice to see him,' I reply. I can sense the mood shifting but I don't know why.

Mom shifts again, crossing and uncrossing her legs. 'I mean of course you can invite Evan . . .'

'Is Linden visiting or something?' I ask the only thing I can think of that would make them this shifty—most summers Linden comes home as a surprise to somebody, but he alternates who he's telling. Last year he surprised Dad by disguising himself as a disgruntled apple picker on the day before his birthday. Dad laughed so hard he cried when Linden peeled off his bald cap.

Neither of them respond, so Linden must not be the reason.

Dad sighs, keeping his eyes on his plate.

'I just think—' But before Mom can finish, Dad cuts her off.

'Just tell her,' he grumbles.

'Tell me what?' I ask, my voice comes out high and strangled. This doesn't seem like a good surprise. My heart starts to race.

'Lou,' Mom says gently, 'I just didn't know if you would want to really soak this one in. You know, without having to host a friend? This might be the last year we help the town with the Fall Festival . . . I think we're selling the farm.'

Chapter Four

Nick

I spend my last day in San Francisco doing my favorite things.

Isaac grumbles but agrees to come hiking with me, through the sandy hills to the rocky dunes of the headlands. We pause at the top to take in the view, listening to the waves crash on the rocks below.

'You'll miss, like, eight games of pickup,' Isaac complains, 'we'll have to find a replacement.'

'It's only two months,' I say as we head back down the hill towards the parking lot. I level a gaze at him. 'My spot better be available in October. Don't give it away.'

We meet Julian and Saber at Hogfish for brunch. All of us order their famous XL breakfast burrito and every single one of us finishes it. We lean back in the chairs and sit as our food digests, shooting the shit about the latest round of NBA trades. My mind wanders as they delve deeper into the world of Bill Simmons and I let my gaze linger on the organized chaos of weekend brunch in San Francisco. There's a pit in my stomach because I have to leave—I like my routine. I love knowing what to expect. It means I can prepare, which means I'm less likely to fail.

We meet up in the afternoon for drinks. This time everyone in the fantasy league is there. Isaac makes no less than six jokes at my expense before Julian pulls me aside to grab me a goodbye beer.

'He's going to miss you.' He jerks his head at Isaac.

'Yeah, I figured as much when he described me arriving at the farm with my shiny shoes and Patagonia vest and he laughed so hard he snorted beer out of his nose. I know that he was really lamenting how much my presence means to him and how lost he'll be with me gone.'

Julian laughs loudly and I see the bartender glance at him out of the corner of her eyes. 'She's checking you out.' I nod towards her. Julian looks her way, and she blushes, returning her gaze to the glass she's polishing to perfection.

I nudge him in her direction and he weaves his way towards the bar with a practiced swagger. Julian is the quietest of the three of us but doesn't need to talk to command attention.

I stare at my friends, congregated at a back table, laughing with each other, every now and then checking the score of various games on their phones. Sure, they fall into the stereotype of San Francisco just as much as I do, with short-sleeved collared shirts and jeans cuffed above the ankle, crisp white sneakers and longer hair than used to be fashionable, but they're good people.

But as much as I'll miss watching games together at my neighborhood Chelsea bar, I'm excited for some fresh air, I'm happy I get a little taste of adventure before I start my adult life. Before I launch myself even deeper into the rat race of climbing the ladder, getting promotions, negotiating for raises, and switching from job to job to get even more leverage than before. A low-pressure environment before I fully dive into a cutthroat career sounds like just what I need.

This is exactly what I tell my mom when we have dinner (apart from the pressure to be successful part, she hates when I complain about that and always reminds me that I'm already successful).

'Who knows,' I say, 'maybe the fresh air will even help my sleep.'

'You're still having trouble sleeping?' She looks at me. 'You didn't tell me that.'

Shit. 'Oh, it's gotten way better,' I lie. 'Don't worry about me.'

'Ronnie's having trouble sleeping now too,' Aunt Martha chimes in, 'because he doesn't have a job and all.'

I nod. *I'm not sure that's why he isn't sleeping*, I think, but I keep my mouth shut.

'Are you sure *that*'s his problem?' my mom asks, squinting at Martha. We all know what she's intimating—Ronnie loves to party. 'Nicky, maybe you'll be so exhausted after putting in all that hard work that you'll be able to sleep just fine.'

'It's just a farm up north,' I say. 'I don't know how much hard work it will be.' But I'm pleased and she knows it. I love that she knows I work hard. She reaches across the table, her arm hovering over the remnants of her famous carbonara and squeezes my cheek.

'Maybe you'll meet a girl up there, Nicky,' Aunt Martha says, sipping her wine with a devious grin.

My mother gasps. 'Don't you say that!' She whacks Martha on the side of her arm. 'Do not do that, Nicky. You meet a nice girl *here*.'

I laugh, throwing up my hands in mock surrender. 'You've got nothing to worry about,' I reassure her.

I'm loading the dishes into the dishwasher when I hear Aunt Martha whisper triumphantly to my mom, 'See? I told you my Ronnie was the ladies' man in our family.'

I'm sitting at the airport waiting for my flight to start boarding about to close my computer and slide it in my bag when I hear the ding of an email landing in my inbox.

Comprehensive Marketing Plan—GRADED

I click straight into the attached file. I can't risk anything jeopardizing my graduation. I haven't worked this hard for so long to let anything derail me. I click into the outline of how I plan to bring the farm back from the brink of bankruptcy. Based on research of the surrounding area, there's no other farms leveraging social media. This seemed so crazy to me that I also asked Julian to see if he could find anything—nope. Everyone out there is still living in the 2000s. I plan to hinge my marketing strategy around TikTok and Instagram. Ten steps over three months:

1. Observe and document, start to create content showcasing the morality of the farm (think granola grandparents, organic rocking chairs, all natural all day). *'Granola grandparents', Nick—really?* my professor has commented in the margin.
2. Based on the rough numbers I was given, increase cash flow through stockpiling goods that can be sold regardless of time of harvest. Apple cider vinegar, apple butter, etc.
3. Interactive content teasers and profiles go live in preparation for soft launch. 'Can you guess where this is?' 'Can you guess the name of ___ farm animal?' Another comment from my professor: *Have you confirmed they have animals?*
4. Soft launch via TikTok and Instagram + hard launch at farmers' markets. Observe competition, red room to spot for weaknesses in strategy
5. Gauge interest in product and prepare owners to capitalize on harvest.
6. Continue to sell in person and open online store with generated buzz from TikTok and Instagram.
7. Take increase in interest and boosted sales to whatever financial institution owner is leveraged with and refinance.
8. Invest capital in online storefront.

9. Create TikTok or Instagram challenge with 'A Day in the Life' as a prize to continue to generate buzz. *I don't know who you think your audience is, but most people aren't in a hurry to sign up for a day of free labor.*
10. Transfer ownership of social media accounts.

It is clear to me from this plan that you have never been to a working farm. Don't prove to me that sending you was a mistake. Best of luck – Professor Adams.

Chapter Five

Eloise

Reasons I Think I'm in the Midst of a Continuous Heatstroke

- My parents want to sell the farm
- I've already drank Mom out of her supply of iced tea
- I saw a hot man at the Parkers' place (this was a heat-induced hallucination)
- I forgot to bring JJ his after-lunch unripe apple
- I almost tripped on our largest (and loudest) chicken, Emily Chickenson
- I can't stop thinking about my hallucination. Like, he was *really* good looking
- My parents want to sell the farm

'You're what?' I splutter.

'You heard your mother,' Dad says, in a voice I've never heard before.

'I don't think I heard her right!' I reply, my voice pole-vaulting into a higher frequency.

'Lou.' Mom reaches a hand towards me. My stomach flips, and I regret eating as much as I did. 'Things have been bad for a while now . . . we thought you would see this coming.'

'I did,' I say. 'I mean, I knew things were bad, but you hadn't said anything about selling.'

They exchange glances.

'We haven't officially decided. We're gonna see how this fall goes, but . . . it's not looking good.'

'What am *I* supposed to do?' I ask quietly, the realization that my future is being taken away from me hitting me like a ton of bricks. All of my hard work this summer, just *gone*.

'We thought about that too.' Mom is gentle, her hand reaching towards me across the table. I catch the glint of a tear in her eye and look away. 'But even if we sell, you'll be fine. You're so smart, and you have this great degree you can put to use anywhere. Didn't you say you liked the research you were doing in the lab? You could . . . do that?'

'Mom.' My voice catches, but I push through. 'That's not how that works . . . I already gave that up . . . I . . . I thought I would be back here with you. I don't understand . . . why didn't you tell me sooner?'

My dad clears his throat but stays quiet.

'Who would you sell it to?'

'Lou,' Dad cuts in, his voice has an edge to it. *Don't go there*, he's saying, but I can't help myself.

'We can't sell out to another big corporation!' I cry out. 'Everyone is doing that. This region will be *ruined*.' My heart starts to beat faster. I glance at Dad, pleading. 'You said you would never sell to them.'

Dad hangs his head and it breaks my heart to see him so defeated. I change the subject. 'If you sell ... then what?' I manage to ask, my voice coming out even more high-pitched.

'We don't know.' Mom shrugs. She glances at Dad. 'Retire, I guess.'

'You can't expect me to believe that's what you want to be doing, you two have been judging retirees for years. You're literally aways asking how they fill their days. And JJ, what about him? And what about—' I stop myself before I ask about the one word we never discuss—*money*.

'Honey, I know we have a lot to figure out, but it's looking like we don't have another choice.'

'But you do have another choice,' I say. 'We only started organic last year. Can't you give it a chance to catch up? The apples sell for more. It works, I *swear*. We did so many case studies on it at school.'

'I don't know if it makes sense to wait that long,' Dad cuts in, finally adding to the conversation. 'I've been running the numbers and we would need to give it another year or two and even then we just max out our orchards and it's still not enough yield.'

'What if I can show you how to make it enough?' I counter.

Dad gazes at me intensely, as if he can read my mind. He's done this since I can remember, and without fail, every time it leads to me telling the truth about something I wasn't quite ready to acknowledge. I fidget in my seat. 'I thought the Parkers' farm would fail,' I confess, 'and I applied for a loan to buy them out.'

Mom goes as white as a sheet.

Dad lets out a breath of air, like the wind has been sapped from his sails.

'It was just an application,' I whisper. 'I don't even know if we'll get it. We can turn it down,' I add, like I'm trying to convince myself that it wasn't the culmination of all my work as a graduate student.

Dad gulps, his Adam's apple bobbing. My gaze travels up his weathered face, snagging on the graying hair at his temples. 'Why don't you walk us through it,' he says. Mom is perfectly still, like she isn't even breathing. I can feel the tension radiating through the air.

'You were right about the margins. We don't have a big enough piece of property. Other farms our size get by on other things—tours, weddings, hayrides, being Instagram-perfect spots to pick apples. They drive in traffic from tourists that keeps them afloat. They sell jams and convert to B & Bs. But that isn't us. We farm apples. And to do it, we need more apples and more land. And—' I take a breath before I add the last part of the puzzle, my pièce de résistance '—we need it to be regenerative.'

Dad rolls his eyes.

'Hey!'

'Regenerative schmenerative,' he grumbles.

'Cal.' Mom levels a look at him.

I give her an appreciative half-smile before continuing. 'I'm serious. Banks are investing in regenerative agriculture because the FAA is pushing them to do it. They get a percentage of loan forgiveness if the farmer is regenerative ag and defaults. I knew you guys hadn't been able to secure a loan in the past . . .' I hesitate, expecting fallout from my knowing something Mom didn't know that I knew, but there is none, she just nods at me, like she expected Dad told me all along.

'I think we just need the Parkers'. We couldn't spin this farm into regenerative ag by itself. We need pigs and cows and sheep and geese, and right now we hardly have enough space for our chickens and bees. We need a whole new round of cover crops, and we need to start growing something other than apples, I'm thinking—'

'You've outlined all of this in the application for the loan?' Dad asks, cutting me off.

I nod.

He settles back in his chair, but an unmistakable flash of pride flickers across his face.

'Did you ask Linden about this?' Mom asks.

My face falls. 'Well . . .' I trail off. 'You know we don't exactly see eye to eye on the farm stuff.'

In truth, I would have loved to get Linden's opinion. But Linden vocalizing that he wants me to do something bigger with my degree than stay at home is a discussion I'm not ready to have. Focusing on what I'm angry about—Linden's choice to make money for other people instead of do his part to protect the planet—is easier than potentially facing his disappointment in me. The last time we talked about the farm our conversation turned into an argument almost immediately.

Dad interrupts my thoughts. 'I bet that was a lot of work,' he says in a low voice.

'It was my Master's thesis,' I admit.

Mom's jaw drops open. 'You wrote your thesis on us buying the Parkers' farm?'

'We need the land!' I argue.

The kitchen is silent. An owl hoots from the backyard, a sound that usually comforts me, but now just raises goosebumps across my skin. I love this place. I don't want to have to give it up. How did everything happen so fast? One minute I'm building my future around saving our family farm, and the next my parents are telling me they want to sell?

'It could work.' Dad sits back in his chair. He doesn't meet Mom's gaze.

It seems, I think, as we clean up dishes silently and trudge to bed, that my dad would consider buying the Parkers' too.

I spend the entire day working with Dad and we don't address the prospect of selling or the loan. Instead, we work harder than usual, filling the silence with productivity. It's all I can do to flop onto the couch in a sweaty heap. 'I'm exhausted,' I say, wiping sweat from my hairline. 'I don't want to move another step today. I think I have heatstroke.'

Mom walks over to the couch and lays a hand on my forehead. 'You seem fine, sweetie. Plus, you'll have to take a couple steps for dinner. I made your favorite.' Dad and I returned from the fields at the same time, and he's sitting next to me, shuffling a deck of cards. His head perks up at my mom's words and she laughs. 'Yes, your favorite too,' she confesses, turning to walk into the kitchen and slide a pan of lasagna into the oven. Before she goes, she stares at me a beat too long. 'I know there's things we need to talk about,' she says, 'but let's try to just enjoy dinner tonight.' Mom *hates* conflict, and I'm exhausted, so I acquiesce, giving her a soft smile while on the inside I feel like crying.

Lily calls me just as my dad deals out a hand of gin rummy. I flash the screen at him, already knowing how he'll respond. 'You should get that,' he says. 'Tell her your mother and I said hello.' For as long as Lily and I have been best friends, he's thought of her as a second daughter.

'My dad says hi!' I say as I pick up.

'Cal!' I can hear Lily's smile through the phone.

'She says hi,' I say to Dad as I leave the room, heading upstairs for some privacy. 'What're you doing?' I ask Lily.

'Making dinner.'

I laugh. 'Crazy that we're three hours apart and still doing things at the same time.'

'Things are so *early* there,' Lily says, like even the mere thought of a 6 p.m. dinner causes her physical pain. 'How is it? Being back?'

'Lily. They want to sell.'

'The Parkers? That's great!'

'No. My parents.'

'What?'

'Yeah.'

'Woah. Damn. I'm so sorry, Lou . . . what does that mean for . . .'

'The loan? My future?' My voice cracks. 'I don't know. I have this fall to prove to them that we should keep it, I guess.'

'What does Linden think?'

A knot forms in my stomach at the idea of talking about it with him. I should be over it by now, the fact that my brother will never return to our small town, the fact that he was destined for bigger things—a bigger city, an illustrious career, a yearning for arts and culture that Carnation just can't fulfill. And my parents wanted Linden to succeed so badly, to achieve his goals, to live his dream life, that it always felt like they never bothered to ask what mine was. Because there was never a discussion, I assumed the responsibility of returning home to take care of the farm and my parents. If I didn't do it, who would? But now there might be no farm to take care of, and where does that leave me?

'Lil, you know as well as I do that I'm not exactly in touch with Linden. And nothing is set in stone, they could still change their minds.'

'Eloise! You said you would call him!'

'You know better than to full-name me!' I retort right back. Everyone I know calls me Lou. It's been that way since I was little. 'I saw a hot guy today.' I change the subject before she can carry on getting angry with me. I don't have the energy to discuss my failings as a little sister.

'You *what*?' she squeals. 'You haven't met a hot guy in *ages*. Here I was starting to think your loins had dried up permanently.'

My momentary wave of guilt at getting her excited about a hallucination recedes immediately. 'Technically, I *saw* the hot guy. In a hallucination. As a result of my heatstroke. And also, my *loins*? Are you reading your regency romance novels again?'

'You did not get a heatstroke,' Lily chastises me, 'it isn't even that hot there. Summer's, like, basically over. You're definitely just stressed about your parents selling the farm. And yes. Not that you care, but the viscount has finally realized he's in love with the neighboring duchess.'

'I swear I did. I forgot to bring JJ his afternoon apple.'

'Hmm,' Lily muses, 'so what did this hallucination look like exactly?'

'Tanned. Muscular. Amazing hair. Like movie-star hair. John Stamos hair. And—' I drop my voice to a whisper '—this is the weird part, but I think he saw me too.'

'OK, so you saw a hot guy and he saw you back and is that what's supposed to make this absolute dreamboat a hallucination?'

'Well, he definitely wasn't a farmer. He was way too put together for that. And the Parkers only have daughters. So there's no reason for someone like that to be there? Plus, like I said before, *I was really hot*. Also, he is like the carbon copy of the protagonist in the latest rom-com I'm reading. So, it's not a big leap that my mind would have made him up. In the heatstroke I was clearly having.'

Lily cackles. 'I can't believe you have the balls to make fun of me for my regency novels while you're binge-reading every rom-com under the sun.'

Our plates aren't cleared from dinner when Mom brings the Parkers up. The pit of dread and guilt that's been sitting in my stomach resurfaces with a vengeance. In the few days I've been home it's only been absent when I've been with JJ.

'I just don't know what they'll do.' Mom sighs at her dinner plate.

Dad glances to his left, out the window towards their farmhouse, lights twinkling on the hill that overlooks our house.

'They'll figure it out. They always do.' Dad pats his belly. 'That was amazing, Haze.'

'You don't think they'll sell? Aren't they worse off than we are?'

Mom arches an eyebrow at me. 'Let's not dwell too much on other people's misfortune,' she says, her intonation reminding me of my late, very Catholic grandmother, and sounding just like the tone she used when I accidentally let a 'Jesus Christ!' slip around her.

'Sorry,' I grumble.

After dinner is cleaned up, we retire to the living room, Mom immediately settling into her favorite chair, a stained-glass Tiffany lamp glowing colorfully next to her.

'That book club of hers has been reading a lot of "romance" lately,' my dad whispers to me, air-quoting 'romance', as he deals out a hand of gin rummy.

'Romance is really in the air today,' I murmur.

'What?' Dad asks, peering over his hand of cards.

I glance at Mom, who's so absorbed in her book she hasn't heard him.

'Is she reading like *romance* romance?' I ask.

He raises his eyebrows in confirmation and nods.

'EW, Dad!'

'What?' Mom asks, looking up from her book.

We both break out into laughter.

A knock on the front door startles all of us. Dad looks at Mom. 'Are we expecting anyone?'

'Hi!' Betsy calls from down the hall. 'I thought I saw Lou walking through the fields yesterday and we wanted to welcome her home.'

A confusing mix of affection and guilt coats my stomach as Mrs. Parker sweeps me into a tight hug. As usual, she smells like rosewater and jasmine.

'Let me look at you,' she says, grabbing my shoulders and stepping half a foot back. 'Every year you get more beautiful. How is that possible?' she asks, looking to my mom for her agreement.

She gives it in spades. 'I know. I pinch myself every time I see her.'

I blush bright red.

'Lay off, Betsy,' Joe chides his wife affectionately. He steps around her to encircle me in a hug.

'So tell us.' Betsy makes herself comfortable without needing to be invited. She sits down at our kitchen table and drums her fingers across the weathered oak. Mom puts a kettle on for tea. 'How was school?' We chat until the conversation turns to our farm and the air in the room stills. Usually this is a practiced topic, one we all resort to when we small talk, but considering I've hardly talked to my parents about them wanting to sell, I don't have much to say.

'It's fine,' Mom offers, her voice going up slightly.

Dad grunts from his chair. Joe does the same, both of them an echo of the other, hunched over the wood ever so slightly.

'How are the girls?' I ask Betsy, taking advantage of the silence as an opportunity to change the subject. She smiles but it doesn't reach her eyes. 'They're good. Don't see them much. Big city living and all.'

This, I think, *is why I didn't want to leave my parents*. It's tangible, the feeling that Betsy is exuding, the acknowledgement that her kids aren't trying nearly as hard as they could be to stay in touch. I never want my parents to say about me, *We never see her. She's in the city now*. But look where that got me.

'And the grandkids?' I ask, surprised I have to prompt her, she usually takes any excuse she has to talk about them.

'Good!' Betsy glances at Joe again and he shakes his head ever so slightly.

Mom sighs. 'Betsy, I've known you long enough to know when you want to tell me something. What is it?'

Betsy smiles, this time it transforms her whole face. She's beaming. 'Do you remember that program we applied for? The business school one?'

Mom nods.

'I was waiting to tell you until I knew for sure, but we got it!' She turns to me. 'And then everything happened so fast. But it's happened. He's resting at the house now. You'll have a friend this summer!' She winks.

So he wasn't a hallucination after all. 'What program?' I ask weakly.

But Mom is already asking Betsy logistical questions about arrivals and plans and grants. Their voices morph into a low buzz.

'Are you okay?' Dad asks me, meeting my eyes across the table. He looks tired again, the glint of excitement gone. I nod. 'Just tired,' I say. 'First week back on the farm, you know how it is,' I add, a little louder, for Betsy and Joe to hear.

'We should go,' Betsy adapts quickly, ever the perfect next-door neighbor. 'Come over soon?' she asks me earnestly, placing her hand on my forearm. 'I can't wait for you two to meet.'

'I will,' I croak out, trying to sound sincere but my voice dies on my tongue and instead, I sound like a pre-pubescent boy.

Mom fills me in after our heavy oak front door has closed behind Joe and Betsy and their footfalls have disappeared down the path that connects our houses. Mom and Dad knew about the program Betsy was applying to. Turns out, they had been the ones to find it. There was an article about it in the paper, about a program to loan out graduate students in business to small, family-owned companies. She told Betsy about it over coffee and she jumped at the idea. She was 'looking for a lifeline', she confided in Mom, looking for anything that would save her favorite place in the world.

Dad reassures me before I head to bed that there's no way a business student can turn around an apple farm on dead soil, but I toss and turn all night anyway. I'm distracted enough from our harvest as it is, and now the Parkers have a 'secret weapon' to turn their business around, *and* their secret weapon is hotter than a firecracker in a hay bale? It's starting to seem like I should have accepted that research job after all . . .

Chapter Six

Nick

It takes all of my willpower to not email Professor Adams immediately.

Mr. Parker *is* a granola grandpa. He picks me up from the airport in a muddy blue pickup truck that looks like it's older than I am, wearing faded Levis and a wrinkled navy T-shirt. George Strait is playing on the car speakers. He tips his hat at me as I swing myself into the car.

San Francisco doesn't really have seasons. It's pretty much eternally foggy, chilly at night, with some days warmer than others. Landing in Seattle was a breath of fresh air. Warmer than I'm used to without the ocean breeze, it felt like the apex of summer standing out in front of the airport. The air was dry and hot, the sidewalk congested with tourists.

Mr. Parker clearly wants none of it, he throws my suitcase in the truck faster than I can blink, surprisingly nimble for someone that looks like he's reaching seventy.

'Glad you made it, son. Mrs. Parker is mighty excited to meet you.'

'Thank you . . . sir?' I hastily tack on to the end of my sentence. Mr. Parker simply grunts and pulls away from the airport, so I take that as confirmation he likes to be addressed as 'sir'.

'Your flight was on time,' he notes.

'Yessir.'

'You from California?'

'Yessir,' I say again. I feel like I'm falling into a rhythm with it. I never grew up calling anyone 'sir'. No one I knew took themselves that seriously. It's kind of fun, I think, sitting back in my seat.

'You can call me Joe.'

Damnit. 'Yessi—I mean, OK, Joe. So . . .' *So much for my politeness.* I search for something to bring up—after all, we do have two hours to get through.

'Let me tell you about the farm,' he says, rescuing me from my thoughts. He proceeds to launch into the most detailed explanation of a business I've ever heard. Halfway through I almost pick up my phone to start taking notes but I second-guess it, worried he'll think I'm texting. By the time we're nearing Carnation I know the names and personality of every pig: Maisy (affectionate), Daisy (stubborn), Princess Peach (loud), and Buttercup (lazy). I know more about his daughters than I know about my cousins. There's two of them, both living in Seattle, one married and the other recently divorced. He has two granddaughters and a grandson, and his grandson, Dev, just learned how to say grandpa. I can tell by the way his eyes crinkle at the corners when he talks about her that his elder granddaughter is his favorite.

He tells me that Mrs. Parker does the crossword every morning and that she's the better cook, although he can make a mean pot roast. He, in turn, manages the business. It takes him a long time, but eventually he works his way up to the financial troubles.

'Boy, we are glad to see you,' he says, his voice a little less gruff than it was an hour and a half ago. 'We had a bad harvest last year that really set us back.'

'That's what I'm here for.' I shrug.

'We're hoping we can get through it. I don't know what else we'll do.'

I stare out the window trying to come up with a response. I hardly know this man at all and I already like him. I don't want to see him fail.

Mr. Parker glances at me. 'You ever worked on a farm before?'

'Not exactly,' I admit.

'Hmmph.'

We don't talk much after that.

I get a text from Anna wishing me luck, accompanied by a photo of her in a pristine white office, smiling coyly at the camera. Even though she was cool after our date, sometimes I feel like she still wants to be something more, and that by continuing our friendship I'm leading her on. I wonder if a clean break while I'm out here is exactly what I need. The more I think about it, the more I'm convinced it's a great idea. In the least presumptuous way possible, I'll just tell Anna that I don't want to be giving her the wrong idea and that I won't have my phone a lot this summer.

Hey, I begin, *just wanted to say I think I'll be off the grid for a bit. Our friendship means a lot to me but I want to really focus on this capstone and to do that I need to unplug.* I'm staring at my phone, wondering if saying our friendship means a lot to me is too opaque. Just as I'm deleting the text to rewrite it, about to add in *I know we went on a date but I think we're better off as friends,* a text comes through from Isaac.

Sweet set up, Anna.

He attaches a picture to the message of himself in his own office.

But do you guys have an in-house barista?

Quick as a flash, there's a photo of Anna with a cappuccino.

Duh.

My service must be crap for group messages to come in one by one, but my annoyance at my cell provider is outweighed by the relief thrumming through my body. I'm such an idiot. *Thank God I didn't send Anna a dumb lets-be-friends message in response to her texting a bunch of her friends in a group chat. Isaac would have never let me live it down.* I have no idea what I was thinking assuming Anna was still so hung up on me. Mamma would slap me if she knew I had gotten such a big head. She hates an ego. I snort out a laugh thinking about it.

'What?' Joe asks.

'Oh.' I grimace. The rumble of the old blue pickup is so loud that I forgot Joe was there. 'Nothing. We almost there?'

'We are here.'

We round a corner and Carnation comes into view. WELCOME TO CARNATION, a sign on our right reads as we speed past it. I feel like I've entered a Hidden Valley Ranch commercial. Everything is green and soft. The truck starts to coast as we journey through undulating hills. Mr. Parker rolls down the windows grunting and muttering that 'The city air just gets worse and worse,' and 'Those hypocrites buy organic and live in a pollution factory.'

I take in a deep lungful and feel the fresh air hit me like pure oxygen. It smells of hay and grass and faintly of manure. It smells exactly as I imagined. I watch the bars of service on my cellphone slowly start to dwindle. *The Parkers must have Wi-FI ... right?* Just as I'm about to ask, we coast to a stop next to a small mailbox and Mr. Parker hops out. 'This'll just be a minute,' he drawls.

I hop out of the truck to take in the view as I wait for him to review his mail. I hear the squawk of a nearby chicken and close my eyes, tilting back my head to feel the sun on my face. When I blink my eyes back open, they snag on a woman walking atop a nearby hill. She's in jeans and a T-shirt, and even from where I'm standing, I can tell she's beautiful. Her hair is golden, lit up by the sun, and her cheeks are full. She's tan, strong, and she looks right at home as she picks her way through the field. She looks up at me and when our gazes meet her steps falter. She cocks her head, like my presence is confusing, and just as she moves to pull her sunglasses down from her face and get a closer look at me, Mr. Parker clears his throat, beckoning me back to the car.

The truck groans so loudly pulling us up the hill that I can't get a word in to ask who she is. Before I know it, we've arrived at the top. We've made it home. I see dollar signs in every window as we approach. This is even more picturesque than I thought. It's so marketable it's almost comical—a wooden A-frame with a wraparound porch and rocking chairs moving gently in the wind. There's a polka-dotted umbrella stand on the porch and a welcome mat that reads, 'Welcome to our home, humans live here with us,' and has pictures of each one of the pigs underneath it—Maisy, Daisy, Princess Peach, and Buttercup. I start laughing and Mr. Parker cracks a smile. 'The girls got that for us last Christmas,' he says.

People would pay anything for what this farm sells, I'm sure of it. The internet goes nuts for pigs. I just need to get Mr. and Mrs. Parker to see it.

Before I can open the front door, Mrs. Parker comes barreling out of the house. Her hair is graying and pulled back from her face. A thick apron is tied around her waist. She is literally holding a spoon in one hand and frantically waving hello with the other. She's beaming.

This might not be so bad after all.

Chapter Seven

Eloise

Anderson Family Farm Running To-Do List

- Harvest eggs from the chickens
- Check on the bees
- Clear out West and Central Barns
- Take inventory of the fertilizer and seeds
- Sharpen the pruning shears
- Figure out a plan for JJ
- Beat Dad at gin rummy

It's my day to get the eggs for breakfast, but the smell of eggs wafting upstairs lets me know that I missed my chance. It took me so long to fall asleep I guess I slept through the rooster. I change quickly, scampering downstairs to find a skillet of scrambled eggs on the stove and coffee in the pot. Mom and Dad are nowhere to be found, Dad is probably tinkering on something in the barn while Mom mucks JJ's stall. Thinking about JJ makes me sit up a little straighter. I can't believe I was even thinking about letting the farm go last night, that taking a job in a lab crossed my mind. My parents don't even *want* to sell, they just feel like they have to. And I have a way to fix it. Plus, if I do, then I get to keep JJ.

I ignore the voice in my ear reminding me that JJ is overdue for a new family, one where he is exercised more often, where a young girl or boy can give him the attention I once did. Instead, I glance at the newspaper lying out on the counter, skimming the headline about a local kindergartner who made national news for an extremely accurate Lego sculpture of a horse, and let myself be happily reminded why I love Carnation so much.

I check on the beehives on my way to find Dad, stopping to listen to their telltale hum, to smell the honey, to lay eyes on some of our most valuable helpers.

'Bees look good!' I call out to Dad as I enter West. He grunts appreciatively before putting me right to work. We start with the barn closest to the house, the biggest one of the three on our property. Every year, before harvest really kicks into gear and the seasonal workers arrive, we do a barn clean-out to get ready for new fertilizer and equipment. We haul out empty buckets and take apart cardboard boxes. We sweep floors and wipe cobwebs. The first steps to prepare for harvest and for the U-Pick weekends—the days that hundreds of people migrate to Carnation to pick apples themselves, our most profitable weekends of the year, exactly what they sound like. On those weekends, our seasonal workers do not pick the apples, the visitors pick the apples.

When we're done with the barn we move outside.

'Do you think Mom will come around to the loan?' I ask him while we inspect trees, both of us crouching down on either side of their slender trunks to check for mites or lumps of a disease. So far, almost all the trees have been clear. A good sign, and one we both needed.

The day is clear, the sun climbing higher in the sky with each passing minute. Birds are loud, squawking and chirping up a storm at all hours of the day. Grass and weeds alike are thriving, hitting my knees as I venture off the gravel paths that crisscross our land. Dry air blows in from the west, keeping the bugs at bay. I stand up, taking a moment to survey the land around us. On every side we're surrounded by fields and hills of bright green trees. The apple blossoms dropped a couple weeks ago and here and there I can still spot white petals littering the dirt.

I swat at a fly that buzzes by my ear. The sun is hot, beating down on our shoulders. I wipe sweat from my hairline. Only a couple more weeks of this before fall truly sets in and the mornings and the evenings get cooler. I can't wait.

'I don't know—' he stands '—your mother is a mystery to me.' He wipes his hands on the front of his jeans. 'She thinks it will jinx us, planning for something bad to happen to people we love. It's the Catholic blood in her.'

'I'm not planning for something bad to happen, I'm being realistic,' I remind him.

'*I* know that,' he says. 'She's the one you have to convince.'

I plod back to the house, intent on doing just that, but my plans are thwarted when I hear laughter unspooling from the back door. There's a waft of blackberry pie penetrating the air. These days Mom saves pie for occasions, like birthdays and graduations. But there is a group she makes it for without any occasion: Book Club.

I'm distracted thinking about pie, and I pause in the door frame for one second too long, just long enough for Peggy to round the corner and squeal with delight.

'Your mother told us you were back!' she cries, pulling me in for a hug. Peggy is old enough to be my grandmother but has enough energy to be in college. She drags me into the living room where women are spread out on our couch. There are extra chairs pulled in from the kitchen, and a blackberry pie sitting in the middle of the fray.

'When is Linden going to come home?' Peggy wheedles at me, clasping her hands together. 'He is such a darling boy.'

'I don't think he's a boy anymore,' I tell her. 'He has wrinkles now.'

'Stop all your chatter and grab a slice.' Marcia beckons me forward. 'You need more meat on your bones.'

'You always say that.' I smile at her, remembering when I came home from college after my first year carrying an extra fifteen pounds with me, and Marcia saying the exact same thing. I love her for it, and I help myself to a piece of pie before perching on an arm of the couch, right next to Peggy. Mercifully, this month's book is so good that I can eat my pie in peace, their conversation immediately sliding back to their romance novel.

'Oh, the ending,' Kathleen says theatrically, placing the back of her hand on her forehead.

'And especially after the family didn't approve!' Marcia crows.

Peggy elbows me. 'You really should read the book.'

'I will,' I reassure her. 'My dad had some choice words about it.'

Peggy shakes with laughter. 'The main character *is* spicy.'

'Hear, hear!' Marcia exclaims. 'George told me I needed to buy the sequel.' She wiggles her eyebrows.

Kathleen explodes into laughter.

'Unfortunately, anything that is even remotely tangential to my parents' sex life is my cue,' I laugh, standing to leave.

'Read it, Eloise!' Peggy reminds me as I go. 'A romance for the ages!'

'More like *smut* for the ages,' Kathleen corrects.

I head into the kitchen to put my dish away with their laughter still bouncing off the walls. I've creaked open the dishwasher when I hear Kathleen catch her breath and add, 'I dare say the main character reminded me of the new guy in town.'

I freeze.

'I agree!' Peggy says happily. 'I saw him at the butcher, and *man*. He is a tall drink of water. Those arms!'

I am as still as a statue, one arm extended halfway into the dishwasher, not wanting to make any noise.

'And that hair. He is so handsome,' Marcia says emphatically.

'You've seen him too?' asks a voice I can't place.

'Well . . . no . . . but everyone keeps saying he is!'

The room explodes into laughter again and I hurry to put my dish away. I turn back towards the living room, wondering if asking about the new guy is worth being teased. Lord knows these women ask about my dating life enough as it is. But before I can decide what to do, Mom walks into the kitchen. She starts when she sees me, clearly expecting me to have gone by now.

'Hanging in there, sweetheart?' she asks.

I nod. My lower lip starts to tremble. All day long I've swung between feeling fiercely determined to make this work, make this fall our best harvest yet, and feeling scared about the future.

Mom's friends get louder, one of them hollering a question at her. 'Sorry—' she smiles, playfully rolling her eyes '—you know how they get.' But before she leaves, she wraps me in a quick hug. 'We'll figure it out,' she whispers.

There's a grocery list on the counter when I come downstairs the next morning.

APPLES
Leeks
Milk
Yogurt
Honey
Oats
Linguine
Canned Tomatoes

I laugh out loud at the list and pour myself a cup of coffee. Apples on the list is a sign that Mom's in a good mood. She always says buying our competitors apples is for 'market research,' but without fail she ends up taking a big bite of each one, theatrically going on and on about how she thinks it looks 'really good' and it 'might be better than ours' before spitting out a chunk with such vitriol you would think I had doused it in rat poison. Sometimes the apple pieces get halfway across the kitchen, landing in mess of spit and mush on the floor. But my dad laughs every time she does the bit, sometimes so hard tears stream down his cheeks.

So, I keep buying the apples, and she keeps doing the bit.

By sending me for groceries, she's giving me an excuse to get off the farm, which I will happily take. I take my coffee to go, heading out the back door to find my dad. I hear him before I see him, the whine of the tractor blocking out all other noise. He shuts off the engine, wasting no time shout-explaining that he needs me in the afternoon—we start pruning today.

I trudge back to the house and pull on jeans and an old apple-farm celebration T-shirt, one of about a hundred that live in my dresser, and head out, adding a few things to the grocery list before I leave. I might as well make the trip last as long as possible.

I remember to bring reusable bags only to realize I forgot to grab my sneakers while I was upstairs. But then I spy a pair of Mom's apple-red Converse by the door and throw those on instead. I peel out of the driveway and head into town, about a twenty-minute drive. I breathe a sigh of relief as I exit the driveway.

I've always enjoyed driving through Carnation. The roads are two-laned and dusty, the town is only about five stoplights long, and there are rolling hills throughout. I often feel like we're stuck in the 1950s, but I don't mind it.

I coast to a stop in the parking lot of Hal's General Store and hop out. I check the clock, plenty of time to grab a latte from the café across the street after I shop. Amie's at the checkout when I walk through the doors. She waves, her red hair catching the sunlight. She started working at Hal's after we graduated and seems to relish her position as the town's reigning gossip queen. When I was home in the winter she caught me up on all the happenings while I'd been away. As long as Amie's working the checkout, I'll never have to attend a high-school reunion.

I go on autopilot through the store, checking things off my list seamlessly until I get to the toiletry aisle. I stop short in front of the razors, wondering if I should pull out my phone to calculate which value pack is the cheapest or just do it mentally. I'm juggling about three packs in my hand when I see movement in my peripherals.

My hallucination is here. But under the fluorescent grocery store lights he's terrifyingly real. His hair is perfectly mussed and doesn't move an inch when he squats down to pick up a can off the bottom shelf. I can't help but notice the way his butt fills out his jeans, firm and strong. But something about his physique doesn't match with the rest of him. His hair is so neat, and his face is clean-shaven. His hands are delicate. He doesn't usually work on a farm, that much is clear.

I bite my lip, wondering if I should introduce myself to the Parkers' secret weapon when he turns to look at me, catching me staring and making the most intimate eye contact I've ever had with anybody, including the time Shari made me play a game where we stared into each other's eyes for four minutes, just to find out if we were really supposed to be best friends (if the test is reliable, we weren't, because we burst out laughing after a minute).

But this man's gaze holds me captive, rooting my feet to the floor. The air is vibrating between us. His eyes are a rich brown, framed by thick lashes. His cheekbones cut his face perfectly, drawing my gaze to his full lips. *You could cut the tension in here with a knife*, I think, only to realize I'm holding three razors in one hand and have stopped mid-reach for the next option. As fast as I can I drop the razors into my cart and duck out of the aisle, my heart hammering in my chest. I can feel my blush creeping up to my hairline.

I pull out my phone to text Lily but then I think better of it. What would I even say? *So actually I wasn't hallucinating and I've FINALLY found someone I think is attractive but he's helping the Parkers so I'm supposed to hate him??* I slide my phone back in my pocket. Better to wait. We haven't even spoken.

The apples are my last stop. I am so focused on my task at hand (being picky about apples comes with the territory) that I don't notice he's approached me until it's too late.

'How do you like them apples?' he asks in a low voice. An invitation of humor edges his question, and I feel for a moment like he's inviting me to share in a secret, illicit game with him. But then Amie's voice rings out over the loudspeaker, reminding shoppers that this Friday there's a canned foods drive, and my mind crashes into reality.

What did he just say to me? I think, panic rising in my chest. *Isn't* 'How do you like them apples?' *an expression about a woman's tits? Why do attractive men think they can get away with anything?* If he's introducing himself to me with a line this racy, no wonder he's been the center of the book club's imaginary small-town smut fairy tale.

I huff a puff of air towards the apples as I wheel around to face him, preparing to dress him down at the impertinence of hitting on someone who's clearly in the middle of grocery shopping. But being so close to him takes my breath away completely. He's devastatingly handsome in the most endearing way I've ever seen. His hair is so lush I want to run my hands through it. I haven't felt this disarmed by anyone since . . . ever. He's smiling at me with an open face, eyes wide, like he's just asked if I want to go pick flowers.

'What?' is all I manage to squeak out, my anger dissolving faster than sugar in sweet tea.

His eyelashes flutter and his eyes get wider. He steps back from me like I'm a hot potato and drops the apple he's holding. He bends to pick it up and while his attention is elsewhere, I scurry to the cash register. There are so many conflicting thoughts pinging back and forth in my brain that I can't focus. He calls something after me softly, but I'm already walking towards the checkout and decide it's better to pretend I don't hear.

I'm still thinking about his comment when Amie asks me when I got back into town. I glance down at my breasts, they're perfectly average. Not too big, not too small. I guess I like them just fine. Not that *he* ever needs to know that.

Chapter Eight

Nick

Mrs. P. (*Oh, sweetheart, please just call me Betsy . . . but I suppose Mrs. P. certainly does have a ring to it*) doesn't send me off to find Mr. Parker this morning when we finish our crossword, instead, she asks if I don't mind running to Hal's General Store. I've been here less than one week and she's already sent me to the hardware store, the butchers, and the bakery. Wrangling their dusty blue pickup into submission has been the hardest part of my time here so far. The pedals are sticky, the wheel is practically fixed in place, and every pothole sends me flying towards the ceiling.

'I don't think he's here to run your errands,' Joe grumbled at dinner last night. Mrs. P just laughed. I was inclined to agree with Joe. Technically, I was *not* here to run her errands. But I'm a mamma's boy through and through, so when she asks I can't help but say yes.

'Is there a gym in town I can check out on my way?' I ask her. I've searched for an Equinox, Lifetime, Planet Fitness and came up empty handed—the local high school can't possibly be the only place to lift weights. I was hoping I had just missed something obvious, but she stares at me like I have three heads. I make a mental note to ask the cashier at the grocery store.

Only when I realize how incredibly tiny the local general store is (*not* grocery store, Mrs. P had corrected me), do I understand why Betsy thought it was so crazy that I asked about a Planet Fitness. But there's a charm to the size. I'm not inundated with choices like I am in the city. I have a silly smile on my face at how relaxing it is not to have to choose between thirteen kinds of canned tomatoes when I see the same woman I saw a few days ago. She's holding so many razors in her hands that I'm wondering how she isn't dropping them when she turns and sees me, my eyes locking with her electric blue ones. She has freckles across the bridge of her nose and her blonde hair is pulled away from her face haphazardly, with tendrils snaking out in every direction. My body is pulling me forward on its own accord, but I can't take even half a step forward before she bolts, ducking out of the aisle like the place was on fire. I pick up my basket. Isaac and Julian may have thought they came up with the world's worst punishment for losing fantasy football but if I end up meeting a girl . . . well . . . who's laughing now? It won't matter that they spent the first quarter of their final year doing capstones at private equity firms and start-up incubators while I ran errands and grimaced through lower back pain if I have a girl by my side while I do it. I shrug my shoulders and straighten up.

I do a perimeter lap of the store trying to spot her, which is incredibly easy seeing as the store seems to be all of twenty square feet. Nothing like the behemoth Whole Foods I usually shop at. I've arrived at the produce section when I see a flash of blonde hair in my peripherals.

She's by the apples—perfect.

I sidle up next to her, but her concentration doesn't waver. Her forearms are lean and tanned, her hands rough. She's picking up apples and putting them down like her life depends on finding the perfect sphere, the perfect weight-to-shine ratio.

I clear my throat. She glances at me, her bright blue eyes sparkling from underneath a fan of eyelashes and my breath hitches in my chest. She glances down so quickly that it catches me off guard. Usually, I have some game when it comes to girls, but for some reason today I flounder, saying the first thing that pops into my head.

'How do you like them apples?' I ask, only to immediately redden after the words come out of my mouth, not sure why I thought choosing an insult from *Good Will Hunting* was a good idea.

She looks up, a wave of an emotion I can't place crossing her face. 'What?' she asks, her eyebrows scrunching together.

I take a step back, fumbling, and I drop the apple I was holding. I bend to pick it up. 'Oh, the movie,' I try to explain, but she's already picked up her groceries and is making her way as fast as she can to the cash register, where she exchanges a few words with the strawberry blonde working the checkout. Her posture is relaxed now, they seem familiar with each other, like they've known each other forever. And, given what I know about this town, they probably have.

I follow meekly and I feign interest in the local honey display until she leaves.

I'm still thinking about how impossibly blue her eyes were when I roll into the Parkers' driveway and realize I completely forgot to ask the checkout lady about a gym.

Chapter Nine

Eloise

Aprons Mom Wears (ranked best to worst)

- Udderly Amazing Chef
- Out Standing in my Field
- Ewe Complete Me
- Silly Goose on the Loose
- Legen-dairy Cook
- It's Pasture Bedtime (honestly, points are only docked here because she always wears this one in the morning, so the pun makes no sense)

'You saw the new guy at Hal's today?' Mom asks before I'm all the way through the back door. I beat the dust of my shoes and set them aside. She's taking up the doorway of the back mudroom, the one that opens up to the sprawling kitchen and dining room combination. I take a deep breath, inhaling the smell of steak, before I turn to her.

'Mom, how on earth do you know that?' I ask in a no-nonsense tone.

'Amie,' she says, in a tone that clearly communicates I should have known the answer.

'How have you already talked to Amie?'

'We text.' She shrugs.

'You text? She's my age!'

'All right, fine. We've been texting about the fall festival. And she happened to mention that she saw you at the store today.'

'Hmm.' I squint at her. 'Well, yes, I did see the new guy.'

'So, what did you think?'

'He seemed . . . fine?' I make to head to the kitchen, but she won't budge.

'He's cute, right?'

'Mom—' I level my gaze at her '—you can't be serious. I don't even know his name.'

'Why not?' She finally pivots from the doorway, letting us both spill out into the kitchen, where she resumes her stance behind the stove. 'And his name is Nick, by the way.'

I glare at her.

'Farming can't be your whole life, Lou. Your longest relationship is with JJ at this point! A horse named after one of those . . .' she pauses, searching for the words '. . . those . . . those brothers!'

'JJ is great!' I retort. 'And look who's talking. Your whole life *is* farming.' I take a seat on my stool, the one in the middle, and gulp down a glass of water.

She puts her hands on her hips, resting them on the sides of her 'Silly Goose on the Loose' apron. 'All I'm saying is that I heard he was nice. And handsome. I want you to have some fun! You're too young to be stuck with us old people all the time.'

I roll my eyes. 'Mom, he commented on my boobs after talking to me for less than a minute.'

Dad steps into the kitchen only to promptly put his hands over his ears and leave. Mom bursts out laughing. 'No he did not. There is no way.'

'You weren't there!'

'What did he say?'

'"How do you like them apples,"' I say slowly, enunciating every word.

'You mean to tell me he commented on your shirt to you and you found that offensive? Why on earth did you think that was about your boobs?'

I look down.

'"Got apples" and "how do you like them apples" are completely different,' I say, but I feel the blush creeping up my cheeks all the same. I am wearing a shirt that reads 'Got Apples' in a clear riff on the 'Got Milk' slogan.

'What were you doing when he asked you?'

'Shopping for apples!' I throw my hands up, exasperated. 'Like you asked me to!'

'Figures.' Mom guffaws and the sound tinkles throughout the kitchen. 'Or maybe he was quoting that movie . . . HAL?' She yells towards the office, where Dad's footsteps had receded. 'WHAT'S THAT MOVIE WITH THE BOSTON KIDS?'

Dad mumble-yells something back that I can't decipher.

'That's it!' Mom says happily. '*Good Will Hunting*. That's the movie. I'm pretty sure it's a line from that.'

I roll my eyes. 'I think I know a line when I hear one.'

'Eloise, you know a lot about a lot of things, but you are hopeless when it comes to romance.'

'Whatever. It's not like I'm going to see him again.' I head towards the stairs. 'I'm going to shower,' I call over my shoulder, at the same times she asks me, 'What makes you say that?'

I freeze. 'Mom . . . what did you do?'

She laughs again, chortling this time. 'You better shower fast!' she calls. 'They'll be here in twenty!'

My hair is dripping, actually more like creating its own weather system, as I make my way downstairs. I wasn't able to blast it with a blow-dryer for more than two minutes before I heard a knock on the door. I catch a faint exchange of hellos, and I clock Dad's introductory grunt. I hurry to pull on jeans and a white T-shirt before I scamper down the stairs, rounding the corner too fast and crashing straight into a man who smells like cinnamon gum and laundry detergent, whose chest is a lot more solid than I was expecting, and who is taller than I thought, seeing as my forehead meets his body a solid two inches below his chin.

'Oof!' he exclaims, stepping back and rubbing his sternum.

Thankfully everyone else has headed down the hallway to the kitchen, so no one has witnessed me bulldozing the visitor.

'I'm so sorry.' I can feel the blush rising in my cheeks.

'You must be Eloise,' he says.

He's just as cute, —no, cuter—than I remember him. He stands straight and confidently. Something about him makes my mouth feel dry.

I shake the feeling off and find my voice enough to say, 'And you're Nick.'

He looks at me curiously, like he's trying to work out how the person who was so stand-offish in the store was somehow spawned by the sweet people who invited him over for dinner.

'Did I offend you today?' he asks me, but I don't realize he's about to speak until it's too late. I've already started, so I end up asking, 'So how long have you been in town?' at the same time he talks.

'No,' I answer. Avoiding the situation is infinitely easier than admitting I could have misinterpreted what he said.

'A few days.' He nods towards the kitchen. 'They've been great.' He smiles.

'I'm sure,' I murmur, my thoughts racing through my head. He's tall, strong, but I tell myself that by the looks of his slim-fit jeans and pressed button down, he's nothing I can't handle. Besides the fact that being in such close proximity to him makes my knees feel like they're turning into jelly.

'Does Nick need a drink?' Mom calls loudly from the kitchen, not so subtly telling me to stop lingering in the hallway.

'Come on.' I wave him after me, wondering under my breath what the hell I'm doing cavorting with Mrs. Parker's 'secret weapon' and how I can extricate myself from this situation as soon as possible.

Chapter Ten

Nick

Cal and Hazel are like younger versions of Joe and Betsy. Instead of granola grandparents, they're more like backwoods boomers... no, that's not right. Maybe they're more like barnyard boomers... but that doesn't feel right either. I'm trying to stay focused on my task at hand, focused on mining anything I come across for socials, but the apple girl, who now I know is Eloise, is very distracting.

I squeeze through a narrow doorway, following her into the kitchen, and as the room opens up around me, I wonder if that's something I can do a bit on—the 'character' of all the houses around here. The doorways of their farmhouse are arched, the furniture is wooden and cozy, and there's richly colored paintings dotting the walls. I walk past a multicolored cow and a still life of apples.

We pop out of the hallway into a large living and dining room, and I'm instantly hit with a familiar smell. *Mmmmm*, I think. Betsy's cooking is good, but it isn't *this* good. Cal or Hazel, whoever cooked, is on my mother's level.

I catch Eloise staring at me, one hand over her mouth, attempting to suppress a giggle that quickly explodes. She coughs to cover it, flushing red.

'What?' I whisper at her as Betsy clucks over the spread. There's fresh bread broken in a basket and butter softening on the table, a heaping salad in the middle. Candles dot the table and there are checkered napkins on each plate.

'Mmm,' Eloise says, her tone lilting, a spark in her eye as she mimics me.

I roll my eyes. 'I didn't think I said that out loud,' I whisper, 'that was an internal thought thing.'

'Is that something you do a lot? Voice your internal thoughts out loud?'

Her remark feels like a veiled reference to our grocery store run-in, which I don't know how to process, so instead I throw caution to the wind and take out my phone to take a picture of the table. If Eloise is already making fun of me, it's not like I can make it worse. Plus, I can *definitely* use this. I just might need to fib and say the butter is apple butter or something.

'So nice to have you, Nick,' Hazel says warmly.

'It looks delicious, Mrs. Anderson.'

'Oh, stop, this is nothing,' she demurs. 'I'm sure you had better food in San Francisco. Did Betsy tell you our son Linden lives there? Also, call me Hazel.'

'She did. Is he coming home over the summer at all? I'd love to meet him.' I swear I see Eloise's eyes roll into the back of her head. She pulls out a chair and plunks herself down at the table.

'I'm sure you've all put this together,' Betsy says as she eases herself into her chair, 'but Nick is our savior from Stanford and he's going to turn the whole farm around.'

Eloise's brows furrow. 'How is he going to do that?' she asks, pointedly looking at Betsy instead of me. Hazel's head snaps towards Eloise.

I clear my throat. 'I guess you'll have to stick around and find out.'

Cal laughs, the first time I've heard him say or do anything since I walked through the door. His smile transforms his whole face, and pretty soon the rest of the table is exchanging generous smiles. When Cal laughs, he looks youthful—and just like Eloise. They share the same light blue eyes, the same nose.

'Well, we certainly plan to stick around, dear,' says Betsy.

Eloise is the only one whose expression remains unchanged.

Chapter Eleven

Eloise

Recipes to Learn from Mom

- Chicken Cacciatore
- Apple Pie
- London Fog Concentrate
- Blackberry Cobbler
- Banana Pumpkin Muffins
- Carrot Cake
- Gnocchi Tomato Soup
- Spritz Cookies
- Sticky Toffee Pudding Cake
- Cheese Crackers

Mom outdid herself with the cacciatore, and still, dinner is slow torture as I try to piece together exactly what Nick is doing here. Mom is the perfect hostess, peppering Nick with questions about San Francisco even though I'm sure she knows the answers seeing as Linden has lived there longer than Nick has, which leaves me to stew in my own conflicting thoughts.

I try not to look at Nick, instead I steal glances at him from under my lashes, watching him appreciate the food. He eats slowly, closing his eyes briefly between bites.

'You used fennel,' he says after his fifth bite. Everyone else's plates are almost clean. Betsy's already gotten up for seconds. Nick, meanwhile, is taking his time. It takes a Herculean effort for me to keep my focus on dinner and not start to think about where else Nick may take his time or whether his mouth can appreciate other things like it clearly appreciates food.

Mom nods. Dad glances at her from under his eyebrows. 'You did?' He winces.

'I hate fennel,' Betsy announces. 'There's no fennel in here.'

Mom and Nick share a glance and they both smile like they're in on a secret. I squint at her. There is no need to be *this* nice to the person sent here to ruin everything I've planned. Even if it does seem like he knows his way around a kitchen.

Mom and Nick talk for so long the streaks across my plate from the chicken cacciatore are completely congealed. He is curious, asking her non-stop questions about Carnation. She's explained the dirt road get-through that shaves a half-hour off of getting to the nearest big box store, she's commiserated with him and Betsy about the butcher's husband taking over the shop while his wife takes maternity leave (the husband *cannot* cut a decent pork belly), and she's forced Nick to recount all his favorite recipes.

The fact that he knows his mom's recipes by heart makes mine do a little flutter. I ignore it. It must be the fennel coming back up.

Mom, on the other hand, is positively gleeful. She grabs a notepad and starts writing things down.

'I can't believe I've been subjecting you to my cooking!' Betsy wrings her hands in her lap. 'We need to get you in the kitchen.'

Nick laughs. 'Your cooking is wonderful,' he says, laying a gentle hand on her forearm in reassurance.

I feign boredom, not wanting Nick to realize I'm focused on his every word. Instead, I trace my fingers slowly over the curves of grain in the wood, remembering snippets of dinners growing up, of Linden complaining about his many responsibilities, of trying to be noticed by my parents while sitting next to him, the golden-haired golden boy. I play with my split ends, wondering how Linden got a vibrant blond color that looks like spun gold, while my hair looks like dishwater.

Mom's chair pushes back from the table with a creak against the floor, and I shoot up, hurriedly grabbing plates to clear.

'Oh, thank you, Lou,' she says sweetly, sitting back down and watching me clear the plates.

Nick tries to help me. 'I got it,' I say, but I clearly don't have it. I reach for another plate and wobble. Wordlessly, Nick jumps up and starts to clear. I hear him behind me as I make my way to the sink.

Slowly, I dip the plates into the suds and stack them in the dishwasher.

Nick clears his throat behind me. 'Do you prefer Lou?'

He's managed to pile the salad bowl, chicken cacciatore remnants, and bread basket all on top of one other, and I have to take them off his hands one by one, leaving us an inordinate amount of time to stand extremely close to each other.

'Eloise is fine,' I say curtly, trying to focus despite being able to smell him again, cinnamon and mint mixing with the Italian scents lingering in the kitchen. His biceps bulge with tension as he stays stock-still, arms at ninety degrees, holding the stack of dishes. I breathe a sigh of relief when I've successfully offloaded the platters without dropping anything. The last thing I need to do is draw any more attention to myself.

'Did you like dinner?' I murmur, offering a conversational olive branch as a thank you for his help. I keep my voice down so my parents can't hear.

'Delicious.' He smiles shyly at me and I glance at his teeth, perfectly square and white, gleaming against his skin. His lips are the color of pink terracotta or a late-blooming rusty dahlia.

He picks up a clean bowl as I set it on the counter next to me, grabs a faded green dishtowel from where it's hanging on the oven handle, and starts to dry. We repeat the process in silence until there's a stack of dry dishes next to the sink. As chatty as he was earlier, he seems just as comfortable with neither of us speaking.

'Guests aren't supposed to clean,' I say, more to myself than to him.

'Am I still a guest if I live across the street?'

I raise an eyebrow at him. 'Technically you're across the hill, and being here for two months is a lot different than living here.'

'Across the hill,' Nick repeats. 'That's got a nice ring to it.'

'Plus, even if you moved here, you would still be a guest.'

'It's nice here—' Nick shrugs '—maybe I will.'

'Something tells me you won't.' I shrug back, leaning against the counter. I glance out the window over the sink, the last dregs of sunlight dapple over the hills. The Parkers' farm gleams on the nearby hilltop.

Before I can second-guess it, I decide the best way to figure out exactly what Nick has planned will be to ask him directly. 'Want a beer?' I offer. 'We could take a quick walk out back?'

Nick's eyes meet mine and linger there, like he's trying to read the expression on my face. 'Sure,' he says. 'That sounds really nice.'

'Mom, I'm going to take Nick on a quick walk around the farm, OK?'

The conversation in the other room completely stills.

'OK!' she calls back. I can hear the smile in her voice. The low buzz of conversation quickly returns, and Betsy laughs, sharp and loud. Nick and I exchange a knowing glance as I hand him a beer. We duck outside into the dim light, stopping to hammer the caps off on the flat edge of a wooden post. We clink our bottles.

'To farming,' Nick says, an eager smile on his face.

Something about his simplicity, his eagerness to please, is extremely endearing. I return his smile. 'To farming,' I say.

We walk in silence along the dirt path to the closest barn. I steal glances at Nick, admiring the way his profile looks in the soft light. He glances back at me and our eyes meet.

'It's gorgeous out here,' Nick says.

'Yeah, it is,' I agree. 'I used to walk this path every night when I was little. My dad would take us through the farm to say goodnight to the animals. Goodnight geese, goodnight bees, goodnight chickens, goodnight JJ, goodnight birds.'

'Damn.' Nick shakes his head. 'Sounds like you were literally living in a storybook.' He pauses. 'Wait—' Nick stills. 'Who's JJ?'

'My horse.'

'That's so cool,' he says wistfully. 'Sounds like the life. Why JJ?'

'Um.' I squirm. 'I don't know, some singer I liked.'

'What singer is named JJ? Isn't her name JoJo?'

'Oh yeah, JoJo.'

Nick squints at me. 'Really? Then why not call her JoJo.'

I sigh. 'Because he's a he,' I admit.

'And you named him JoJo?' Nick is thoroughly confused now.

'Ugh,' I groan. 'Fine. You caught me. I named my horse Joe Jonas,' I mumble.

Nick bursts out laughing. It's easy, generous, like it wouldn't take much to bring him joy. 'No you didn't.'

'In my defense,' I say, crossing my arms, 'I was ten.'

He holds up his hands. 'That's fair. Can't say anyone has great taste at ten.'

I swallow back a smile. Nick is being generous. Many people have better taste at ten than to name their horse after Joe Jonas. 'Did you have good taste at ten?' I ask.

'I was voted most likely to smile in middle school, so . . . yes? I mean, I guess? I was smiling at everything, so . . .'

'Somehow I don't think much has changed since now and then.'

Nick smiles, catches himself, tries to frown and then smiles even bigger.

I start laughing, so distracted that I almost trip on the trail I've been walking since I could remember.

He reaches out and grabs my forearm to steady me. 'Thanks,' I murmur. His touch on my arm is enough to make my heart beat faster, and for a moment I have to keep my gaze trained on the ground as I try to relax. He releases his hand from my elbow, but I can still feel the heat of his fingerprints. A thought explodes in my mind with the nuance of a firecracker—I haven't felt like this in a long time. I decide it's the beer, that's what's making me so light-headed.

Nick clears his throat.

'So, what do you have planned while you're here?' I ask, breaking the silence. It's as good a time as any to find out what he's up to.

'I'm really just here to help out the Parkers.'

'Doing what exactly?'

'Well, as you've already guessed, I don't farm.'

I nod. We're about halfway to the North Barn, cresting over the gentle slope of a hill. I know Nick will hesitate before he does because I know this view by heart, and right in between our house and the barn there's a lookout over a swell of land about half a mile away that looks like a dragon's back. I've always felt like the land looks alive from here, undulating into the distance.

Like clockwork, his footsteps slow. 'Not too shabby,' he breathes.

We stop, perching our arms over the wooden fence that borders the path, and stand, staring into the distance. There's a choir of cicadas humming in the air around us.

After a quiet minute of enjoying the view, Nick continues explaining. 'I provide marketing and branding expertise. I'm in my last semester of graduate school at Stanford. I'll graduate early—in January. I'm getting a degree in Marketing and Brand Strategy.'

'So you won't actually be farming?'

'No.' Nick laughs in a self-deprecating way. 'But I'll have to learn about it to market it well. I'm not contracted hourly to the Parkers or anything. All I'm obligated to do is give them a business and marketing plan. The rest of my time I'm free to do what I want.'

'And this business plan is like a school test for you?'

'We call it a capstone, but I guess you could view it as a test.'

'So, if the Parkers' farm doesn't come back from bankruptcy, you'll fail your course?'

'Well, no.'

He's got to be kidding me. He's out here for nothing?

'So then what's your incentive?'

He hesitates. I can see it in the set of his shoulders, a little more tense, higher than usual, closer to his earlobes. 'I mean—' he shrugs '—I want to help them. Figured I would use what I've been learning to make a difference . . . I suppose I *could* fail. But it's unlikely.' When I don't say anything right away, he takes a deep breath. 'I appreciate a job well done.'

'Ah, so it's less about altruism and more about being a perfectionist.'

Nick tilts his head back, staring at the evening sky. The stars have just started to wink to life. 'Hmm, I'm not really a perfectionist. More like a successionist.'

'That sounds like the name for a person who loves the show *Succession*.'

Nick laughs. 'I like success. I like to succeed.' He smiles again, but this time it doesn't reach his eyes. 'I was that kid growing up who really wanted a gold star,' he admits.

'Ah, so a teacher's pet. I will note down gold stars as your love language.'

'It's a good thing I also like you busting my balls.'

'Well then, it's a great thing that's one of my love languages. So, this little stint on the Parkers' farm is just to practice charity before you go into the world and make a ton of money convincing people to buy things they don't need?' As soon as the words are out of my mouth,

I know they're too harsh, but my frustration is starting to feel like a living, breathing thing within me.

Nick recoils. 'Well, we can't all make a living the old-fashioned way. Even if we want to. Anyway, enough about me,' he says, his voice tight. 'How did you know they were bankrupt?' He swings his gaze to meet mine. His eyes are so intensely brown that my heart flutters.

'Everyone knows,' I say, trying to keep my cool. The truth is everyone kind of knows, but it's supposed to be unspoken. The tension in the air feels heavy. 'It's getting dark,' I say before turning on a heel and heading towards the house.

With every step I feel my frustration grow. *Why did he have to pick this town? His capstone project doesn't even matter! He already has a job! How dare he be so cute while doing it! Didn't he stop to think who he would be affecting? He can just leave afterwards, but some people have to stay. Some people have to look out for their family.*

I'm breathing hard when we get to the house, frustration simmering in my gut.

'Eloise.' Nick lays a hand on my arm as I reach out for the handle to the back door.

I spin around.

'I feel like I keep offending you,' he says. He glances at the ground, and I watch the way his long eyelashes flutter.

I feel his charm worming its way through my defenses. 'You're not,' I say. I duck inside, motioning for him to follow me through the mudroom to the kitchen. I'm embarrassed at the way I'm acting, knowing I probably seem like a child, and exhausted that I have to explain my feelings to someone I don't know.

'I did in the grocery store,' he murmurs.

'First of all, it's a general store. Second of all, you said something offensive.'

'I asked how you liked your apples!' Nick cries in exasperation. 'You sniffed, like, every single one.'

'No!' I exclaim, not ready to let him off the hook so easily. 'You asked me how I liked my . . .' I gesture at my chest. Nick pales. 'My boobs!' I finish loudly.

Nick's jaw goes slack with surprise. 'It's a movie quote!'

Fuck. Mom was definitely right. Why didn't I google it before he came over? 'I think "how do you like them apples" is slang for tits,' I say, doubling down as frankly as I can manage.

He chuckles, and his grin gets even wider. 'Clearly you need to watch *Good Will Hunting*. And you do realize what you were wearing, right?'

'Not the point,' I huff.

'You picked up and smelled every single apple. You were wearing bright red shoes and an apple-emblazoned T-shirt. I am here to learn about apple farming. I thought it was the perfect reference. I'm a nice guy, I swear.' He holds his hands up.

I raise an eyebrow at him.

'You just tell me when you want to come over and watch *Good Will Hunting*, OK? It's the least I can do to repay you for taking me for a walk.'

'You don't need to repay me,' I manage to say despite my insides screaming *GO WATCH THE DAMN MOVIE, ELOISE.*

Nick's smile gets bigger and bigger, like he can't contain his grin anymore. He bursts into laughter, his entire body shaking with it.

I can't help but start to laugh too. I laugh so hard I start to cry. Nick is wheezing next to me, slapping his hand on the kitchen counter. 'You thought I asked about your boobs,' he says, in between breaths. 'Me!'

Chapter Twelve

Nick

WEEK TWO

I've hardy sat down the next morning when Mrs. Parker asks, 'Nick, what's a four-letter summer?' She's sitting across from me at the kitchen table, morning sun streaming in from the window behind the sink. 'And did your friends ever answer about visiting?'

'They would love to come,' I tell her. Upon my arrival, Mrs. Parker made one thing clear—U-Pick weekend (the first weekend the farm will have visitors) is a huge deal. In fact, she insisted I invite my friends up to the farm. Julian and Isaac both jumped at the chance; even though Isaac grumbled about having to reschedule a weekend tournament, he booked his flights in under fifteen minutes. Ever since he's been texting me things like 'How goes it from where the other half lives?' and 'Is the Wi-Fi good enough to stream the Giants game?'

I tap my index finger to my chin. 'OK, Mrs. Parker . . . is the four-letter summer a seasonal clue? Something to do with fruits or veggies?'

'Betsy,' she corrects me. She gets up and pours me a coffee, setting down a plate of scrambled eggs and toast despite my protests that she doesn't have to cook every meal for me. 'Pear summer? No, that doesn't make sense,' she mutters to herself. 'Farm summer? Donna Summer! That's it! Oh wait, that's five letters . . .'

When I come back downstairs changed and ready for the day, Betsy is still working away at her crossword. 'Nick, it starts with a B,' she says as I pull on my work boots. 'Baby summer? This makes no sense.'

'Oh!' I start to laugh having finally realized the clue. 'It's BRAT summer, Mrs. P.'

'Brat? Like a bratwurst?'

'Um.' I try to swallow my laughter. 'Kind of. Spelled like a bratty kid.'

'Hmmm.' She turns back towards her crossword. 'Brat summer . . .'

'It's from a music album,' I try to explain, but she's already absorbed with the next clue, a soft smile on her face.

While I am better at guessing crossword answers than I gave myself credit for, everything else is much worse than I thought. Not that I've told Isaac or Julian that.

Isaac: Guys, they're taking our cohort to Nobu this Thursday for lunch.

Julian: Stop bragging.

Julian: But they're taking us to a Giants game. In the Owner's suite.

Isaac: NO WAY.

Me: Have fun eating previously frozen stadium mystery meat. I'll just be here.

I send a selfie of me with Daisy from the day before, her bubblegum-pink snout pointed at the camera.

Julian: That pig looks like it's AI-generated.

Julian: Damn, I can't wait to visit in September.

Isaac: LOL I can't believe we're at desks while you're in a literal pigsty. Odds you fall in love with a hot farm chick like that girl from that movie.

Me: Isaac, you don't need to bring up *THE LONGEST RIDE* every day. We know it's your favorite.

Mrs. Parker, Betsy, Mrs. P., is delightful. I've been at the house for under two weeks, but we've fallen into an easy pattern—every morning I help her with the crossword. When I throw out a suggestion that sticks, she acts like I won the Olympics. The house is charming and quirky, but I'm used to old spaces with 'character' as my mom likes to call it, so I don't mind that the shower blips with ice water every now and then and that when the heaters crank on at night it sounds like there is a cat stuck in the walls. I quite like Mrs. Parker's crochet coasters, which seem to dot every surface.

I'm in one of their daughter's old rooms and there's still Nancy Drew books on the bookshelf and NSYNC posters on the wall. It feels like a time machine. As much as I would prefer not to wake up and immediately be confronted with historic boy bands, the bed is comfortable and the room is clean, and I've been so exhausted by the time I reach my bed at night that I'm asleep before my head hits the pillow. I'm only a little over a week in but I'm wondering if my mom was right, if the fresh air will be good for my insomnia.

After last week, I think my time trailing Mr. Parker around the farm is up. I have no idea where the man finds his energy. I start after him (by the grace of God, Mrs. Parker keeps me around until the crossword is finished) and I'm practically begging to go home by the time the sun is setting. Mr. Parker thoughtfully checks on every tree we pass. He tries to explain to me what he's looking for, but a lot of it goes over my head.

'Which pest is that again?' I find myself asking, when we've passed the third tree with tiny holes in its leaves.

'Remind me the plan to irrigate this?' When we pass a row that's especially dry.

'The workers come on which day?' When Mr. Parker laments again how much things will cost.

Even though I haven't been able to get them a printout of my new and improved marketing plan, Mr. Parker and I did discuss the financials a few days ago. It was clear he did not expect me to follow him around like a Labrador all summer. I think he was starting to wonder what the point was in teaching *me* about farming when I was supposed to be teaching *him* about business. When he finally beckoned me into his office to show me the books, I saw the glance he snuck at his wife. The shame on his face made my heart crack. I've seen the same look on my mom's face when she couldn't pay for the school field trip or afford to get me the new pair of shoes I wanted.

'No matter what it is, it's fixable,' I lied through my teeth. 'I'm here for a reason. And I think we both know it's not to help with the farming.'

That got a chuckle out of Mr. Parker. When he handed me the bucket of pig feed on the first day, I didn't pour it out fast enough and Daisy headbutted me so hard I fell down. He laughed for about an hour after that.

The figures on his spreadsheets matched up exactly with what he'd told me in the car and aligned with the brief I'd got from my professor. The farm is so low on cash flow that they will have to foreclose. The Parkers will be OK—their land is worth a lot of money, they just can't afford to keep it. I'm comforted that no matter what happens they'll be all right, but I can tell by the anxious looks they've been exchanging that selling the land is the last thing they want to do.

I walked them through how I'll start to capture content, videotaping Mr. Parker around the farm and Mrs. Parker at home, and how I hoped that will drive up sales of their non-perishable products.

'The only non-perishable we have is apple butter,' Mrs. Parker told me.

'That works just fine,' I replied, although I was beginning to feel like things were in fact not fine. 'Everybody loves old people on the internet,' I told them. 'You will be universal grandparents before you know it.'

I'm replaying that conversation in my head as I watch Betsy move from her crossword to her crotchet. It's only nine in the morning and she's already fulfilling her grandparent duties to a T. Maybe my plan will work after all.

'I'm headed to the Andersons',' I tell Mr. Parker. 'Some research on the competition is in order.'

Mrs. P. laughs. 'Is that what the kids are calling it these days?'

'Do you realize that you're acting like you don't like me or is your personality just naturally stand-offish?'

I know enough about Eloise's personality to know that even though she's intimidating when she talks about the farm, and she certainly likes to give me a hard time, she's not actually stand-offish—the Parkers, for one, describe her as 'sweet as sugar' and 'as nice as pie'. I saw her greet the cashier at Hal's General Store with a warmth I never see in the city; I saw her 'I've-got-this' hand her dad's shoulder when he tried to get up and help with the dishes last night; I saw her eyes light up when she told me about JJ. And in the little amount of time I've been with her so far, I've seen her handle her apple trees with a level of care usually reserved for newborn babies.

Eloise stutters for a good minute before straightening up to her full height and crossing her arms across her chest. Her honey-colored hair is pulled back into twin braids today and is frizzing up around her face in a golden halo, framing her impossibly blue eyes. I press my lips together, trying not to laugh at her indignation. If she only knew how often my mother does this to me, asking me seemingly innocent questions in such a passive-aggressive manner that it can only be explained as plain aggressive.

She stares at me some more, squinting into the sun. It's 10 a.m., and I've only been at the Andersons' farm for twenty minutes, most of which I've spent tailing Eloise trying to ask her questions about life on the farm. My education with Mr. Parker can only go so far when he mostly responds in grunts of acknowledgment. Now that the hired hands are about to arrive, he's busy preparing their tasks. I feel like I'm bothering him, but I also need more information if I want to be able to really tell the story on socials. Therein lies my competitive research—Eloise.

The divot between her eyebrows deepens. 'What in God's name kind of question is that?' she finally spits out.

My concentration breaks and I start to laugh. 'I'm just giving you a hard time.'

She's relieved I wasn't serious, I can tell by the way her face immediately relaxes, her cheeks rounding out into a smile. 'Giving me a hard time while asking for favors?' She gives me a pointed look.

'I was hoping for more of an exchanging of favors.'

'I'm listening.' She's wearing jeans, farm boots, and a black T-shirt that bears zigzags of dust marks. She glances at my tennis shoes. They used to be white. After a week they're already a dusty brown. I wonder how long until they're fully earth-colored.

'Well, you could just explain to me how to help you. And then the little productivity you lose by talking to me won't matter.'

Eloise surveys her surroundings. She's standing in the middle of a row of trees holding what looks to be a giant pair of scissors. She sighs, her shoulders loosening down her back. She's strong, but sexy, her collarbones protruding ever so slightly from the collar of her shirt. She wipes the sweat off of her brow with the back of her hand.

'I guess it doesn't seem like you're going anywhere so I might as well put you to work.' She hands me the giant scissors. 'I also wouldn't hate the company.' Her lips quirk up into a half-smile.

I grab them. 'Oof,' I say, the weight pulling down on my forearm unexpectedly. 'These are heavy.'

She raises her eyebrows at me in a challenge. 'And?'

Grinning, I just follow her as she walks down the rut in between neatly ordered trees. She comes to a stop in front of a small one, barely any small apples on the branches. If I squint through the sparse smattering of leaves, I can barely see the Parkers' house. Cal is off somewhere nearby doing the same thing Eloise is doing. Hacking trees with giant scissors, if appearances are any indication.

Eagerly, I follow her lead and start plucking tiny apples from the tree. She explains hand-thinning to me methodically.

'First, you pluck off any clearly damaged or misshapen fruits,' she instructs. 'Next, we give each remaining apple room to grow.' She steps back from the tree, surveying it. 'You need to leave about four to five inches between each apple, and you only want one apple on each spur.'

'Spur?'

'This little woody guy.' She grabs at a branch and shows me a thick stem. 'They can only support one apple each.'

I stare at the tree with her. 'Is this like some sort of messed-up Sudoku puzzle? How do you manage to make sure every apple has enough space while taking away the bad ones while making sure it's only one apple to one stem.'

Eloise chuckles and the thought that I've just said something to make her laugh fills me with excited energy. She's like a breath of fresh air. 'It'll get easier.' She shrugs. 'But yeah, hand-thinning sucks.'

As we work, my finishing one tree in the time it takes Eloise to do three, she tells me that hand-thinning happens around the second week of August every year. It's her least favorite part of the harvest cycle because it is tedious and exhausting.

I completely understand why hand-thinning is exhausting. In fact, I can't imagine anything *more* exhausting. I can't take it anymore. I finally put down the scissors I've been holding. My forearms are screaming at me. 'What are these for?' I ask, confused as to why we haven't used them since I got here and yet it seems to be important to lug them around.

'Pruning emergencies.' Eloise shrugs.

'So, no one has to be carrying them around?' I watch Eloise's face as she fights back a smile.

'No one has to carry them around,' she admits, 'we usually leave them at the end of the row.'

I rub my shoulders. 'Damnit, Eloise,' I mutter. 'And to think I was starting to like you!'

She laughs, bright and clear. 'I'm sorry! It wasn't very nice of me.' A shadow of contrition passes over her face. 'Consider it farm hazing. And you passed.'

'I'm not believing anything you say anymore.' I shake my head at her.

'Fine by me,' she says, 'but things were just about to get interesting.'

I roll my eyes. When I look back at her, she's spinning a small golden apple gently in her hands. 'Even though sometimes I hate the work, I love the way the orchard looks when the first apples have just begun to appear. When I was little, I thought it was magic. Their colors are so mellow early in the season that I used to think they were tiny little orbs guiding fairies home.'

I pull out my notebook and frantically try to capture what she just said.

'*That's* what you write down? That is the least useful thing I've said so far.' She shakes her head. 'Business people are so confusing.'

But despite the gentle teasing, Eloise is more helpful in two hours than Mr. Parker has been since I arrived. She's patient and clear when she explains things to me, like the never-ending cycle of weeding, mulching, pruning, and watering. She walks me through the science of dirt, how regenerative agriculture can help build back up farms that have depleted the natural biodiversity of their soils. She's so excited to tell me about cover crops and contour farming that I can't get a word in edgewise.

'RA—' she stops short '—regenerative agriculture,' she corrects herself, 'is what I want to start doing.' She sighs, planting her hands on her hips and gazing out at the fields. I think I see a wrinkle of worry appear between her eyes, but she gets right back to work after a deep breath.

It's not just her words that don't stop, she also never stops for a break. I've sweat right through my shirt, my shoulders are aching from reaching for apples, my lower back is groaning at me for bending down so much, and my skin feels sticky from fruit.

'LUNCH!' Cal calls for Eloise loudly, his voice ringing out over the trees.

'Thank God. I'm starving.' She stands up, wiping her hands on the front of her jeans. She wipes her forehead with the bottom of her shirt and I catch a glimpse of the smooth skin of her belly. I can see her abs. *Damn.*

'What?' she asks, self-consciously pulling her shirt back down across her stomach. But her gaze lingers on my face for a second longer than it has to, and I swear she can feel it too, the magnetic energy pulling us closer to each other.

'Nothing.'

She gives me a suspicious look. 'I still don't understand why you need all this information. Not to mention, you're kind of helping out the wrong farm.'

I raise an eyebrow. 'Look, I am not obligated to give the Parkers anything but the plan, which you already know. You think that what is going to save the Parkers is an extra farmhand? What's going to really help them is marketing. Plus, Mr. P. wasn't exactly loving my questions.'

'So what is this grand marketing plan of yours? We could certainly use an improvement on that front.'

'TikTok.'

She bursts out laughing, startling a nearby swallow from a tree, before she claps her hand over her mouth. 'You're serious?'

I nod, meeting her gaze. People underestimate social media all the time. 'Yep. All I need to do is capitalize on the buying local trends and capture momentum.'

'Mhmm,' Eloise says, but there's a glint in her eye. I can't tell whether she's happy or upset. I felt like that a lot with her today, like I *really* want to know what she's thinking, but I have absolutely no idea.

'It'll work,' I say with as much confidence as I can muster. 'I just need some content to start posting. You'll see.'

'You know nature isn't like social media. You can't hack the algorithm here.' She spreads one arm out in a wide, sweeping gesture. 'It's wild.'

'You can manifest good outcomes with optimism,' I counter.

Her lips press together in a tight line. 'I think the struggling farmers out here would beg to differ.' She pauses, gesturing towards her house. 'I should probably go grab lunch, do you—?'

'I'll eat at the Parkers',' I cut in, not wanting to overstep. 'Thanks for letting me tag along this morning.' I step back to let her pass and as I do I step on a line of sprinklers, tripping over it and dislodging it in the process. Water erupts from the broken sprinkler line, spraying everywhere. Eloise shrieks and I scream too, both of us lunging for, and missing, the sprinkler head. The pressure of the water casts the hose around chaotically, soaking Eloise and I every couple of seconds as it thrashes around. By the time she's able to grab it, we're both dripping wet, dust streaking in rivulets down our faces.

I glance up at Eloise, panting, worried she'll be angry. She seems to care so much about keeping things at the farm in line. 'I'm so sorry,' I pant out. When she looks up and sees my wide-eyed gaze, she frowns. Then, before I can even clock it, she's whipped out the hose and is pointing it at me, completely soaking me head to toe, and cackling manically as she does it.

I shriek like a little kid as the water blasts through my hair and I lunge at her, our arms entangling as we each try to gain control of the hose. Suddenly our faces are so close I can see droplets clinging to her eyelashes. I wipe a drop of water off her cheek, my thumb stroking her constellation of freckles. We both still. Her face is upturned towards me, and I feel her hips give into mine. I tilt my face towards her, my gaze lingering on her Cupid's bow, her perfect, upturned lips.

'LOU!' I hear Cal's yell cut across the fields. 'Your mom's making fried green tomatoes! You better hurry or I'll eat them all!'

We break apart, breathing heavy, and Eloise lets the hose drop to her side, not meeting my gaze. 'I guess I better get this reattached,' she says, bending down and reconnecting the hose.

I feel like I've lost her, without her looking at me it's like the sun's been hidden behind clouds. 'Hey, how do you feel about me coming by tomorrow? I promise I won't mess up the sprinklers system again.'

Eloise looks up at me with a glint in her eye. She smiles softly. 'I guess that'd be OK,' she says. 'Our water fight was hands down the best part of my morning . . .' She pauses. 'But before you go thinking you got a gold star, remember it was either our water fight or hand-thinning.'

And with that, she heads towards her house, leaving me staring at her retreating figure. Even with the sun beating down on her shoulders, she carries herself with her head held high, shoulders square. She fits in perfectly with her surroundings, the heat of the bright blue sky contrasting with her black shirt. Her blonde hair gleaming in the sun. I like late summer here, the way the lush green seems to dry out just a bit, everything parched in the sun, suspended in a state of waiting for fall to really kick in, for the promise of cooler weather and longer nights. The Parkers keep saying fall is just around the corner, but it's so hot today I can't see how they'll be right.

Like magic, I've forgotten all about my back pain and my sore shoulders. I'm filled with so much energy it's like I haven't worked at all. Tomorrow can't come soon enough.

Chapter Thirteen

Eloise

What I Would Do if I Could Do Anything*

- Work in an agricultural research lab
- Hang out with Lily in New York City
- Backpack across Asia (Linden swears it changed his life)
- Run the Anderson Family Apple Farm Operation
- Open up my own regenerative farming consultancy

*Topic by Nick Russo

One of my teeth drops into my palm. It's not bloody, instead it's as white as snow, the roots perfectly molded, like it got plucked from a pair of dentures. But despite its pretty appearance, it makes me panic. I feel with my tongue for the hole in my mouth where it used to be, and in doing so I pop out another tooth.

I'm in my bedroom but it feels vaguely unfamiliar. I realize why as I'm looking for the tooth that fell out of my mouth. The rug I had all throughout middle school is on the floor. It's a purple shag rug and my tooth has been lost to its tentacle-like depths. What am I going to do if I can't find my tooth?

'Lou!' I hear someone say.

I open my mouth to ask them for help, but no sound comes out.

'Lou!' they say again.

I have the moment where I realize I'm dreaming, I can feel myself detaching from my childhood bedroom, and I run towards whatever edge of my brain is pulling away. I don't want to be in this dream anymore. I want my teeth.

'LOU!' Mom yells louder. 'Wake up! You have a visitor!'

Damnit.

I pull my hair into a messy bun and throw on a T-shirt and jeans as fast as I can, patting color into my cheeks as I brush my teeth. It's 7.30 on a Sunday. Whoever is here, I'm going to kill them.

Weekends are an odd beast when you live on a farm. There's always more than enough work to go around, and the operating hours other businesses live by don't apply. Sometimes I wonder if that's why farmers stay religious. If they didn't have a mandated day of rest, they would never take a break. We stopped going to church when I was six because Linden lost control of his bladder and peed during the sermon and Mom never had enough courage to return. Linden blames it on the Red Bull-chugging competition his friends made him do beforehand. Story goes that every single one of those boys was hopping from one foot to the other for the entire sixty minutes. Only after it was over did the other boys notice Linden had stopped hopping.

He still blushes when that story comes up. I don't remember it; I was too young. But I do remember that we used to get donuts after church as our treat for dressing up and sitting still. There's a bakery about twenty minutes away, a mom-and-pop shop that's been open as long as my parents can remember. They make the *best* apple fritters come apple season, and every other month of the year they sell out of their sticky cinnamon buns before noon. I make a mental note to drive out there and pick up some goodies soon. I always love seeing the baker, Mr. Bernard. He tells a different joke every time I'm there and never fails to make me laugh.

But seeing as Sundays are the holy grail of rest, I have no idea who is here to wake me up before eight in the morning. It could be Lily's mom, she usually stops by when she knows I'm home (she has no social awareness, something Lily endlessly makes fun of her for), and we catch up and send a selfie to Lily.

I scamper down the stairs praying someone has made coffee. Sunlight streams into the windows. The kitchen smells faintly like pumpkin, and I wonder if Mom has started making muffins. My mouth waters. Reflexively, I poke my tongue around to make sure I have all my teeth.

'He's on the front porch,' she says with a knowing smile, inclining her head to our wide front door.

'He?' I ask, as I turn and squint out the window.

Nick is sitting on the front step staring out onto the horizon, a to-go coffee cup at his side.

I turn back to Mom. 'What is he doing here? Did you invite him?' I expect to find her smirking, but she only shrugs.

'Beats me.'

'Morning,' I say softly, as I ease myself out onto the front porch. I immediately wish I had a sweatshirt. There's a bite of chill in the air signifying fall is only weeks away.

'Morning.' Nick smiles at me and hands me the coffee cup that was sitting next to him. He looks so at ease on my front porch that my breath catches in my chest.

'Lavender latte,' Nick tells me.

'You remembered!' I exclaim.

Nick laughs. 'I don't know whether to be insulted or pleased that you're so happy I remember something you told me twelve hours ago.'

I roll my eyes at him and take a sip. Warmth blooms in my insides despite goosebumps freckling my arms. 'Wow, that's good. I had terrible dreams last night.' I set the coffee down beside me. 'I needed this.'

'I'm sorry,' Nick says, the touch of tenderness in his voice so earnest I feel my insides turn to goo. 'What about?'

'Nothing glamorous,' I demur, not wanting to paint a picture of myself as toothless. Not exactly the sexy vibe I'm going for. Not that I've been able to make Nick see me as anything but a sweaty farmhand. Plus, it's definitely an anxiety dream, and one I'll most likely have again as I wait for the verdict on the loan. The way this summer plays out will determine my whole life. And it's becoming a bigger and bigger thing to keep from Nick as we spend more time together.

'I usually don't sleep well either,' he confesses.

'But?'

'I've been sleeping better since I got out here. It's the air, I think . . .'

'Maybe it's the hard work too,' I suggest, knowing from experience how much better I sleep when I'm bone-tired after a day in the field than the days I've spent sitting behind a desk. I excuse myself to grab a blanket, stealing one off the couch and wrapping it around my shoulders before coming back outside.

'Much better,' Nick says, registering my outfit addition with approval. 'It's cold out here in the mornings now.'

'Now?' I tease. 'You've only been here, like, two weeks!'

'Almost three,' he reminds me.

I can't believe Nick's only been here three weeks. His presence has started to feel so *normal* that I hardly register it anymore, the last thing I thought would happen after our disastrous first meeting. At first I was so annoyed by him, didn't understand how he had any right to be here. But his curiosity, the way he works all day without asking for a break, how every morning he's *happy*—its growing on me. *And* he's handsome. I was doomed from the start, a fact that definitely hasn't escaped Mom, who thinks it's hilarious that Mrs. Parker's secret weapon is spending more time with me than he is doing anything useful. She's even started to make comments about how I must be sabotaging him somehow.

Every day Nick and I have done slow laps around the farm as we work. While we navigate the dusty tracks of roads that are littered with potholes, Nick asks about everything that has to do with regenerative agriculture, he even tries to follow the really science-y stuff, but he asks about trivial stuff too, like how often I get stung by bees (roughly once a year) and what my favorite thing is to make with apples (pie). He asks Mom about recipes for apple cider. He asks Dad how often he needs to repair the tractors. We pop our heads into Central and West Barns.

He usually leaves when I head in for lunch. I'm not sure what he's doing in the afternoon, working on his marketing plan, I guess. I haven't told him how crazy I think his TikTok idea is. Social media won't repair the Parkers' soil, but at the end of the day, that's what I want—the Parkers' farm needs to fail. But Nick seems so eager and earnest I can't bear to tell him how much I think his plan sucks. Plus, if I did that then he wouldn't be sharing useful tidbits with me like how to use hashtags and what times to post. Instead, I talk him through what apple blossoms smell like and what it feels like when the bees arrive to pollenate the trees.

He clears his throat, bringing me back to the present moment—the two of us on the front porch, the swallows waking up the rolling hills with their cheerful songs.

'Did I wake you?' he asks, breaking the silence. 'Everyone who lives here is up so early all the time. I feel like I'm always the last one awake.'

'No.' The lie rolls off my tongue. I register the new impulse—the need for me to protect Nick's feelings—with mild surprise. 'We're always awake. We're farmers.' A bird chirps happily in the distance.

'That's what Betsy said!' he exclaims happily. 'Anyway, I was hoping we could talk about the start of the season again. I'm just trying to conceptualize the story from the beginning.'

'Hmm,' I say. I know I shouldn't help him at all, especially when the last thing I want is for him to succeed. But I can't help myself when it comes to him. I can see him grinning in my peripheral vision. He has a great smile. At least that's what Mom keeps saying. I haven't figured out if she keeps bringing him up to distract me from wanting to talk about the potential sale of the farm or what, but either way I replace every nice thing she says about him in my head with *Nick is moving back to San Francisco* or *Nick is helping the PARKERS*, just so I don't lose my focus over something so fleeting.

I keep my gaze focused on the driveway, letting my eyes dance over the curve of the road. 'March is when trees are planted.'

Nick starts to scribble in his notepad.

'But technically we start prepping before March . . .'

Nick strikes through what he just wrote down.

'Let's call it November.'

'November it is.' Nick grins.

I have a crick in my neck by the time I stand up. It's past ten in the morning, and Nick and I have been talking for hours.

He glances at his notepad, which is full of scribbled notes.

'So next week,' he confirms with me one more time, 'the farms will be in full swing?'

'Yep,' I sigh, 'our seasonal workers are about to arrive, and that's when things get really crazy.'

'Thanks, Eloise.' Nick wipes his palms across the front of his jeans. 'This was really helpful.'

'Hey, the coffee was thanks enough,' I tell him.

There's a tiny piece of dust caught on one of his impossibly long lashes and my gaze lingers on it. Seconds pass before we both realize, at the same time, that we've just been staring at each other. I wonder if there's dust on my eyelashes too.

'Well.' Nick glances towards the driveway. 'I better get going.'

My heart tugs. Sunday suddenly stretches ahead of me—empty. I don't want him to go. 'Actually,' I say, before I lose my nerve, 'I was just about to head to let JJ out. Do you want to come?'

'You mean I get to meet Joe Jonas?' Nick asks, incredulous.

I swat his arm. 'We do not use his full name. JJ only . . . You also don't have to come if you have—' I gesture at his notepad '—you know, like, things to do.'

'Are you kidding?' Nick asks happily. 'Lead the way! Get it, like don't horses go on leads or whatever.'

I laugh. 'I'm surprised you knew that.'

Nick stills as soon as we step into North Barn. I hear JJ paw at the floor in his stall. 'He's excited to meet you,' I tell Nick.

When JJ sticks his head out of his stall, nuzzling at my cheek, Nick's jaw drops open.

'Can I?' He reaches his hand towards his neck.

'Of course,' I say, mirroring his motions on the other side, both of us stroking JJ's coat.

'He's beautiful,' Nick breathes.

JJ nickers. 'He likes you,' I say, feeling a rush of pleasure in my chest. 'Here.' I hand Nick an unripe apple. 'He loves these.'

'Really?' Nick looks at me with so much gratitude in his eyes that I feel like I'm seeing what he was like as a little kid, and my heart squeezes.

'Really. Just hold it up to his mouth.'

JJ chomps away happily as we lead him to the paddock and let him run around.

'How long have you had him?' Nick asks, his gaze tracking JJ as he canters about.

'Almost fifteen years . . . my parents gave him to me in a last-ditch attempt to cure my loneliness. Linden had just hit puberty and decided I wasn't a cool sidekick anymore.' I laugh. 'The irony of it was that right after I got JJ, I met Lily, and—' I shrug '—well, you know how that ended.'

Nick grins. 'By the frequency with which she calls you, I sure do know how that ended.'

I smile, but watching JJ my smile quickly falls. 'He got hurt a few years ago,' I explain to Nick. 'We really shouldn't be keeping him here—he's lonely. But I can't seem to let him go.' Just then, he stops prancing and comes up to where we are on the fence.

'I see why,' Nick says, reaching out to pet him.

'It's no excuse,' I admit. 'It's on my list of things to do.'

'Ah yes, Eloise and her infamous lists.' Nick elbows me gently.

'Who told you about those?'

Nick's eyebrows knit together as he looks at me. 'You? You reference a list like every day. Yesterday I'm pretty sure it was something about the places you still needed to clean.'

I roll my eyes, but I'm secretly pleased that Nick pays so much attention to what I say.

After making sure JJ will be happy in his paddock for a few hours, we walk back to the path that joins our two houses.

'What would you do if you could do anything?' Nick asks me. We're walking close, our shoulders bumping every now and then, and each time I want to make touching him last longer. I wish our hands would start brushing against each other too.

'Work in a lab,' I answer, 'like an agricultural research lab.'

'No way, really?'

'Really. What's so surprising about that?'

Nick laughs. 'I don't know, I thought you'd say you would travel or, like, open a café or a plant store or a bookshop . . . something more . . . aspirational?'

I can't help but laugh at his confused expression, the little divot that appears between his eyebrows when he furrows them. I shrug. 'I worked in a lab this summer and really loved it.'

'Why'd you stop?'

I gesture at the hills around us, the rows and rows of perfectly spaced apple trees. 'This won't take care of itself.'

'Isn't that why you hire seasonal workers?'

'Well, my parents need me too,' I remind him.

'You need you also,' Nick tells me. 'If working in a lab is putting your dream first, maybe you do that for a couple years and then come back if you still want to. Your parents will be fine.'

He says it so casually, *your parents will be fine*, but I can still feel my face fall. 'I think they need me here,' I say, but my voice catches, betraying my emotion.

Nick's fingertips graze my forearm as he reaches for me. 'Oh, Eloise, I didn't mean it like that. I'm sure that's true.'

'You can call me Lou, you know. You don't have to call me Eloise.' I switch subjects, not wanting to have to face Nick's pity.

Nick's nose wrinkles. 'Really?'

'What? My brother gave me the nickname ages ago. He couldn't say Eloise when I was born so instead he called me "Ee-lou" and over the years it morphed into

Lou.' I pause. 'You think it's weird because it's usually a guy's name?'

'No!' he exclaims, his face flushing red.

Nick blushes, I think, *another thing to add to the Things I Like About Nick list.*

'Well . . . yes. I have an uncle, Luigi. We call him Lou.'

'Luigi?' I laugh. 'Wow, you are so much more Italian than I thought.'

'Is that a bad thing?' Nick asks, batting his eyes at me.

God, no. No, it really isn't. Nick is moving! I remind myself, trying to fend off the butterflies that wage a war in my stomach every time Nick looks at me. 'I think you can deal with two Lou's in your life. I can't bear that much similarity to your uncle.'

'You'd be surprised.' Nick waggles his eyebrows.

'Isn't Nick a nickname?'

Nick shakes his head. 'No.'

'Do you have a nickname?'

Another shake. 'No.'

'We can fix that,' I assure him. 'Give me a day to think on it.'

Nick beams. 'I'd like that,' he says, and pauses at the fork in the path. He turns back to me, holding a hand over his eyes to block the sun. 'But I'll keep Eloise if it's all the same to you.'

I feel the same tug in my heart at the prospect of him leaving as I did earlier, but I can tell by how high the sun is in the sky that I'm getting a very late start to my day. I promised Lily I would call her and I promised Mom I would help her in the garden this afternoon. But I'm not ready to tell Nick goodbye. 'I still don't understand what you'll do with all this information . . . you know . . . in October . . . when you leave here to never return.'

'Never say never.' Nick winks.

There it is again—that swoop in my stomach when he jokes that he won't leave.

'Seriously,' Nick says, oblivious to my thoughts, 'thank you.' He places a hand on my forearm as he says it, and a jolt of electricity runs up my spine.

'Anytime,' I squeak out. I smell cinnamon and mint and *damn*, he looks even better up close. I bite my lip.

Nick inhales, his hand lingering on my forearm. A bird stirs in a nearby tree and we both start. 'So, I'll see you soon then?'

'Soon,' I say.

'Your mom invited me to the big dinner on Tuesday.'

'Of course she did.'

He pauses. 'You don't want me to come?'

'No. I'd like it if you came.'

He smiles. I turn to head inside before my telltale blush rises to my cheeks.

Evan: How is our budding romance coming along? Get it? BUDDING *laugh-cry emoji*

Shari: The sexy farmer of my dreams. I cannot WAIT until you get to meet him. Do you think he dresses like Luke from *Gilmore Girls* or more like the cowboy from that Nicholas Sparks movie?

Evan: Hmmm, probably neither because Luke is literally a diner owner and the cowboy is a... cowboy. You need to be thinking FARMER.

Shari: Got it, so overalls and a piece of wheat between his teeth?

Evan: Exactly. The wheat is perfect for Lou. Maybe that's the key to her FINALLY finding someone she's into.

Shari: LOL

Me: Can you stop. You both know I haven't asked if he's single. And he's not a farmer. He dresses like someone that lives in San Francisco.

Me: Also, Evan, just so you're prepared. We are WORKING at the Fall Festival. I know you're not used to real work at your new cushy job so this gives you ample time to prepare.

Evan: He's definitely single. He's sending you all the signs.

Evan: You're acting like I don't already have my work outfit picked out. I bought the cutest new boots.

Shari: This is criminally unfair.

APPLE OF MY EYE

Evan: Two weeks until I'm King of Carnation.

Me: Hate to break it to you but the people at the old folks' home are always king and queen. Last year it was Betty and Roger.

Evan: THERE'S ACTUALLY A KING AND QUEEN. STOP IT.

Shari: No, like can we actually stop. I was jealous enough already. I cannot bear to miss a sweet old lady and man pair get crowns. Can we go back to farm boy. Hasn't he come by the farm like every day this week?

Me: Evan, ilysm. Also, yes, he has. *Sent with invisible ink*

Evan: YAAAAS.

Shari: *Celebration emoji*

Me: You two are forgetting about a key piece of this.

Shari: And that would be??

Me: Um?! That I hope the farm he's trying to save fails.

Evan: He doesn't actually care about the farm. Hasn't he hardly been doing anything? He's been too busy 'interviewing' you!

Shari: LOL!!!!

Shari: Can you get a picture of him?

Me: Are you kidding.

**Evan: Just find out his last name!
Me: Guys, he is leaving in October. This is not happening so can we CUT IT OUT.**

Shari: Did you mean prune it out? *Laugh-crying emoji*

Chapter Fourteen

Nick

WEEK THREE

There's a current of emotion I can't quite place when I sit down for dinner on Monday. I can't tell if it's nervousness because I have to ask the Parkers if they'll film a video, excitement because I'm starting to really want this to work in a way I haven't felt about my career in a long time, or relief that my hands have *finally* stopped hurting.

I have open blisters on both palms and cracked skin along the backs of both my hands from helping Eloise in the field. Even though I lift, I'm not used to carrying these types of tools for so long each day, and my skin definitely isn't used to the dust. I wasn't trying to hide the state of my skin, but I also didn't want to give anyone more reason to think I was just another city guy that couldn't tough it. I didn't think anyone noticed until Eloise wordlessly produced a small tin from her pocket before going into lunch today.

'For your hands,' she said simply, her clear blue eyes shining in the afternoon sun.

When I reached out to take it, our fingertips brushed and I swear I saw her stand up a little straighter. *So it isn't just me that thinks it's unbearable to not be touching each other?* 'Thanks,' I managed to say, opening the plain aluminum capsule to find a clear gel-like substance.

'Apples have really high water content. They're hydrating.' She shrugged, like the gesture was no big deal. 'My mom makes it.'

It's only been a few hours but the state of my hands has improved tenfold. I'll have to thank her and Hazel tomorrow night at dinner.

Betsy clears her throat, bringing my focus back to the kitchen table. Summer produce is in full swing at the farm and Betsy tends to a mean garden. Tonight, we're eating freshly picked zucchini and tomatoes bursting with flavor. I showed Betsy a trick to slow cooking tomatoes that she can't stop making. Joe loves it.

'I would like to film a video of the two of you,' I announce.

Joe starts. 'No way,' he says quickly. 'I am all for you doing whatever it is you think you need to do, but I don't want to be wrangled in front of some camera.'

I try to keep my posture relaxed, my face nonchalant. 'It's no big deal.' I shrug. 'I think it'll take a second, we can do it tonight even, when we sit out on the porch. I'd like you two to be the first thing people see.' I desperately need to go live on socials ahead of the farmers' market this weekend, and this is the last piece of the puzzle. There hasn't been a buzz around any farmers' markets yet because the produce hasn't been ready, but there's some early harvest and some canned goods to sell this weekend, so the Parkers are excited.

We've been sitting on the porch every night to watch the sun dip behind the hills. The sun is setting earlier and earlier as the days shorten and fall approaches. It's relaxing to sit outside with them. The world feels so slow. It's the perfect backdrop to an introductory video.

Joe grunts.

'I'll do it,' says Betsy. 'It'll be fun.'

I want to wait until golden hour, so to waste time I cycle through the photos I've taken so far. I've been capturing the Parkers without them knowing in the mornings before I head over to see Eloise, and in the afternoon when the slanted sunlight hits the kitchen just right. I flip through photographs of Betsy sitting on the porch swing doing her crossword, stirring something on the stove with her apron crisscrossed around her waist, and one of her smiling towards the fields, where Joe was headed to work.

Joe has been more difficult to capture, but I managed to get some good shots of him pulling up weeds, driving a tractor, and one of him in a squat, with a handful of soil slowly draining through his fingers towards the earth. I'm no photographer, but I think these photos have a special quality I don't see on social media anymore—they're real.

I'm startled when Betsy appears on the porch, the door creaking loudly to announce her arrival. My heart melts when I see that she's changed from her usual flannel and T-shirt to a plain cotton blue dress. Her hair is combed back from her face a little neater than usual for this time of day.

Joe beams when he sees her, and I instinctively snap a photo of his face upon seeing his wife. I've just lowered my phone when he turns to look at me. 'I guess this means we're doing it,' he grunts.

I instruct them to sit in their rocking chairs like normal. Eloise has been dropping hints about fitting into small-town life while she's been teaching me about farming. She warned me how proud farm folk can be, how I should be careful not to step on toes. I need to make them feel like what they were doing was already the right thing to do before I suggest they change.

'Eloise,' I pointed out, 'you know that isn't just farm folk, right? Nobody wants to be told they're wrong.'

She pulled a face at me. 'Didn't I just tell you not to tell farm folk when you think they're incorrect?'

Soon Joe and Betsy are set up in their chairs. I take a few videos from the POV of someone walking up to their porch for the first time, then one of Betsy opening up the front door and welcoming me in. I don't have to rewatch them to know that with a couple edits they'll be gold—exactly what people want to watch when they've finally clocked out of their desk job at 8 p.m. and are ready to disassociate from the day.

I can hardly wait to show Eloise tomorrow. She seems skeptical, always emphasizing that 'you can't control nature' and 'farming is unpredictable,' but what she hasn't come around to yet is that *people* are predictable, and you can sure as hell control a lot of aspects of farming by harnessing marketing power. As a bonus, maybe this will help me thank her for the salve—driving business to the Parker's farm will mean more business to the Anderson farm too.

On Tuesday morning the thunderclouds roll in quickly, building up a powerful line across the distant hills. One moment and the clouds are white and fluffy and the next time I've looked up they're looming on the horizon like an angry gray army. It doesn't storm a lot here, but I've heard that when it does, it's bad.

'Shit,' I mutter under my breath. Eloise was specific—we have three more rows to go before we're finished for lunch. She never cuts corners, never wants to turn in early. I admire that about her—her dedication. It's how I feel in class, wanting to go the extra mile, not take the easy way out like Isaac would. 'We'd better hurry,' I call over to her. She's on her hands and knees a couple trees over, inspecting the trunk for fungus or rot.

'Oh no!' she exclaims when she looks up, following my gaze. 'We gotta finish the three rows,' she yells.

'Like I wasn't already doing that,' I shout back. I wish she was this easy to predict in other areas . . . sometimes her gaze lingers on my arm or snags on my face when she thinks I'm not looking. Sometimes her jokes edge into flirtation, but just as quickly she'll pull back into being serious again, as if she's embarrassed she tried to be anything else. There's something making her hesitate, that much I can tell, and I'm almost one hundred percent confident it's the fact that I'm moving. And if she doesn't want to waste her time with someone who can't stick around, I can't very well fault her for it.

We work as fast as we can, but we aren't done when the first raindrops hit us. They're fat and powerful, thudding against our clothes. We have two more trees to check.

Eloise holds up a hand, making a visor against her face. 'You game?' she asks, pointing to the last two trees in the line. 'You take left, I'll take right?'

I nod. We get to work as the rain turns the ground around us to mud. It only takes us a couple minutes, but it's a couple minutes too many and when we both straighten up it's pouring, with thunder cracking in the distance.

'Come on,' Eloise grabs my hand, 'let's get inside.' She leads me to the nearest barn, one I haven't been in yet, crisscrossing through the orchard, dodging between trees until we arrive, breathless and soaking wet, crashing together under the overhang. The rushing is so chaotic that I don't have time to enjoy how right it feels—Eloise's hand nestled in mine. The sound of the rain is relentless and loud against the roof.

As soon as we've squeezed inside, she pulls out her phone to text her dad, letting him know she'll be late for lunch. 'We can wait out the storm in here.' She stops, glancing at me. 'If that's OK with you? Or I can ask Dad to come pick you up, but—'

'I'm happy here,' I interrupt her, knowing she's about to start rambling in an effort both to make sure I'm comfortable and cover up any potential awkwardness because we're alone.

'OK.' She clams up, walking absent-mindedly across the length of the barn, which is small. There's a scattering of grass across the cement floor, dry and brown with age, remnants of when this place was last used. Eloise stalls in the center of the space, the A-frame ceiling lofted high above her, right in front of a rope swing. Her blonde hair is damp, clinging to the sides of her face and her shoulders and she shivers, her hands fluttering up and down her arms. Goosebumps freckle the backs of her legs. I'm pinned to the floor where I stand staring at her. She has no idea how beautiful she looks. I open my mouth to tell her but something about being alone inside feels wildly different from the amount of time we've spent alone together under the open sky. I don't want to disturb the peace. I make up my mind to tell her the next time, to give her a real intentional compliment, not one that could feel sleazy, especially since her nipples have peaked with the cold and I can see them through her shirt. I would give anything to close my mouth around one, to tease her slowly, to lick every inch of her until her toes curl in her work boots. My heart thuds in my chest.

'I used to spend so much time in here,' Eloise says quietly, nudging the rope swing with an outstretched finger. It sways gently, responding to her touch.

'I-It seems like a really cool space to hang out as a kid . . .' I cough out, momentarily embarrassed at how dirty my own mind is. I force myself to look around and take in my surroundings so I stop imagining what Eloise would look like with me inside her, back arched, mouth agape. Instead, I take in the rusted rake hanging on one wall and spot a rickety ladder leading up the side of another and take a deep breath. 'Is there a loft?' I ask, trying desperately to make my voice as normal-sounding as possible.

'Yeah.' Eloise lights up. 'It's tiny. I used to read up there when I was a kid.' She climbs up the ladder nimbly and pulls herself over the top, disappearing from view. 'Come on,' she calls me. I pull myself up after her, the wood creaking, until I too am perched up on a narrow shelf. It's so small that both of our legs are dangling off and our shoulders are touching, cool wet skin to cool wet skin.

I wonder if I imagined it, but when I leaned in closer to Eloise, I think she leaned right back.

'Linden would try to jump from here and grab the rope swing. He missed a lot.'

'Ouch.' We're about ten feet above the ground. Those falls had to hurt.

'Tell me about it.'

'You don't talk about him a lot.'

She runs a hand through her damp hair, thinking. 'I guess I don't. I think about him a lot now.' She pauses. 'Things have been . . . strained . . . between us.' She turns to look at me. 'You don't have siblings, so I don't know if you have something like this—' She pauses, as if wondering if I'll correct her.

'You're right,' I reassure her. 'I don't have siblings. Tell me.'

'We were *so* close growing up. Siblings are like your built-in best friends. We spent all our time together, we pranked our parents together, we told each other everything. Linden hitting puberty was hard for me, we drifted apart for a while. I became his loser sister and he became this golden child . . .' She trails off again, gazing out into the empty space of the barn. 'Anyways, I thought we would eventually get close again, you know, when we both came back home to the farm. But he never did.'

'But he comes home?' I ask. 'To visit?'

'I would call it coming home to gloat but yes, he does. My parents love it. But then he gets to leave.' She sighs. 'Just like you do. And I'm left here being the one to worry about how my parents will ever be financially in the clear. I don't understand how he does it so casually . . . I don't understand how anyone does it really . . . how they think their happiness is more important than a sustainable future for all.' Eloise stops abruptly. 'I sound like a PBS special,' she grumbles.

'Hey—' I nudge her '—I love PBS specials.'

Her lips quirk upwards.

'I get why you have resentment towards him up and leaving, especially while you don't feel like it's as easy for you to do. But—' I lean into her shoulder '—it's good he's happy, right?'

Eloise bobs her head in agreement, her shoulders slumping. 'I don't like holding a grudge, it's just infuriating that I'm the one that has to care about the environment. I'm the one that has to stay in a small town with no good bagel places. I'm the one that has to take care of my parents.'

'Yeah,' I sigh. 'I feel like that too. I'm worried about my mom being alone. And because I'm her only son, I'm the only one who carries that burden. Not that she's a burden at all . . .' I feel my cheeks redden as I notice I'm babbling, but Eloise turns to look at me, her blue eyes burning.

'See,' she breathes. 'You get it then, why it's so important, what I'm doing here. It's hard when you're the only one worried about the people who raised you.'

'Exactly. And my mom, she's fine, but she's had some health scares in the past. She's had a couple bouts of chest pain that we thought could have been heart attacks, we called an ambulance and everything, and it ended up being heartburn.'

'Oh, that's so scary.'

'Yeah, it was. It's hard to see her get older.' I shrug. 'She's the reason I care so much about being successful. My mom means more to me than anything.'

Eloise sighs. She mumbles something unintelligible. Something that sounds a lot like *Of course you're doing this for your mom.*

'What?'

'Nothing.'

'She'd like you, you know.' The thought pops out of my mouth before I can think it through. 'My mom, I mean.'

Eloise blushes. 'You think?'

'I know. She loves a hard-working woman.'

'Takes one to know one.'

'I didn't even tell you what she does.'

'I can tell she works hard. She raised you.' Eloise leans back into my shoulder. My insides feel all warm and tingly. An Anderson saying you're a hard worker is a big compliment, maybe the nicest thing Eloise has ever said to me.

Eloise stills, cocking an ear up towards the ceiling. 'Still raining,' she confirms, 'we might have a while.'

'Truth or dare?' I suggest.

Eloise laughs. 'Something about me telling you I used to come here when I was younger must have really stuck. I haven't played truth or dare in, like . . . a decade?'

'That's the magic of it.'

'OK—' Eloise turns to me '—I'm game. You go first.'

'OK.' I take a minute to think about what to say. We're so cozy in this barn, so close and so intimate. 'Truth,' I decide.

She smiles. 'Tell me a secret.'

'What! That's not a truth. You have to ask me something.'

'OK,' Eloise teases, 'can you please tell me a secret?'

I laugh. 'Touché.' I rack my brain, swinging my feet back and forth while I think. A secret for Eloise. I don't have many. I don't want to tell her anything cliché about a first kiss or the first time I had sex. I don't have any family secrets. I'm definitely not going to tell her about losing the fantasy football bet. I haven't told anyone that's what got me here. Everyone assumes it was so altruistic of me, and I can't bear to tell them I was forced to do it. Suddenly, it comes to me.

'I hate football,' I say. It's the first time I've ever said it out loud.

'What?' Eloise asks. 'That's your secret?'

'Eloise,' I say, turning towards her so our eyes meet. 'If you met my friends, you would understand what a big deal that was.'

'That you hate football.' She crosses her arms, eyebrows raised with skepticism.

'Yes. You cannot tell them. I mean it. Ever.'

She snorts. 'You're acting like they're on their way here as we speak.'

'Isaac and Julian are visiting for the first U-Pick weekend,' I explain. I can't help but smile thinking about it. 'I'm excited.'

'I can see that.' Eloise grins. 'That's cool of them. One of my best friends from graduate school is visiting for Fall Festival—Evan. You'll like him, I think. I wish you could meet Shari but she's in Italy.'

'Awesome,' I reply. Trying to play it off that I'm not completely thrilled Eloise wants me to meet her friends. 'I'd love to meet him.'

'Wait, so back to football. You're actually pretending to like it?'

'Well.' I squirm, beginning to regret telling her. 'Yes?'

'Nick!' She playfully swats at my arm. 'Boys are so dumb.'

'OK, I did it. Your turn. Truth or dare?' *Is it so lame if I dare her to kiss me*, I think.

'You know what?' she says, squinting towards the window at the far side of the barn where the sun is just beginning to peek through. 'It actually looks like it stopped raining.'

As quick as lightning she jumps to her feet and scurries down the ladder. 'Better get back out there!'

'Eloise!' I shout after her. She lets out a peal of laughter and I can't help but join in, running after her back into the sunshine, the earth smelling like fresh rain.

Chapter Fifteen

Eloise

Possible Nicknames for Nick (and his reaction to them)

- Nick-O—'Why would I want to rhyme with Jell-O?'
- Nickerdoodle—'I mean, I love those cookies, but no.'
- Nickel—'Why would you even suggest that?'
- Nickeroni—'You are terrible at this.'
- Nick Knack—he didn't even bother responding to this one

'We're just friends,' I repeat to Mom. She rolls her eyes. I'm saying it more for myself at this point. *We technically are just friends, aren't we?* I still haven't told him about the loan, about what him succeeding in his capstone project will mean for me. I flip-flop between being worried I've helped Nick too much and feeling confident there's no way social media alone can turn things around. It doesn't matter how much I help him; the Parkers still go bankrupt. But in case they don't, I've started working on a contingency plan—weddings. Even though the thought of repurposing land that's perfect for farming into a venue makes me want to gag, I can't ignore the financial upside to obtaining an events permit. I even brought it up to Dad. We both think that West Barn could hold one hundred people.

Despite being 'just friends' with Nick, I'm still spending longer getting ready for dinner than I ever have. We throw an annual welcome dinner for the seasonal workers every year. Mom makes her lasagna, and over the large meal introductions are made, shifts are bargained for, and return workers stake out their claim to the best jobs. Usually I walk to dinner still sweaty from a long day on the farm. This year I'm showered and blow-drying my hair before I shimmy into a gauzy sundress and a cardigan.

Dinner marks the entrance into fall. After this week, we're basically in September, the days get shorter and the cool breeze welcomes in London fog lattes and sticky toffee pudding cakes. Mom switches out her bathrobes, wrapping herself in thick terrycloth every morning. Dad starts to wear his flannel pajamas. I feel a thrill of excitement thinking about fall, it's my favorite season. Fall somehow feels both like swirling change and relaxed coziness.

By the end of the week, having the workers here will feel normal. But until everyone has settled into the rhythm, the farm feels chaotic, buzzing with energy, just like our beehives.

Nick arrives for dinner in a button-down shirt and jeans. I feel my heart skip a beat when I open the door for him. I can't pull my gaze away.

'What? Is there something on my shirt?' He picks it up by the hem and examines the line of buttons. By the time he looks up I've regained my composure.

'Your shirt is great,' I reassure him. Just then, Mom sweeps by.

'Nick!' she exclaims. 'Don't you look handsome.'

Nick reddens and it's so endearing that I feel a tingle all the way down to my toes. I haven't stopped thinking about how it felt to grab his hand and pull him towards East Barn, how I felt like my heart was hammering so loud I didn't know how he couldn't hear it.

'You don't look a day over twenty, Hazel.' Nick smiles at Mom before glancing my way, his eyes raking over my blue patterned dress. I shift my white cardigan and it falls off one shoulder, leaving it exposed to the breeze of chilly night air that flits through the door.

Nick places a hand gently on my bare shoulder as he walks into the house. His fingertips leave heat marks on my bare skin. My breath catches in my throat.

'And you,' he says, turning to look at me once more, 'you look beautiful.'

I can't even begin to hide my grin. My chest feels like it's full of champagne bubbles. I'm rooted to the entryway as I listen to Nick make his way towards the kitchen. I hear a muffled thank you for the apple salve I gave him a few days ago and an immediate request as to what he can do to help. Mom puts him to work without a moment's hesitation. Seconds later I hear 'Lou, can you grab the salad?' Not even a chore can make the fizzy feeling leave my chest.

'Eloise Anderson?' Nick sidles up behind me, speaking louder than he normally would to counteract the noise of the crowd. My pulse quickens. I smooth out my dress with my hands.

There's about fifty people scattered at folding tables behind us. I'm standing at the food table with my back to the crowd, getting my second helping. The evening has been smooth sailing so far. Nick has fit right in, so much so that no one questioned why he was here. I'd like to think it's because of the hints I've been dropping him about how to fit into a small-town dynamic, but he would fit in without my advice. People love to talk around here, and Nick is ready to listen.

'My full name this time?' I say. Secretly, I think we both know I love that he doesn't use my nickname. Eloise sounds so rich in his mouth, so special, like we share a secret language. *Eloise*.

'I'm glad you made it, Nicky!' I raise my plastic cup full of red wine to cheers him, my drink sloshing precariously close to the rim.

'Nice try, but only my mother calls me that.'

We sit next to each other on foldout chairs. 'I've been meaning to ask you,' I say between mouthfuls, 'have you started your TikTok?' I haven't been able to bring myself to google it. If it's going badly, that means it can't help me in the future. But if his TikTok has taken off that means the Parkers may stave off their bankruptcy.

'Wouldn't you like to know,' Nick says, a devious smile spreading across his face. 'Nothing's up yet, but I'm launching before this weekend.' He walks me through an explanation of the algorithm, when it makes sense to pay for ads, how to maximize your reach, and how to determine your target audience. Eventually he clocks my expression. 'You're not the only one who knows things, Eloise. I'm gonna drive a crowd to the farmers' market this weekend, you'll see.'

'We'll see about that,' I try to mumble playfully, but his plans have me feeling overwhelmed at the prospect of his TikTok blowing up in popularity. I wonder how quickly I can get the events permit. Maybe I need to email town hall to expedite it.

He whips out his phone and passes it across the table towards me. 'That's what I have so far,' he explains, but right as he says it, a huge dollop of red sauce starts to slide off his fork. His eyes widen but his reflexes are too slow, and it splats in his lap.

I can't help but laugh and he joins right in. 'Goddammit,' he says, with a twinkle in his eye, 'you can't take me anywhere.'

I push back from the table. 'Follow me,' I say, leading him towards the house.

As soon as the door shuts behind us, we're enveloped in quiet. I can still hear the faint hum of the crowd outside, but the house is silent. 'There's stain remover in the laundry room,' I say, knowing he's still following me as I weave through the downstairs.

Even though we've spent a lot of time together, something about being alone in my house at night makes my heart beat faster. Nick steps into the laundry room right behind me, and when I turn around to find the stain remover we're standing chest to chest, as close as we were that very first day on the farm, when the hose exploded everywhere and I thought, just for a second, that he might kiss me.

'Eloise?' he prompts gently.

'It's just back there,' I say, managing to recover my voice. I point to a shelf behind Nick. Suddenly, I'm parched. My mouth is so dry that I lick my lips.

Nick glances at my mouth. When he looks back up at me, and our eyes meet, I feel my knees go weak. I've wanted to kiss him since I saw him in the general store. Even when he pissed me off. Especially because he pissed me off. Even though I've tried to ignore it, I've wanted to rip off his shirt every time he delicately handled an apple like it was made of glass. And even though I know it's a terrible idea, even though I know he's leaving *and* I haven't been honest with him about the Parkers . . . Well, maybe that's the silver lining of his leaving, right?

He leans in closer to me and I breathe in his familiar cinnamon smell. My thoughts dissipate like the softest cloud of morning fog. Ever so gently, he wraps a hand around my waist, reaching his palm to my lower back, and he tugs me closer to him. Heat builds beneath my belly. Instead of thoughts I just have desires. *Him. Closer. More.*

Our chests press together and I can feel his heartbeat. My nipples tighten. Nick's eyes stray to my lips, hungry and dark.

'Eloise,' he whispers, almost breathless. 'Can I—?'

I'm nodding before he can finish his sentence, the glass of wine having knocked down the last remains of the crumbling walls I had tried (and failed) to build to keep this from happening. It's such a dumb idea. And yet I can't help but tilt my hips forward, our bodies melding as his mouth crashes into mine. His lips are strong and sure, his tongue expertly claiming my mouth as our kiss deepens and my insides melt, my knees weak. *Damn.* My mind can't form any coherent thoughts except *Damn*.

His mouth is hungry and before I know it, I'm panting as his lips press soft kisses down my throat. In an easy movement he grips my ass and hauls me on top of the laundry room counter. I wrap my legs around his waist and intertwine my fingers in his hair. *Damn.* A breathless moan escapes my mouth and he answers with a low grumble in his throat. He nips at my bottom lip and my hips arch forward, the increased contact letting me feel the size, the hardness of him. 'God,' I whisper in between kisses. I feel his smile against my collarbone, his lips as light as feathers as he kisses my throat. The washing machine rumbles next to me, shaking with the movement of a spin cycle and *God* if Nick had placed me on top of that vibration I think I might have exploded already. I lean back, exposing my chest to him, feeling like my body is acting entirely on its own accord, when I hear it. I freeze. *No. No. No.*

'Lou?' I hear again. My eyes fly open.

'Are you in here?' Mom's voice rings out through the house.

I jump down from the counter as Nick hastily re-tucks in his shirt, smoothing back his hair with a hand.

'Here!' I try to call out, but my voice comes out strangled. I clear my throat and try again. 'In the laundry room, Mom! Nick spilled!'

'Thanks for that,' Nick whispers. I can still see a hint of blush dappled across his cheeks.

Nick seems to have recovered but I still can't see straight when Mom steps in behind me and aggressively directs Nick to the stain remover, tsk-ing as she does so about how he's let the stain sit for too long already. Nick catches my eye as I walk out the door and smiles so big it almost runs off his face.

I brace myself once I get into the hallway, resting a palm on the wall. My heart is thundering. On one hand, that was bad. I should not have done that, not when there's so much at stake. But on the other hand ... damn, that was *incredible*.

Chapter Sixteen

Nick

I keep thinking about her before I sleep, the way she sounded when I kissed her neck, the way it felt to grab her ass and pull her closer to me, her legs wrapped around my waist, her hands in my hair. I can almost feel the dip in the small of her back when I leaned in to hug her goodnight. The night was quiet around us, moonlight shining down onto her wooden front porch, a rocking chair creaking in the wind. Everyone else had gone home and I had lingered, wanting more time with her, wanting her alone, but not sure how to get there. Her piercing gaze pinned me in place. A wisp of her hair was loose from her ponytail. She hates having hair in her face, so I tucked it behind her ear instinctively, my fingertips grazing the soft part of her temple. The incline of her chin towards my lips, expecting me to kiss her again. The way her eyelashes fluttered when I leaned in closer, so ready to press my lips to hers. I would have given anything for another moment out there alone. But then the porch door swung open, screaming on its hinges, Cal jolting us out of the moment.

I stumbled to head back, barely hearing her murmur when I left, 'Look up on your way home. The stars here aren't like they are in the city.' If I'm not mistaken, her voice was as shaky as my hand had been when I smoothed her wayward curl down.

Either the lack of socialization out here is getting to me or not being able to get Eloise alone is driving me crazy. Because even though I've been sleeping well, I wake up with a headache. Maybe it's because I finally bit the bullet and started a TikTok account for the Parkers late on Tuesday night, still buzzing with energy from kissing Eloise. My first few videos were pretty standard, an introduction to the farm, 'meeting the grandparents,' and what amounted to a little infomercial about their products. But then I posted a video introducing everyone to the pigs. I paid to promote it, deciding I wouldn't even tell the Parkers about it. I could afford a $50 ad placement. It worked. The internet *loved* it. We're already at over five thousand followers, a number that I think I can keep driving up.

Eloise hasn't followed the account yet. I've checked. But I'm not sure if she's seen it. I thought she would be excited about the prospect of more folks visiting the farm, but she always seems uneasy when we talk about it. I've only seen her once since the big dinner and her dad was tending to apples a row over from us, so we only talked about two things—how the apples are doing, and how excited she is to see her friend Evan, who's coming into town for the Fall Festival. Every time she mentions Evan I feel a tug in my chest. I can't decide if I want to meet him or pretend he doesn't exist. He seems to make Eloise really happy. I decide that, for now, I don't need to like the guy. He's coming in from Seattle and is probably some stuck-up city butthole. Not that I'm any better, but at least I'm out here in the fields every day.

'The town really goes all out,' Eloise explains after she reminds me again that Evan's coming, her voice interrupting my descent into hypocrisy. We're out in the orchard netting trees to protect them from pests. Cal is infuriatingly nearby again. Five minutes ago I tried to mouth to Eloise, 'Can we go somewhere to talk,' but she said 'What?' so loudly that I saw Cal's hat move out of my peripheral vision.

'All out as in I can expect Joe to wear something other than his flannel?'

Eloise laughs. 'You're never going to see Joe in something other than a flannel. But I meant the apple pie contest.'

I go still. 'Eloise Anderson. Did you just say *apple pie contest?*'

She laughs. 'Yes, my mom won two years ago and she's looking to repeat.'

'Who gets to judge?'

'Locals.' Eloise emphasizes the word so heavily I wonder if she's about to tell me that non-residents can't participate, but then she says, 'I'll sneak you a piece of my mom's, don't worry. And . . .' Eloise pauses, a shy smile creeping across her face '. . . we're doing something different at our tent this year, we're giving out growing kits for kids.'

A smile tugs at my lips.

'What?' she asks, self-conscious.

'I love how much you love teaching kids to farm,' I admit, thinking back to the first time she told me about how much she loved volunteering at their summer camp.

'It's not teaching them how to farm really,' she corrects me, but I can tell by the way her face lit up that she's pleased. 'This summer we were more teaching them how to garden.' Her shoulders drop a little. 'It would have been better if it could have been farming. We need more farmers,' she sighs, 'but it is *really* cute to see a little kid get so excited about a tomato.'

'So, what are the growing kits?'

'They're radish seedlings that have already germinated. A radish can grow in about a month. All they need to do is water it. And the best part is that the containers are clear, so the kids can watch the radish grow!'

'But don't the radishes grow in dirt?'

Eloise's bright blue eyes narrow just slightly, like they always do when she's surprised I don't understand something. 'Well, not these ones . . . it's a hydroponic system,' she explains, 'they only need water to grow. It's magical to watch, really.'

I reach my hand towards hers and squeeze it. 'That sounds so cool.' There's dirt between our fingers, and our hands are sweaty from hard work, but she intertwines her fingers with mine and squeezes back.

'I can save you one,' she promises.

'I'd like that.' I wonder if she would want to go to the festival together, but before I have the chance to, she lets go of my hand and drops to her knees.

'I saw a worm,' she exclaims, digging up a scoop of dark soil in her palm and letting it run through her fingers. We've talked a lot about soil lately. I didn't realize how essential it was to the farm until I met Eloise. She is always feeling the dirt. Sometimes it's dry and sandy, her shoulders sag when that happens. Sometimes it's rich and moist, like it is today, and before her face turns towards mine I already know she'll be beaming. This is the first time she's mentioned worms, though.

'Last year we filled this in with clover on the off season,' she says happily, 'and now, look!' Excitedly, she picks up an earthworm that was wriggling in the dirt she just upended. 'Hey, little guy,' she whispers, 'you're welcome here.'

She sighs. 'Sometimes I think my dad doesn't believe me,' she says loudly, emphasizing *dad* enough for Cal to hear from a row over. 'But I don't get how he doesn't see it. The proof is right here!'

That's when it hits me. It's lack of socialization, it has to be. There's no other explanation for why I like a girl who talks to worms.

We spend the rest of the morning finishing the netting. Like most other days, we fall into an easy rhythm. She hands me a new piece of mesh without asking if I need it. I carry the supplies with us to the next tree without either of us asking the other if we're ready to move on. As the sun soars higher into the sky, we both build up a sheen of sweat on our faces. Without thinking, I tuck a damp curl behind Eloise's ear while she's netting the final tree of the morning.

I can't tell if it's a glow from the midday sun or a blush that colors her cheeks.

'Thanks,' she says.

I resist the urge to tuck back another flyaway that isn't even there, I just want an excuse to touch her again. As I walk back to the farmhouse it crosses my mind that I've never been that in sync with anyone except when I'm cooking with my mamma in the kitchen.

I call her when I get back to the Parkers', the porch door creaking behind me as I slip in.

'Hi, sweetheart,' she answers. I can hear her smile.

'Hi, Mamma.' I feel both a rush of relief at hearing her voice, knowing she's OK, and a rush of guilt for being away from her, for starting to imagine a life with Eloise, one where I don't live as close to my mother, where I can't support her so fully.

I ask her how she is and she tells me about Ronnie and her cousin Vienna (who has reappeared on the scene since I've been gone). She gives me the vegetable garden update and laughs when I tell her I'll have some advice for her when I get home.

'How are Julian and Isaac? Did you tell them they could come over for dinner while you're gone?'

'Mamma, you don't need to feed my friends while I'm away.' I laugh. 'They're good. They're liking their internships.'

She harrumphs. 'And how are *you*?' she asks after a beat of quiet.

'I'm good. It's nice here.'

'But not too nice,' she says, 'not as nice as home. You better not be getting too skinny.'

'Not too nice,' I agree, although when I say it my heart sinks just a little. It is better than too nice, it just happens to be so far away from her. 'I'm eating enough,' I promise, 'but the cooking here is nothing compared to yours.'

Chapter Seventeen

Eloise

Observed About Nick (in Chronological Order)

- He must use eyelash serum
- He smells like cinnamon
- He has dimples
- He blushes easily
- He notices spiderwebs before I do and clears them out of the way without ever saying anything
- He is deferentially polite to Dad
- He is way too comfortable with Mom (why doesn't he find her intimidating?)

I've known the days leading up to the Fall Festival will be tough for weeks, but when Thursday arrives, I groan. I drank too much wine last night at dinner, something my parents only bring out when they are having a tough week, and my head feels fuzzy. My alarm is blaring. 5:30 a.m. and I know Dad will already have started his day. Evan arrives tomorrow afternoon and the festival is on Saturday. It kicks off with the farmers' market. Usually, one of our largest of the season. Like clockwork, just as I'm doing the backwards math in my head, the smell of pie crusts wafts under my bedroom door. Mom has started baking her blue-ribbon pies.

I fumble around my room in the dark for my alarm. At the beginning of August, it was still light out when I woke up, making the early mornings infinitely easier, but as fall approaches, the mornings have gotten progressively darker. A shame, really, because the daylight gives us much more time to get ready for our orchards to churn out hundreds of thousands of crisp red apples. I pause, thinking momentarily of Nick, and how I promised I would take him up here soon. He told me yesterday that he won't be by the house today. Today he has to 'work on the campaign' to turn around the Parkers' farm. I haven't dared check the social media accounts he's told me about. I can't look. I feel all sorts of tangled feelings for him—annoyance that he's trying to fix something he won't be around to see through, frustration that he's made me sympathize with leaving Carnation for San Francisco, something I've never been able to look kindly upon until now, and . . . well . . . lust.

I spend my day working but distracted. The Parkers' swells with workers in late August too. When I hear their voices catching on the breeze, floating down the hill towards us, Dad and I exchange glances. *The Parkers must really be putting their eggs in Nick's basket hiring all these people.*

Dad shakes his head ever so slightly in the Parkers' direction, a clear hint of his disapproval. What he's disapproving of I'm not quite sure, it could be my plan to buy the farm or it could be the potential sale of our farm. I've tried not to be frustrated with their lack of willingness to talk about either thing. Neither of my parents want to talk about the sale or the loan, both demurring with 'no use in talking about it before we see how this harvest goes.' Which is insanely frustrating given that my future and theirs is at stake.

A strand of hair comes loose from my ponytail and annoyingly falls in front of my eyes, building frustration to anger. I can't help but think it's too bad Nick isn't around to tenderly tuck it behind my ear. He's figured out how to dissipate my moods with a smile. He's the only person who's ever made me wish that days on the farm would last *longer*. As much as I hate to admit it, I could use him next to me today. With each branch I prune, I analyze the kiss in the laundry room from a new angle. *Should I have ignored Mom calling my name? Should I have invited him to stay the night? Will we get to do that again? Why hasn't he tried anything else? It's Dad . . . suddenly lingering when it's inconvenient.*

I've been undressing him more and more with my mind lately, especially now that I know what he feels like. When he walks across the field towards me with that casual, loping, sexy stride of his it makes me tingle with want all over. I want to feel the butt that looks so good in jeans. Hell, I want to nibble his ears with my teeth.

I haven't said a word about it to Evan or Shari, I've only denied it. I'm waiting for Evan to meet him, curious to see what he thinks, trying not to think about how disappointed I'll be if Evan doesn't approve. But then I remember, Nick's leaving. And it's not like I'll be visiting him in San Francisco. I'll be busy here. But even as I think it, I wonder if a visit would really be so bad, it would be a chance to see Linden too . . . I shake my head to clear my thoughts. A farmer in a long-distance relationship is a recipe for disaster. Sometimes I don't even have the energy to wash my hair, I would never be able to give the energy late-night phone calls require.

When 6 p.m. rolls around, the sun is sinking below the hills. I gaze at the Parkers' one last time, squinting into the sun, before I head in towards the house. I think about Nick, about the way he calls me by my full name, *Eloise Anderson*. I think about how I really need to *stop* thinking about Nick.

Amie clears her throat awkwardly as I'm checking out my groceries. I'm at Hal's for the second time today. Mom keeps running out of flour. She says her crusts aren't baking right. I've tried six pies today and they've all been delicious. I make a mental note to tell Evan not to eat on his way here. Mom has already told me she expects him to try all twelve pies to help her choose which recipe to submit.

'Hey, Lou?' Amie asks. The scanner beeps as she rings up the flour.

'Hey, Amie,' I reply, digging through my purse for my card.

'So, you know Nick?'

I freeze. 'Yeah,' I say slowly. 'What about him?'

'Well—' Amie twists the ring she wears on her right middle finger '—I was wondering . . . is he nice?'

I relax. Everyone is *so* curious about the new guy in town. 'Yeah.' I feel my cheeks widen with my smile. 'He's really nice.'

'Are you guys seeing each other?'

'Me and Nick? Um . . .' *Technically, we're not, but* . . . When I glance back at Amie she's staring at me. 'No. We're not,' I say. The last thing I want to do is tell everyone in the town my business and Amie is a huge gossip. No one faults her for it. Everyone knows her checkout line is the best place to hear about the goings-on in town. Even Hal admits it helps with business.

'Oh really?' Amie leans forward slightly. 'OK, well do you think he would say yes if I asked him out?'

It is all I can do to keep my face from falling. 'Um,' I say through my strained smile. *Amie wants to ask him out?* I do my best to keep my voice even. 'I don't really know.'

Her face falls. 'Oh really? Why?'

'Um . . .' I trail off, panicked. 'I mean, I guess he might? You might as well shoot your shot,' I offer as casually as I can manage.

Amie beams. 'OK. Cool. I'm glad I asked you. From the way he talks about you I totally thought you might be a thing! But he's so cute I feel like I might as well see if he'd go to dinner. We never get new people in town and . . .'

I can't focus on what she's saying. *From the way he talks about you I totally thought you might be a thing?* What does that mean? *Nick is talking about* me?

'Lou?' Amie interrupts my train of thought, holding out the receipt for me to take.

'Sorry.' I take the receipt, forcing myself to smile again.

'I'll let you know how it goes!' she calls after me as I leave.

My heart sinks. Amie is cute. She's bubbly and fun and the picture-perfect farm girl. Her red hair is almost always in twin braids that somehow don't make her look childish. Her legs are impossibly long and tan. If she worked behind a bank counter, she'd be Jolene.

I shake my head. I can't keep thinking about Amie. Or Nick. I need to focus. I have basically one month to convince my parents not to sell. I should be using my brain space to figure out how we can start to host weddings. Thank God Evan is coming. He has the most distracting personality in the absolute best way. He'll set me back on track.

Evan: T-minus five hours until I am living the American Dream!!! Getting in the car now.

Evan: Shari, we will miss you!

Shari: I'm in Rome living the Hilary Duff Dream.

Shari: Sorry, I'm clearly bitter. Have fun, you guys. Miss you more.

Eloise: Thank God for you, Evan. Mom has made twelve pies. A dozen. Literally. Bring your appetite.

Evan: I bet Rome doesn't have good pies *Sent with invisible ink*

Shari: Shut. Up.

Evan gasps so loud when he gets out of the car that he startles a nearby barn swallow that's been nesting in one of the maple trees in our front yard.

'I love it here,' he gushes immediately, gulping in a deep breath of air. 'Ohmygod, it's like I can *feel* my lungs relaxing.' He takes another deep lungful. 'Wow.' He pauses to look me over. 'Look at your tanned legs. You look good,' he says, wrapping his arms around me in a tight hug. 'Healthy. Strong.'

I smile in his embrace, our cheeks pressing together. 'I feel healthy and strong,' I admit, hugging him tighter. 'I missed you.'

He pulls away to survey the barn. 'I'm so happy I'm here,' he says.

'I'm so happy you're here,' I say at the exact same time. We both laugh. Excitedly, he gestures towards the front door. 'Hazel and Cal home?' Evan and my parents love each other.

'I'll get your bags,' I tell him, nudging him inside.

In the five minutes it takes me to bring his bag to the guest room, Mom has called Dad in from wherever he was and the three of them are laughing at the kitchen table. Dad and Evan are both sipping an Old Fashioned and Mom has a hefty glass of red wine in front of her. She pours me one too and we all cheers.

'To the Fall Festival!' Evan announces excitedly. We clink glasses.

'Evan,' Mom says as we lower our glasses, 'when will Eloise introduce you to our new neighbor?'

'He's not exactly a neighbor,' I grumble.

Evan perks up. 'Nick?'

Mom's face splits into a grin.

'Guys,' I protest. I feel my cheeks reddening. 'I'm sure Evan will meet Nick tomorrow.'

Mom ignores me. 'You know they've been spending a lot of time together,' she says to Evan. 'Right, Cal?' She nudges Dad, who has been staring off into the distance, clearly not listening.

'Mhmm,' he grunts.

She leans in closer to Evan like she's about to tell him a secret. 'You know he comes over every morning.'

'He just needs to learn more about farming for his capstone thing. Can we change the subject?'

'He seems to be doing an awful lot of work for it,' Mom says. She turns to Evan. 'Did Lou tell you how handsome he is?'

'No!' Evan exclaims. 'Tell me someone has a picture.'

Mom pulls out her phone and starts typing, furrowing her brow at the screen.

'Mom,' I wail, 'can we not? Dad, help me out here.'

Dad grunts non-committally again, exactly zero help. Meanwhile Evan is practically sliding off his seat leaning closer to Mom. 'Got it!' she says triumphantly. She pulls up a grainy photo of Nick clearly taken off the Stanford webpage. Despite the poor quality Nick looks like himself, which is to say, very cute.

'Lou!' Evan gasps loudly. 'You did *not* say he was that cute.'

I can feel my face redden at the thought of how cute Nick is, and how not-cute Nick *feels*. I squirm. 'When is dinner?' I ask Mom, pointedly changing the subject.

'Where has Nick been this week?' Mom asks, ignoring my question. 'I haven't seen him around the past couple of days.'

'He's been working, Mom.'

'Working on helping the Parkers?' Evan supplies. But he emphasizes 'the Parkers' too heavily. Mom whips her head towards him. I glare.

'So, you knew about this plan too?' She shakes her head. 'I don't like scheming to steal from neighbors.'

'It is not stealing, Mom. They're going to go under.'

'Does Nick know you feel this way?'

'We've already talked about this,' I grumble through clenched teeth.

'Now that you say that,' Dad jumps in, 'Nick did come by yesterday.'

'He did?' Mom and I ask together.

'Yeah. He was asking me how to fix the potholes in the Parkers' driveway. Says Betsy keeps complaining about how they jostle her around so much she spills her coffee if she tries to leave the house in the morning.'

My heart swells. I shake my head to clear away any positive thoughts of Nick. I've already given Amie the green light. And it's not even like Amie is the problem. The Nick ship has already sailed for San Francisco.

'So, he's an angel?' Evan volunteers.

I've had enough of this conversation. Thankfully I know exactly what to do to change the subject. 'Mom, what time do we have to leave?' I ask. 'I don't want to forget to set my alarm.' Mom *hates* waking up her children, she claims it makes them lazy and grumpy. Forgetting to set an alarm is not an option and is something she will always try to avoid.

'Oh,' she says, immediately pulling out her phone, 'let's do . . . five thirty?'

'Works for me,' I pretend to toggle my alarm—it was already on. 'And what time do we need to finish setting up? That way Evan knows when to get there.'

Like clockwork, Mom launches into plans for the day.

Evan narrows his eyes at me. I smirk back at him as Mom outlines into our detailed schedule, starting with all she expects from booth setup and when she's slated to drop off her pie.

All of the stalls that frequent the farmers' market have a dedicated street during the Fall Festival. Despite the harvest not coming in full yet, it is usually our second busiest day of the year behind the opening of U-Pick in late September. I tried to explain that to Nick, how big of a deal it was, but I'm not sure if he understands. He kept harping about his TikTok, how it would drive more people to come visit, but he didn't seem to realize how many people already turn out at the festival. I don't know why he thinks a couple videos will make such a big difference.

Evan flops on my bed after dinner, tossing a paperweight apple I've had since I was little in one hand. He recites Mom's plan. 'So, tomorrow we do the farmers' market stall in the morning, then we shower and go to the carnival?' He smiles at me, pure glee on his face. 'I *love* a carnival.'

I laugh. 'You've only told me that ten times,' I say, reaching over to give his arm a squeeze. 'Thank you, seriously, for being here. I'm sorry we have to work. At least you don't have to wake up super early tomorrow, I'll get everything set up alone. You can come later with Dad.'

'Alone?' Evan asks, a devilish grin widening across his face. 'Or maybe with . . . Nick?'

I narrow my eyes at him. 'No,' I correct him, 'Nick will be setting up the Parkers'. And my mom will be there.'

Evan flips onto his stomach. 'What *is* going on with Nick?'

'Nothing.'

He raises his eyebrows at me.

'Seriously. Nothing. Amie, a girl I went to high school with, she's asking him out.' I busy myself tidying up the clothes strewn about my room.

'Mhmm, and how do you know that?'

'She asked me.'

'Wait, so you're telling me *nothing* is going on, but someone asked you if they could ask Nick out? That doesn't track.'

'I said yes.' I shrug my shoulders. 'She can do whatever she wants.'

'Have you told Nick about his admirer?'

'No.'

'Hmm.'

'He'll find out when she asks him.'

'Yeah.' Evan tosses the paperweight apple into the air and it lands in his hand with a thud. 'Have you told him that you wanted to buy the Parkers' land?'

'No,' I admit. I turn away, pretending to focus on putting my clothes in a drawer.

'OK, so you aren't going to go out with him because some random wants to date him or because you've purposely kept something pretty big from him?'

'He's also moving, Evan. You'll see when you meet him, he's just . . . he's . . . he's not my type.'

Evan snorts. 'I don't think someone I was lying to would be my type either, but OK.'

'I'm not lying!'

'You're not being honest.'

'I don't have to tell him.'

'Don't think I don't know what you're doing,' Evan cautions, abruptly halting his game of toss. His voice softens. 'Your life can be bigger than this farm, you know.' And with that, he gives me a loving hug and goes to bed, leaving me tossing and turning all night long.

Chapter Eighteen

Nick

WEEK FOUR

'We didn't bring too much,' I tell Betsy for the thousandth time this morning. We're setting up the stand in the back corner of the town farmers' market. The last weekend of August has brought a chill to the air and slight haze of fog on the hills around the town, fall arriving in perfect timing for the Fall Festival. I'm looking forward to a steaming cup of coffee as soon as we get everything squared away.

Buttercup squeals loudly from the pen we've put her in next to the tent. Bringing her was my idea. Joe was reluctant at first, but Betsy convinced him. And I convinced her when I showed her how many views the video of the pigs had.

'Fifty thousand?' she exclaimed. I thought she might faint right there in the kitchen.

It took a lot of convincing, but I finally got Betsy to agree to unpack all the apple butter, apple jam, and apple cider vinegar they had in storage.

'We used to sell lots of these,' she said, blowing the dust off the tops of the lids.

'You're sure they're still good?' I asked, surveying the damp underground storage hatch filled to the brim with jars.

'You tell me.' Betsy cracked open a jar of jam and stuck in her pinky.

I did the same. The flavor was incredible. It tasted just like a crisp fall afternoon. 'Wow,' I said, 'you've been hiding this from me all this time? Why have I been eating blackberry jam at breakfast?'

Betsy laughed, a sound that has been more frequent lately. 'Oh, stop.' She swatted at my arm, blushing.

I glance at the table we've set up, jam jars arranged in neat lines behind little placards. Betsy squirms from her seat behind the table.

'It looks like we expect to sell *all* of this stuff,' she says.

'We do.'

She squirms again. 'It just seems . . .' She trails off, looking at the other stalls in the vicinity.

'It has nothing to do with being humble,' I tell her firmly. 'We are giving the people what they want.' I cross my fingers behind my back. I *really* hope I'm right.

It's still early in the day and other farms are just starting to set up their stands. I'm looking around the Main Street when I spot Eloise hauling boxes with her mom. They must have gotten here earlier than we did, because while we are sequestered away, left to the back corner of the market, Eloise and her mother are front and center, their booth in the best location.

Betsy catches my eye.

'Go help them,' she shoos me off. 'I've got it here. We won't open for another hour anyway.'

I nod and dash towards the truck.

'Nick!' Hazel says warmly, immediately depositing a pie in my hand. There's a few slices taken out of it already. 'Bring that to Betsy, will you?'

'Sure.' I place it on a nearby table to free up my hands to help Eloise with a box she's lugging towards their tent.

'Anderson Family Farm' is emblazoned in red across the top of a banner.

'Thank you.' Eloise relaxes a bit. The box is heavy but easy to carry with both of us doing the lifting. She cranes her neck around from one side of the box and smiles at me, but it doesn't reach the corner of her eyes. Something feels off.

'Is Evan here?' I ask.

She smiles for real this time, rolling her eyes. 'He's coming later. He's terrible at alarms.'

I bite my tongue from saying something judgmental, like asking aloud how Eloise would ever think someone terrible at alarms would be a good match for her. We put the box down and repeat the process with three more crates, lugging them to the tent in silence.

'Lou?' Hazel asks, peeking her head around the front of the truck. It's amazing to me how much they look alike, even though Eloise doesn't think so. Hazel has the same tendrils of hair that curl up around her face. She has the same dynamic smile, the one that completely betrays her if she isn't actually happy.

'Could you grab me a coffee? I think Carnation Cup just opened.' She nods in the direction of the nearby intersection and sure enough there is already a line forming in front of the coffee stand.

Eloise jerks her head at me. 'Do you want anything?'

'You two just go together.' Hazel waves us off.

If I'm not mistaken, she winks at Eloise as we walk away.

Eloise tugs at her shirtsleeves. She's wearing a long-sleeve flannel over her jean overalls and Anderson Farm T-shirt. We're halfway across the road when she whirls around to look at me.

'Did you really ask my dad how to fix potholes?'

That's what's on her mind? 'Yeah.' I shrug. 'Betsy hates them.'

Eloise murmurs an acknowledgment and keeps walking. She takes five steps before she turns around again. 'And you're really just trying to be successful to take care of your mom?'

'Yes? Eloise, what's this about?' I'm reaching out to grab her arm and ask her to tell me what's wrong, to tell her that I've wanted to be alone with her every second of every day since Tuesday night, when she turns around for the third time, coming to a full stop about ten feet from the coffee stand. I shudder to a halt behind her, barely stopping from running into her. We're inches from each other. Her eyes are so blue up close it's like looking into ice. She looks away and I glance down.

'I have to tell you something,' she says softly, glancing at the line to make sure no one else can hear. She fidgets awkwardly. My stomach flips.

'OK,' I say, 'I don't know what you'll have to tell me that has to do with those questions, but . . .'

Eloise wrings out her hands. 'You're just so . . . perfect,' she says in a small voice.

Gently, I nudge the bottom of her chin up with my fingers so she looks me in the eye. 'No, I'm not.'

She groans. 'It's Amie,' she sighs, 'she's going to ask you out.' She crosses her arms in front of her chest. 'I just thought you should know.'

I laugh. 'That's what you have to tell me? What does that have to do with me being "perfect." Amie's nice but . . .' I trail off, leaving what I'm thinking unsaid, that I like Eloise *more*, that when I'm around her I'm not thinking of anyone else. Eloise is still standing still and looking somewhat pained. 'I thought it was going to be bad,' I say, realizing too late that maybe the fact that Amie is asking me out *is* bad. That could mean Eloise doesn't want to go out with me. 'Wait. Are you wanting us to go on a double date with you and Evan?'

'God no.' Eloise barks out a laugh before her expression shifts. She bites her bottom lip, her eyebrows drawing together. 'Um.'

'Wait . . . is there something else that is bad?' My stomach flips again. What if something's wrong with Hazel or Cal . . . or Eloise. I reach for her hand instinctively. 'You can tell me,' I say softly.

'OK, so here's the thing.' She can't meet my gaze and I notice her hand is trembling in mine. 'I kind of need the Parkers' farm to—'

I'm listening as closely as I can but she's talking so softly I can't hear the end of her sentence over the 'your order is ready' announcements.

'The Parkers' farm to what?'

'The Parkers' farm to fail.' Eloise says glumly.

'To fail?' I repeat, wondering what I heard incorrectly because that doesn't make any sense. But she nods, finally meeting my eyes. 'I'm so sorry I didn't tell you sooner. But then I got to know you and you're well . . . you're you . . . doing things for the good of other people and . . . and the Parkers don't even know this,' she whispers, 'but we need to buy their farm if ours is going to survive.'

I stumble back from Eloise. 'Surely that can't be right . . . but you've been helping me this whole time. I thought I was helping you too. You know . . . driving business to the farm and stuff.'

'I mean.' Eloise grimaces.

'You're saying that if the Parkers don't fail your family's farm will?'

'Well, not exactly, but I think in the future, yes. My parents will sell.'

She sounds so broken-hearted at the idea that my own heart aches. 'Do Betsy and Joe know?'

Eloise shakes her head. 'My own parents didn't know until, like, four weeks ago.'

'OK.' I take a deep breath. My brain is struggling to put together the pieces of the girl I really like rooting for my failure and the worry that, based on my TikTok numbers, I may have already succeeded. What does that mean for her . . . for us? 'I think need a cup of coffee.'

Chapter Nineteen

Eloise

[FOR EVAN] List of Must-Trys at the Fall Festival

- Mom's apple pie (I guess you can get this at home, but yk what I mean)
- Apple cider donuts from DeeDee's Donuts (we can go get these Sunday, but you will want to get them twice)
- Cherry hand pies (Mrs. Marple makes a great one)
- Kettle corn (Lyle and Son's Potato Farm, don't ask me how they execute on this, but trust it)
- Apple cinnamon barbecue (ribs or brisket sandwich)
- Carmel apples (Moody's or Hal's)

'I told him.'

'What?' Evan's mouth drops open, revealing a mouth full of kettle corn. He is carrying a half-eaten cherry hand pie and the remnants of a brisket sandwich. He swallows. 'Which thing? You told him about the farm? Or Amie? Was it Amie? You're such a martyr.'

I roll my eyes. 'I am *not*. I told him both.' I raise my eyebrows. *See*, I think, *I can have hard conversations*.

Evan's eyes widen. 'Damn, girl, you executed quick.'

'Well, you got in my head! I had a nightmare about him finding out. And then I saw him this morning and he was helping my mom, and I thought about him fixing Mrs. Parker's potholes and how much he loves his mom, and . . . well . . . it just kind of came out.'

Evan completely stops moving, unable to talk and walk and eat. 'OK,' he processes, 'so you felt bad lying to an angel, which for the record, I would have too.' He creates a small pileup behind us as we take up most of the sidewalk. 'What did he say when you told him the truth?'

'Come on—' I tug his elbow "—we've got to get back to our stand. I'll tell you on the way.'

I start by explaining how confused Nick seemed by the idea of Amie asking him out.

'Confused as in he's into you—you know that, right? Don't be another one of those dumb girls who can't read the obvious signs.'

'Well, we did make out in the laundry room last week,' I mumble.

'Eloise!' Evan gasps so loudly the woman in front of us jumps. 'You made out with him and then told him someone else was going to ask him out? That's insane behavior.'

'Ugh,' I groan. I cover my face with my hands, peeling apart two fingers to stare at Evan with one eye. 'He is a really good kisser,' I whisper.

'I could have told you that,' Evan declares 'and I haven't even met the guy!'

'It doesn't matter. He doesn't even live here!'

'Exactly. He's only here for the summer, so maybe the two of you should consider a no-strings-attached summer fling.'

I sigh but I don't try to fight it. 'It was just weird,' I admit, 'the way he reacted to me wanting to buy the Parkers' farm.'

'I don't blame him at all. If what you're telling me is right, and who knows these days because you're hiding some stuff as of late, you made out with him, never discussed it, told him a different girl wanted to ask him out, *and then* you also told him you have all these weird feelings about his job.'

I squirm.

'So,' Evan prompts.

We swing around a gaggle of teens queuing for donuts. 'He was so . . . nice about it.'

'Why is that weird? Everyone has been practically screaming about how nice he is. God, I can't wait to meet him,' Evan adds the last part under his breath. 'Nick Russo, Adonis extraordinaire.'

'He *is* nice,' I say, 'but something felt different about it. Like he was nice and also sad? I'm not sure . . . I'm definitely overthinking it.'

'Definitely,' Evan agrees. 'Maybe he was just bummed you hadn't told him sooner?'

'Maybe.' I shrug. 'He said "business is business, right?" and I just sort of agreed and that was it. Then we drank our coffee.'

Evan slows down, glancing at me curiously. 'Do you really believe that? That business is business?'

'I guess . . . I mean . . . it has to be. I think it's both of our first priorities.'

'It sounds like something only rich people say.'

'Nick isn't rich,' I say quickly.

Evan raises his eyebrows at me. 'Coming to his defense pretty quick for someone you have such mixed feelings about.'

'All I'm saying is he has a point about the business is business thing. We probably need to have some sort of truce while we each try our best.'

'Business just happens to also be your family,' Evan reminds me, like there's any chance I could forget. 'But I guess if that'll work for you guys—' he elbows me '—and leaves things open.'

'It's already feeling messy without opening up that can of worms, no matter how much I want to. Plus, it's not like he'll actually accomplish anything. He'll leave, and I'll get what I want.'

'That's the confidence I've been wanting to see!' Evan fist pumps into the air.

I can't help but smile as we near our tent. The chilly early morning turned into a balmy afternoon. The sun is high in the sky, but the air is dry and a gentle breeze ruffles the row of white tents. The whole place smells like fall—fried food, apples, and fruit. I reach around Evan's shoulders and give him a hug. I'm happy he's here to see this, a larger version of the farmers' market where I'll spend my weekends all through September.

I spot my mom sitting at the front of our tent, fiddling with the brim of her hat, her twin braids thrown over her shoulders. She's in our farmers' market uniform—a loose pair of denim overalls over a white branded T-shirt. Mom and I upgraded a few years back after Lily convinced us to 'capitalize on the hippie moms.' It worked. We instantly sold more apple butter and apple marmalade. Women in pigtails and with long braids flocked to our stall.

Evan and I pass Dahlia, whose stall is next to ours, and I have to tug on his elbow gently to keep him from stopping. Dahlia tries a new thing every year. Last year it was crystals, the year before it was essential oils. One year she sold soap, the next she sold jewelry. This year, it seems, she's doing candles. And she'll talk anyone's ear off. If I let Evan linger, he'll be there for hours.

'You're back!' Mom says excitedly. 'It's gotten really . . .'

'Crowded,' I finish for her, looking around. It's markedly different than it was when Evan and I left an hour ago. Snippets of conversation float in the air towards us. I see various groups of young adults I don't recognize, most of them women, and the street is congested with people.

Mom and I are still looking at each other, confused, when a young woman approaches our booth, glances at the sign and squeals, 'Apples!' before she asks happily 'Are you guys the Parker farm?'

We shake our heads. The girl apologizes and leaves, exiting the shade of the tent and returning to her cluster of friends. I watch as she communicates the news and they move on.

Mom and I look at each other. She eases herself out of her chair and stands in front of our tent to crane her neck down the street. Something she sees makes her go completely still. 'Lou,' she says, 'come see this.'

I'm by her side in seconds. My jaw drops.

There is a line snaking from our tent down about two blocks, ending at a dinky, off-white tent at the end of the farmers' market. In all my years at the market I have never seen a line so long.

'You have to go see.' Mom elbows me sharply in the side.

'Ow!' I cry out. But I obey. I can't help myself. I'm being pulled towards the line like I'm magnetized, Evan following hesitantly behind me. I'm beginning to realize the mass of people all look to be about the same age. Younger than me, late teens, early twenties, dressed like they googled farm chic beforehand. About half are in overalls. One girl is in cutoff jean shorts that show the goosebumps dotting her legs. Impatiently, I weave around them. I know what I'll see beyond the line but I'm unprepared anyway. At the very front, manning the helm of the Parkers' tent, preoccupied with helping a teenage girl get a selfie with a pig, smiling from ear to ear, is Nick Russo. Beside him, Betsy is beaming.

My stomach drops. 'I'm going to kill him,' I seethe.

'Lou?' Evan says slowly. 'What happened to business is business?'

Chapter Twenty

Nick

I have only seen Betsy this happy the time Joe pulled her into an impromptu dance across the scratched wooden floor in the kitchen, somehow making their farmhouse look more romantic than any scene in *The Notebook*. The spin around the room lasted less than a minute and Betsy smiled from ear to ear for days. The next morning, she came downstairs with curled hair and blushed when Joe said good morning. For some reason it made me think of my mamma. All she wants is for me to have a love like that. All I want for her is to be loved that way.

Today, Betsy is just as happy, her smile practically splitting her face in two. It overtakes me as well; I can't help but feel as elated as she does.

'I can't believe this,' she whispers breathlessly to me as we unpack the last of the crates we tucked under the table. 'This is our stock for half of the year. It's gone.' Her eyes are wet when she looks up at me.

'This is just the beginning,' I say.

'I know, I know,' she mutters, busying herself by unpacking the apple butter. 'I won't get ahead of myself.'

I was actually trying to tell her to get more excited, but I don't correct her. The last thing I want to do is overpromise and underdeliver. I still have to run the numbers to determine how much profit we've made and I need to model out the rest of the year. How much product can Besty and Joe produce, their paths to expansion, how can they continue to advertise. I need to walk Joe through all those things. Betsy keeps muttering about how much Joe will hate that it was the pig that finally made their business work—I didn't learn until today that Betsy's soft heart is the reason they have all the pigs to begin with.

Everyone's been asking me where Princess Peach is, so I jot down a note to remember to bring her next time. Almost half of the people who stand in line to take a photo end up buying something from Betsy. Her hit rate for people who buy the apple butter after trying it is almost one hundred percent. Our problem now is that we've run out of crackers for them to try it on. Another thing I make note of.

The line is still snaking out of our tent when the sun crests high in the sky. Betsy told me the farmers' market winds down around 2 p.m. so the town can rest and prepare for the evening carnival, so I pop my head out to check and see how many more people we have to get through before we get a break. There's a gaggle of girls in baggy jeans and T-shirts holding up the end of the line but thankfully things appear to be cooling down.

A blonde head catches my eye as I'm about to duck back into the tent. I'd know those braids anywhere—Eloise. I linger outside the tent hoping that Betsy can pick up the slack while I dawdle. That's another thing I need to think through. Betsy and Joe will need help—more than just seasonal help. They'll need someone to help them run the tent all year.

Eloise is slowing as she approaches our stand. I see someone behind her. A man with brown hair spiked with blond highlights in an Anderson Farm T-shirt emblazoned with a bright red apple.

Eloise comes to a jerky stop, taking a half-step before she sees me. When our eyes meet she doesn't move even an inch closer. Her eyebrows furrow, her nose scrunching up in anger. Irritation flares through me, hot and strong. She has no right to be annoyed that I'm succeeding. We agreed this morning that business was business.

I walk towards her quickly, closing the distance between us in fifteen steps. Even when she's angry she makes me smile, so I come to a stop in front of her, grinning. 'You didn't think I had it in me?' I ask, elbowing her gently in the ribs. I don't know what I'm expecting, but it isn't what I get, which is Eloise huffing air out of her nose and turning around sharply.

'Evan,' she says, just as he catches up to where we're standing. 'We're going.'

I close my mouth just in time to say, 'Hi,' to Evan but he's already walking away. He gives me a wide-eyed look that says *sorry, man* before he turns to follow Eloise.

I watch them go, growing angrier by the minute. Eloise seemed so cool about things earlier, so apologetic that she didn't want the Parkers to be able to keep their farm. Now she's acting like this is personal, like I designed this project to hurt her.

After Eloise dips her head into her tent I reluctantly turn back to Betsy. Thankfully when I get back, she's laughing, trying to take a selfie with two teens who keep telling her how adorable she is. At least something is right in the world.

As soon as the line dies down to dawdlers, I ask Betsy if I can go help Hazel.

'Sure, honey,' she says with a wink, 'Eloise sure is pretty, isn't she?'

I give Betsy a stern look. 'I'm just being a good neighbor.'

'Mhmm.'

Eloise, Hazel, and Evan are packing up their tent when I walk over. Their folding chairs and table are already in the truck. I feel a pang of jealousy that Evan was the person who helped them pack up. But of course they don't need me, they were doing this long before Evan or I got here. I spot boxes of unsold goods in the back of the truck and wince.

'Hi.' I wave. 'Need any help?'

Hazel clears her throat. 'I'm going to go drop off my pies,' she says, scurrying out of the back of the tent and towards the neighboring stand.

'How was your afternoon?' I ask. I feel awkward now, like the charm I had all afternoon has drained out of me. 'How did handing out the radish-growing kits go? Did the kids like them?'

'Fine,' Eloise says tersely.

Evan clears his throat. 'I think I'm just going to get one more apple cider donut.'

Eloise's cheeks redden as he walks away.

Evan stops at the door and turns. 'Anyone . . . um . . . want anything?'

'No thanks,' I muster. It's taking everything I can to not immediately wrap my arms around Eloise. She looks completely deflated.

'You don't need to help us,' she says after Evan leaves. 'You must have a lot to do.' Her tone has a bite to it.

'We're all packed. Betsy's grabbing some stuff from Hal's. I'm happy to help.' I absent-mindedly scratch the back of my neck. Eloise and I never feel this . . . stilted.

'It's OK. You've done enough already.'

It couldn't be any more clear that Eloise is *not* paying me a compliment. 'I think the business will be good for you too,' I say in a soft voice, the same one I use with my mom when I don't want her to be mad at me. 'Even if it isn't what you wanted, maybe more people coming to your farm will change things.'

'You know what, Nick, it won't work like you think it will. The Parkers don't have the soil health to keep their farm going no matter how much you market their pet pigs. But that's none of your business. It's not like you'll stick around here long enough to know what the impact of anything you're doing actually is.'

I take a step back. 'That's not fair. I'm making a plan for them. They'll be taken care of.'

'A plan?' Eloise throws her hands up in the air. 'Farms don't work with *plans*, that's like Farming 101. Plans get ruined like that.' She snaps her fingers in the air. 'One drought, two days of too much rain, three days of an early frost. *Plans* can't fix those things. Good farming can. I thought I explained that to you—' she lets out an exasperated sigh '—but you clearly didn't listen. This is why I should have never—' She stops herself short, her cheeks reddening. 'I should never have assumed you were different! Men only ever think about themselves!'

I feel myself bristle. This is bigger than me and I'm not sure if she's talking about Linden or something else. Given the hurt in her voice, I think it might be more than Linden, it probably has to do with her parents wanting to sell their farm, but either way, it isn't *my* fault

'Selling product can help,' I grumble under my breath. Eloise treated me like I didn't know anything when I met her because I didn't know anything, but things have changed. 'Look, it isn't my fault that your plan hinged on someone else failing.'

'Low blow,' she mutters.

'Look, I don't want to hurt you,' I say, 'but I can't let the Parkers down either. Whether you like it or not this is about more than just them. My future is at stake here too. What do you expect me to do?'

She sighs, some of the anger disappearing from her expression. 'I know. I know you're doing this for your mom. I can't ask you to sacrifice the future you've planned for her, but I can't exactly keep helping you hurt me either.'

My heart clenches in my chest. 'But, Eloise,' I say, 'I like you more than for your farming help. Can't we just separate the two?'

She shakes her head. 'Maybe it's a good thing Amie wants to ask you out. Whatever happened between us was a mistake.'

'This isn't fair,' I argue. 'You're punishing me for something you would do in my position.'

'You're leaving soon anyways, so I suppose we can be cordial until then.'

I can't believe what I'm hearing. How did we go from spending every morning together to *cordial*. 'Cordial? For something that isn't even my fault?'

'OK.' She crosses her arms in front of her chest, her light blue eyes piercing. 'Whose fault is it?'

I raise my eyebrows at her.

She huffs.

'Eloise, what happened to "business is business"?'

'What happened? What happened is that business *isn't* business to me. This is my *family* we're talking about. This is my *life*. You're just doing a fall fling. There are no repercussions for you. I know you feel pressure to succeed at everything to make your mom proud, but . . .'

'You're acting like I'm not doing this for my degree,' I say, but even I know the argument is weak.

'You said it yourself it didn't matter if you succeeded or failed, you'll still graduate. You have a job! Nick, you don't understand. I don't know why I expected you to. But this matters to me. This is everything to me.' Eloise voice cracks. Her eyes start to fill with tears. 'You know what, just go.'

'Eloise.' I step towards her.

'Go.' She turns around, her shoulders curving inward. I watch as she scoops up a germinated radish seed, the only container left on the otherwise empty table and dumps it into the trash. Clearly it was the one she had saved for me. My heart seizes.

Just as I'm taking a step towards her I hear the clear of a throat behind me. Hazel appears. 'I think it's best if you leave,' she says softly.

Reluctantly, I obey.

Chapter Twenty-One

Eloise

Things About Myself I Am Embracing This Fall

- I am my father's daughter—I have his grit (never mind that we are both lacking in the charm department)
- I am a damn good farmer
- I am a petty person, who always wants to prove my worth and avenge my wrongs
- If I can teach little kids how to plant a baby seedling without squishing it, then I can do pretty much anything

Lily: Hi cutie peach, I miss you! JW but is that video of the Parkers' pig? Apparently it's trending. That guy is SOOOO cute. You should totally meet him.

Lily: OK wait . . . this is DEFINITELY Buttercup. Get your ass to the Fall celebration thingy STAT!

Lily: Can you respond to me please. I have friends over and we are INVESTED.

Two hours later:

> **Lily: Hello???**
>
> **Me: Hi!!! What are you talking about LOL**
>
> **Me: Also, miss you too.**
>
> **Lily: Lily Shared a TikTok!**

I click on the group chat with Evan and Shari:

> **Evan: . . . ELOISE ARE YOU THERE *sent with slam effect***
>
> **Shari: What am I, chopped liver?**
>
> **Evan: *Pâté**
>
> **Evan: I can't be bothered to care as much about you while you're in Italy. I'm too jealous.**
>
> **Shari: Jealousy is the best compliment!**
>
> **Evan: That isn't a saying.**
>
> **Me: Evan stop texting me from the bathroom when you're IN my house. Shari, we miss you.**
>
> **Evan: Thank GOD. I was waiting for you to be active in this chat to send.**

Evan: Shared a TikTok.

Shari: OMG IS THAT Nick?

Evan: Shouldn't you be sleeping?

Shari: SHUTUP

Me: Evan, if I have to see this video again I will claw my own eyes out.

I am frozen with reluctance at the kitchen table when I press play. A glass of iced tea sweats on the counter in front of me. Mom is stirring at something on the stove. Dad is in his office. We're supposed to be heading back out for the Fall Festival Carnival in two hours. It's the first break I've had all day. We're all beat.

Sure enough, when I click on the video Lily sent me, Nick's face fills the screen. And he looks . . . incredible. His jaw seems even stronger, the light is hitting him *just* right, and he's wearing a plaid button-down I've never seen, but one that hugs his arms perfectly.

The only thing out of place is the piece of wheat he's stuck between his teeth.

Anger roils in the pit of my stomach. He can't be serious. Is this about to be a video caricature of farmers? *I hate men.*

I press play.

'Howdy, y'all!'

Dread blooms in my gut. *No no no no no no*. This can't be happening. I cannot have fallen for this . . . I move my finger to navigate away from the page to text Evan and say *I told you so! Why do you think I hate this guy now? Nobody takes f*cking farmers seriously!!!* but before I can, Nick's laughter fills the room.

He takes the piece of wheat away from his lips. 'I'm kidding!' he exclaims. 'I've been here two weeks and haven't seen one person chewing on wheat. I think I've been lied to my whole life.' Nick laughs again. It's different from how he laughs when we're together. On video it's louder, less charismatic.

'Thanks for all the love you've sent the Parkers this past week. They love you too! While you've been doting on our favorite grandparents, I've been prepping something special for you guys. The big announcement . . .' Nick trails off, and a picture of Buttercup the pig fills the screen.

Mom stops stirring and turns around. 'What are you watching?'

I motion for her to come over and she does so, wrapping an arm around my shoulder for balance and leaning even closer to the phone.

'Is that . . .'

'Yep.'

I press play again.

'I'll be at the Carnation Fall Festival farmers' market this weekend! Come and see us, we'll be ringing in fall in this beautiful weather.' Footage of the rolling hills around Carnation fill the screen. I'm pretty sure the footage was taken from a spot on our property, the dip in the hills between the Parkers' farm and ours. Anger pulses in my veins.

The video continues. 'This fall, I have the pleasure of working on the Parker family's farm . . . and the pleasure of meeting this cutie.' The frame switches to a video of Nick and Buttercup together. She's a soft pale pink with a perfectly cute snout. She's adorable. I've always loved Buttercup. Nick's done a good job, I have to give him that.

He reaches a muscled arm around Buttercup. 'This little lady is going to be at our farmers' market stand this weekend,' Nick narrates. 'And if you come see us, you can get a picture with her. She loves people, isn't that right?' He turns to Buttercup who snorts right on cue.

'Is this why they had so many people at their stand?' Mom asks.

I press on the screen to see how many people viewed the video, a knot forming in my stomach. The video was posted two days ago and already has over six hundred *thousand* views.

My jaw drops open.

Evan and I make it back to the carnival in just enough time to check the results of the apple pie contest before settling on a picnic blanket. Mom was awarded first place, and the huge smile on her face took some sting out of the day. We wave goodbye to her, ducking out of the gaggle of bakers wanting to know her secret, heading to grab barbecue sandwiches before the fireworks start.

'I'll get us beers,' Evan says, while I lay out a picnic blanket.

I press a twenty into his hand. 'Please let me pay,' I say. 'I'm so happy you're here. I don't know what I would have done without you today.'

'I'll listen to you complain about a hot farm boy any day.' Evan winks, before walking towards the alcohol tent. Fireflies are flickering and the field smells like freshly mowed grass. I sit down on the blanket, sinking into the soft earth, and let out a long sigh.

I get everything set up on the blanket—our sandwiches, napkins, and the apple pie Mom packed us for dessert—but Evan still hasn't returned. I scan the crowd, looking for his mop of blond-tinged hair by the alcohol tent. My body goes rigid when I spot Evan and recognize the head he's leaning towards—Nick. As if he can see me, just then he whips around and gives me a cheery wave, instantly heading in my direction. Nick disappears the other way, fading into the crowd.

'What were you talking about?' I ask Evan suspiciously when he reaches earshot.

'Nothing!' Evan chirps. 'I know you're mad at him. And, like, I get it. But he's really hot. And nice.'

I glower at Evan. 'I'm not thinking about that anymore. He does not exist to me except to ruin.'

Evan laughs so hard he snorts into his beer. 'Except to ruin? What are you—a heroine of a romantasy series?'

'It's not funny. He *cannot* succeed.'

Evan softens. 'I know. I'll help you plan.'

'Good, I need it.'

'Eloise, your petty ass probably does not need help planning. But I think it's fun, so I'll do it anyways.' He grins, and we tuck into our food. A full belly and an hour of fireworks later and I'm feeling a little better. I can outsmart Nick with Evan at my back . . . I think.

I dream about Nick. We're sitting together at a picnic table out back. His profile is lit by the setting sun, showcasing his Cupid's bow just so. His eyelashes flutter when he looks at me. I'm thinking about how smart and thoughtful he is, and how much my parents like him. He's ambitious. He's sexy and interesting. I can't help but think about how much I want to sleep with him. Just as I'm thinking it, as if he can read my mind, he leans in to kiss me. I'm so eager for it to happen again, I lean forward, closing my eyes. And right in that moment I wake up with a start.

Nick. Nick. *Stupid motherfucking Nick.* What if his plan works. And what if he's the reason my plan doesn't.

I toss and turn the whole night through.

When I wake up in the morning, my sheets are twisted but my thoughts are clear. I will not let Nick take my family farm down.

'Evan?' I call down the hallway as soon as I hear his door creak open. 'We have some planning to do.'

Thirty minutes and two full cups of hot and strong coffee later and I'm pacing back and forth in my room, walking through the puddle of light that pools through the stained-glass window and back again. Every time my shadow crosses it I get more and more annoyed. I'm practically stomping.

'Eloise,' Evan demands from his spot on my bed. 'Can you *please* stop doing that. It's driving me insane. You're walking around like an elephant.' He pauses, smirking at his phone. 'Also, you need to stop doing that because I'm ready to show you *my* plan.'

Evan's Plan

- Do better than his TikTok. Educate people. You'd be surprised, but some people find that more interesting. Those people are your people. Find them. The only thing people like better than a hot man is a hot girl. I don't want to objectify you, but if you got it, flaunt it.
- Make the *better* farmers' market stand every Sunday. Get there early. Get the best spot. Leverage things people will want to take a picture in front of. Think 'perfect Instagram background' and set your tent up that way. Then offer to take pictures of the girls walking to Nick's tent.
- Buy a pig. Or a baby animal of any kind. Take to farmers' market.
- Put the stuff Nick uses for the farmers' market on Craigslist next Friday so he's distracted fending off pickups and can't focus.

- Steal the pigs. Or let them loose. Check if this is animal cruelty?
- Win *every* competition. Hazel winning the apple pie competition was a great start. Next is applesauce, right? Win that too. Use it to advertise.
- Advertise U-Pick season like crazy. Double what you usually do. I'll help. Add a photo backdrop to your U-Pick layout and say you'll help people take Holiday Card photos.
- Do you know how the Potato Farm makes that popcorn so good? Maybe you should sell it.
- Lean into what Nick *doesn't* have. <u>Real farming experience.</u>
- Nick maybe looks like a god, but we both know he can't fix soil in two months. You got this.

Chapter Twenty-Two

Nick

WEEK FIVE

Julian: Nick, you gotta get back here, man. We're getting swamped in pickup.

Isaac: Dude no were not. We're doing fine.

Julian: We've lost the past three weeks in a row.

Isaac: But that's because those teams had Bryan and that other guy that just graduated from LSU.

Nick: If I could come back tomorrow I would.

Isaac: Trouble in paradise?

Nick: Didn't say that.

Julian, in a separate thread without Isaac: Everything good, man?

Nick: Yeah, just tiring out here. Long days.

Julian: Well, I can't wait to visit!

Nick: I'm excited for that too.

Julian: Three weeks until we're there. Then you're basically home.

Nick: Yeah.

Julian: If it makes you feel any better, not that Isaac will admit it, but his internship is running him into the ground. He's been working twelve-hour days.

Nick: Haha. Makes me feel a bit better. Thanks, dude.

Julian: Np.

Isaac would have a field day if he knew how much trouble there was in paradise.

It's been three days since the farmers' market and Eloise has not spoken to me once, despite my going over to her house *every* morning. On Tuesday I left her a lavender latte on the porch, a gesture of goodwill, with a note that said *Hey, can we talk?* and had my phone number scrawled across it. All day I was glued to my phone. I felt in my bones she would reach out. But the day ticked along, a chilly morning making way for another bright fall afternoon, a crisp breeze floating through the apple trees, which turned into a brisk evening, only for my phone to stubbornly stay silent.

This morning when I woke up I decided I'd had enough of her freezing me out. If this is the way she wants to play it, then I'll let her know who she decided to play against.

I was iffy on whether or not to release this campaign at all—it does involve significant work on Mrs. Parker's part, but now I have nothing to lose and everything (revenge on Eloise) to gain. In a flurry of TikTok's I announce the 'Day in the Life' competition, where a lucky winner will be chosen from the list of people who like the video and follow our account. They'll get a chance to come up to the farm, meet the pigs and Mr. and Mrs. Parker, and they'll get to take home a basket of home-made goods. To top it off, Mrs. Parker will cook every single meal, as farm to table as you can get it. *And* the lucky winner can bring a guest with them.

Mrs. Parker, for her part, is thrilled. When I show her how many people have entered the competition so far she claps her hands together with glee.

'You'll have to tell me what to make,' she says, putting down her crotchet.

We're on the porch, as we are every evening, all three of us gently rocking back and forth in rocking chairs. Heat emanates from the cups of apple cider that rest at our sides, a fall tradition for the Parkers. I've already asked Betsy for the recipe, although recreating this type of fall magic in my studio apartment in San Francisco will be impossible. Betsy looks so small under the chunky quilt that she's pulled up so high it almost reaches her chin, and I feel a swell of affection for her.

'All of your meals are delicious,' I say emphatically.

'I could do my roast chicken.'

Joe grunts from his chair. He *loves* her roast chicken. Betsy glances at me for approval.

'That's a perfect idea,' I say.

I only let the competition run for one full day before I enter the applicants into a random generator at the end of Wednesday night. I'm exhausted, but I sit straight up, my eyes almost popping out of my head when I read the name the generator outputs: *Anna Park*.

No. No. No. Anna of all people? How on earth did she win this? I let my mouse hover over the 'spin again' button wondering how unethical it would be to just pick someone else. The last thing I want is for Anna to come up here sniffing around, making small talk with Mrs. Parker. For all I know Anna will probably reach out to my mother and bring her *too*. Suddenly I feel like I bit off way more than I can chew.

But when I go to click the mouse, I hesitate. It doesn't sit right with me to manipulate the contest so much. Maybe having Anna won't be as bad as I thought. A familiar face could be nice. Plus, I know what I'm getting myself into. I type out a message to her: *You'll never believe it!* . . . ignoring the nagging feeling that I'm allowing the winner to be Anna for an entirely different reason than it could be nice to see a familiar face—a reason that has everything to do with the fact that this is the perfect way to irritate the hell out of Eloise, who just so happens to be irritating the hell out of me.

Chapter Twenty-Three

Eloise

The Best Things About Fall on a Farm

- London fog lattes
- Seeing your breath in the morning
- The sun (and the roosters) rising a little later
- Golden turmeric chai lattes (in my opinion, this should be a year-round thing, but the coffee shop has always branded them as 'their alternative to pumpkin spice')
- Cardigans
- Home-made sticky toffee pudding cake

Every three years the Fall Festival coincides with a drop of about five degrees in the daily temperature, everyone starts to wear flannel, even the people that insist on wearing shorts in the winter, and Carnation truly comes alive.

There are yellow mums blooming in front door pots and garlands of dried orange daisies hanging from inside windows. Rocking chairs are draped with thick blankets on front porches and chunky knit sweaters are unearthed from the back of the cabinet. Every year Mom spends a whole day pulling out our fall wardrobes, which are home to an embarrassing amount of red sweaters and plaid scarves and way too many *Anderson Farm*-emblazoned beanies. But when she does the closet switch, she also makes spritz cookies shaped like pumpkins and the smell takes over the whole house, filling us all up with the cozy fall joy.

This year the cookies smell just as good, but everything else feels a little less joyous. It's been six days since I last talked to Nick. We have three weeks left before U-Pick season officially kicks off at the end of September. Which means about a month until Nick leaves. I convince myself the contraction in my gut when I think about him leaving is because I dread having to be around him until then, *not* because I don't want him to leave.

I take refuge in the field to distract myself, putting in a longer day of work than I have in ages, especially for a Saturday. I survey every single line of the orchard for misshapen apples—it's critical they're all removed so the trees can direct all their energy to growing the apples we can sell. I lose track of time and end up rushing back in towards the house, hoping to squeeze in a hand or two of gin rummy before dinner. The sun is almost completely set when I head home, the fields rolling endlessly into a dark haze of twilight.

'Eloise?' I hear a familiar voice ring out.

I freeze. I'm right at the part of the path where it splits, one direction heading towards the Parkers'. I know that voice. I look around but I can't make out anything in my rapidly darkening surroundings. It's dark enough that he may not have seen me, but eventually the outside lights will click on, the ones that stay on for thirty minutes to help guide workers out of the field when it's dark. If I can hide before the lights turn on, then maybe I can avoid him. I've been doing a lot of that lately. I duck behind a tree.

I wait a minute, then two, before I decide the coast is clear. Nick doesn't call out for me again. I stand up and start striding towards the house when the lights blaze on, bathing the whole field in fluorescent white light.

Nick is standing on the opposite hillside. A black-haired woman stands at his side. My stomach drops right as he waves hello.

'Hi,' he says, his voice friendly but his gait hesitant, not the usual sloping, confident walk that I'm used to. 'I wasn't sure if that was you.'

'Hi.' I muster up enough decency to wave, approaching them slowly. I'm opening my mouth to apologize to them, to tell them that I'm so sorry but I need to head inside for dinner, but Nick speaks before I can get a word out.

'This is Anna,' he says with a sweeping gesture as a cheery-faced woman steps forward. 'She won our "Day on the Farm" competition. I was just showing her what it looks like at night.'

'Over two *thousand* people applied,' Anna gushes.

'That's great,' I say dumbly. My mind wanders, wondering how on earth this woman manages to look so good under fluorescent lighting. I am all too aware of how I look after a day of hard work—my face flushed, dried sweat around my temple, frizzing hair and dirt caked under my fingernails. *I never used to care about this around Nick*, I realize with a sinking feeling. *He used to make me feel sexy no matter what. The fact that I worked hard was sexy, my untamable hair was sexy,* sweat *was sexy.* I make the mistake of glancing at her manicured nails, which are perfectly square and pale pink. She seems nice enough, launching into chatter about how good her day has been and how excited she is for Mrs. Parker's cooking after the lunch they had.

I reach to a nearby tree and pluck an apple. 'Have you tried one from Andersons' farm yet?' I ask her. 'They're the best.'

Nick narrows his eyes at me. 'I wouldn't say that,' he counters. But Anna is already happily reaching out to take the apple. 'Mmm,' she says, as she takes a satisfyingly crunchy bite, 'this is amazing.'

'You have to be careful at the Parker farm,' I confide in a faux whisper, 'there are some rotten apples over there.'

Nick forces out a laugh. 'Very funny, Eloise.' His forced smile wavers, the corners of his mouth pulling down slightly. 'I guess we can let you get home.'

I stare at Nick a beat too long, wondering how we got from the laundry room to here, this feeling of insurmountable distance when there's only a few feet between us.

Anna protests, gently swatting at Nick's arm. 'I'd love to talk to a female farmer. I haven't seen one all day!' she exclaims. 'Well, unless you need to get home?'

I notice with a little flare of satisfaction the way Nick steps back from Anna ever so slightly, putting distance between them.

'Oh, that's all right, you're not keeping me,' I reply, warming up to her as my jealousy subsides. 'How long are you in town?'

'Just until tomorrow. Then I head back to Seattle.'

'You live there?' It seems like Anna and Nick are more familiar than having met this morning, but that's the thing about Nick—he can really put people at ease. I wouldn't put it past him if he did in fact only meet Anna hours ago and he's already bewitched her.

'I actually live in San Francisco, but I'm doing my capstone project in Seattle.'

Oh. 'Capstone? So you go to school with Nick?'

There's a flash of confusion across Anna's features, like she's surprised Nick hadn't filled me in on that, but she brushes past it, confirming pleasantly that she does go to school with Nick.

'How are you liking your capstone?' I ask her.

'It's great. But compared to this, it's pretty boring. Not all of us are saving the world like Nick here.'

I raise my eyebrows at Nick, who at least has the decency to look sheepish. 'I never said that. Anna, why don't you tell Eloise what happened with the pigs today.'

Anna leans forward like she's confiding a great secret to me and explains, through cackles of laughter, that when Nick brought her to meet the pigs Daisy got so possessive she headbutted Anna's shins and Anna fell into the slop of the pigsty. She gestures to her outfit, which now that I take a better look at, is definitely Mrs. Parker's clothes. I can't help but laugh at her own ability to laugh at herself, and I catch Nick's expression relaxing just a bit.

'I was just showing her how fast the stars come out,' Nick explains, 'we didn't mean to bother you.'

'Why don't we walk you home?' Anna says happily. 'Your house is just over this way, right? That way you can get to dinner *and* tell me what it's like being one of the only women out here. That's something I'm working on this summer actually, the impact the #MeToo movement has had on women in male workspaces.'

'That's so cool that you're doing that. I wish I had more to say, but I've done this all my life, so I don't notice it too much, that I'm the only woman out here . . . that's not a very helpful answer is it?'

Anna smiles warmly. 'It's a data point that you don't notice, so it's for sure helpful! Does your mom farm too?'

'She used to. She threw her back out a while ago and had to stop doing heavy labor. I think she really misses it.'

'And will you do this as your career?'

'Probably,' I say, 'I'm born and raised here. It feels like I should take up the mantle. Enough about me, I'd love to hear more about your internship, Anna. It sounds so interesting!'

'You should be in a lab, not out here,' Nick interjects before Anna can answer.

'Excuse me?' I say. 'Where I work is not your decision to make. Especially not when you clearly should be behind a computer screen.'

'Yeah, jeez, Nick,' Anna says. 'Men,' she whispers conspiratorially in my direction. 'Eloise did more than you today I'll bet.' Nick's glare is lost on her because she continues to babble on about how great of a farmer I am and how cool it is to see a young woman doing this kind of work. I stand there smirking happily. *Take that, Nick Russo*. I'm warming up to Anna, I decide. Although she has questionable taste in acquaintances.

'Unfortunately, this is about the only thing I'm good at,' I say to Anna, thinking about how terrible I am at filming TikToks—I can't seem to make it past what my own voice sounds like being played back. Not that I'll get into that with Anna in front of Nick.

I turn to Nick. 'I like her,' I say, 'let's not send her home tomorrow.'

Nick runs a hand through his thick hair and murmurs something I don't quite catch, but sounds suspiciously like *Why did I think introducing you two was a good idea*?

'Nick says you're in some sort of rivalry,' Anna says. Nick shoots her another glare, this times she catches it and blushes. 'Whoops,' she murmurs, 'was I not supposed to say?'

'A rivalry? That's what we're calling it?'

I stare at Nick for a beat too long before turning to Anna. 'The problem with Nick,' I say, loud enough for him to hear, 'is that he never understands when he should be taking things more seriously.'

Chapter Twenty-Four

Nick

WEEK SIX

Something's not right. I tried to tell Betsy but she waved me off, instead directing the conversation towards Eloise, which is a sure shot at making me clam up. I swear I saw a flashlight around the equipment barn when I was working last night. I looked out my window and saw a flicker, next thing I knew it was gone. I rushed downstairs to see if Betsy and Joe were both home—they were, Joe was reading the paper and Betsy was knitting. I almost stopped to take a picture of them, content of the two of them together does really well. They are both relationship and lifestyle goals apparently. I've even managed to put some up of Betsy talking through her outfits, 'These boots are from . . . well . . . I think my own mother,' she says, as she sticks her foot out in a an extremely worn and muddy boot. 'These jeans are from the Gap. And my shirt—' she turns around trying to check the tag '—well, it's just cute isn't it?' she asks the camera. The shirt reads 'Don't Go Bacon my Heart,' with a picture of Buttercup.

As soon as I realized Joe and Betsy were both inside, I rushed to the window. 'I think I saw someone out back,' I told Joe, who grunted at the newspaper non-committally.

'I'm sure it was just a firefly,' Betsy said cheerily, not taking her eyes off the knitting. 'Have more of Hazel's cookies.' Hazel's been dropping off pies and goodies all week, part of some fall thing she said they do at their house every year where she makes all their favorite recipes to usher in a new season. I dragged myself away from the windowsill. 'OK,' I said, helping myself to a few. I looked out the window every minute or so until my plate was completely clean. Nothing.

But this morning a strange truck drove by the farm at breakfast and turned into the Anderson farm. Nobody has a reason to be on these back roads unless they live here, so if a new car arrives it's odd. I try and dismiss it, maybe Eloise's older brother Linden has come home?

But by the time I'm heading to help Joe with harvesting a hand-pick only row of specialty apples, a varietal he grafted himself, I've seen two more trucks drive by. Both of them turned into the Andersons' driveway. They're delivering something . . . but what?

It's been three days since I ran into Eloise with Anna. I don't know why I thought someone from the city could make Eloise jealous. She warmed up to Anna right away, as friendly and genuine as ever. The entire time they talked I missed Eloise so badly I could feel my desire to hold her close buzzing underneath my skin. I've tried not to think about her, but I haven't succeeded. Everything reminds me of her. Each apple I see, every tree branch swaying in the morning breeze, the smell of the apple blossoms and the low chatter of the other workers in the field, even the hum of machinery can remind me of her, dredging up something she's told me before about why she likes John Deere tractors better than Kubota.

Anna could tell something was up, zeroing in on Eloise right after they met and asking me a zillion questions about her, pestering me about what the rivalry really was because 'it's clear there's something there, Nick.' Thankfully Anna also talked my ear off about a new guy she was seeing, someone she met in Seattle. Although my mamma would be disappointed, I was elated. One less complication on my plate. Plus, I love having Anna as a friend. She's friendly and ambitious and smart as a whip. The next morning when as Anna was leaving she said, 'You must think she's cute right, I mean she's *beautiful*,' while staring wistfully in the Andersons' direction. I knew what she was doing, luring me into admitting how breathtaking I thought Eloise was, and I still couldn't avoid it. I nodded. Anna punched her fist in the air. 'I knew it!' she cried triumphantly. Since she left I have gotten no less than five texts from her asking if I've made up with Eloise yet. What Anna doesn't know is her texts are somehow making me angrier and sadder at the same time.

They send me into a spiral where I start thinking about how Eloise's bright blue eyes narrow just so when she knows I still don't understand something even though it's the second time she's explained it. I miss how she angles her head towards me when a piece of hair has come loose from her braid, knowing I'll tuck it behind her ear. I miss the way she smells like sweet grass and the way her laugh rings out over the fields if I've said something funny.

I keep fighting off the desire to text her to tell her about what Betsy cooked for dinner or how many times Joe said 'in my day,' which as of this morning, is already three today alone. But thinking of her also makes my blood boil in frustration. The only thing I hate more than her being mad at me is the fact that she has no reason to be angry. I don't understand when 'business is business' stopped applying. When did our stupid rivalry turn into something so much more serious?

When the fourth truck of the day rumbles past, I stop wondering *if* she's up to something and start wondering *what* she's up to—I wouldn't put it past her to do something to make sure I don't succeed. All I need to do is make sure I outsmart her. My Instagram account is gaining more followers by the day. The best part is that I'm starting to love the pigs as much as the internet does. Maisy breaks into grunts as soon as she sees me, Princess Peach squeals just once, but loud enough to make the nearby chickens squawk, Buttercup even pulls herself up to her hooves to amble by and say hello, and Daisy, the most stubborn of them all, has started to accept me as one of her caretakers.

The pigs aren't my only good news—Scott's Orchards, a large farm in the neighboring county that's owned by an even bigger conglomerate, is looking for ways to diversify. I reached out to them to see what they think about investing in the Parkers' farm and they said they want to come down for a meeting. I haven't told Joe and Betsy yet, I don't want to get their hopes up, but an investment from a bigger farm and an opening to sell down the road is a big deal. It's the only silver lining to not talking to Eloise. I know she'll disapprove.

She'll have to do more than get some random deliveries sent to her farm to derail me now.

Smiling, I head into the field. Time to put in a good day's work.

Chapter Twenty-Five

Eloise

My Go-To Karaoke Setlist

- 'Sweet Caroline'
- 'Dancing Queen'
- 'Linger'
- 'Redneck Woman' (Lily is fantastic at this one)
- 'Party in the USA'
- '. . . Baby One More Time'

'I'll be posting a new video every day while I'm here for the fall with a fun farm tidbit, so you all can learn more about farming. Then, when the apples are ready to eat, I expect you to visit! Stay tuned, Mrs. Parker will be sharing some of her classic family recipes.' The screen blurs and text appears on top of the video.

> **Every June, bees are hauled out to the orchards en masse to pollinate the trees. Multiple hives! The farmers say the beats of their wings sound like rolling thunder.**

'That was *me!*' I yell at the phone. 'I said that!'

'What was you, dear?' Mom asks, spinning around from where she is sitting. She's leaning over her iPad, playing a card game on her phone at the kitchen island. As soon as I showed her there was a gin rummy app, she's been intent on practicing. But she refuses to tell Dad. She's too excited about the possibility of a surprise win.

'Another one of Nick's videos,' I say with an exasperated sigh.

'Gosh, that boy is busy. I feel like you've shown me a new video every day this week. And you helped him with one?' She lowers her reading glasses to the bottom of her nose. 'Finally! I was wondering when the two of you would make up. Is that what you were doing with all those supplies you got delivered to the garage.'

'I didn't help him,' I mutter, 'he stole it. And I'm sorry I'm cluttering up the garage, it'll be worth it.'

'I know it will.' She walks towards where I'm sitting on the couch and peers over my shoulder, reading the text. 'That's so pretty,' she muses. 'You could have been a poet.'

'Thank you, but that is not the point.' I glower. 'He used it without telling me. He shouldn't be allowed to do that.'

'He did?' Her eyebrows crease together.

'I mean, he told me he was interviewing me for his work but . . . yeah, kind of . . .'

'Hmm.' She gets up and makes her way back to the stove. 'Well, did he send it to you? Maybe that was his way of asking you.'

'Mom,' I say, 'Lily sent it to me. If he was going to ask, he should have asked a million views ago.'

'How *is* Lily?' she asks, a smile brightening her face. 'I miss that girl.'

'She's home this weekend,' I say. 'She wants to go to karaoke.'

'At Tractor Tavern? How fun!' She claps her hands.

'I guess . . .'

'You love karaoke.'

'I know,' I agree glumly. 'I haven't been feeling so much like myself lately,' I admit, 'so I don't know if I'll want to sing in front of a huge crowd.'

She crosses the room to squeeze my shoulder. 'Maybe it's just the thing you need then. Oh, Linden called,' she says, returning to the island to continue playing her game. 'He says hello. He asked how you were doing. Did you know, he finally got over his hatred for green peas?' She beams.

My ribs will be sore tomorrow, but a hug from Lily is worth it. I give her strict instructions as soon as she stops squeezing the life out of me.

'Barn first, remember?' I say, reminding her of the deal we made when I picked her up from the airport. We both know I would have picked her up no matter what, but I figured I might as well call in a favor.

'Right, right,' she says, but she looks wistfully at my front door. I know she wants to say hello to Mom, but I also know Mom will talk her ear off and then she won't be able to help me. I smuggle her across the yard and into the side door to the barn instead.

'Lou!' she squeals when she steps inside. 'Cuh-ute!'

'You think?' I grin. 'I was hoping you would like it.' I twist my hair around my finger. Lily has long been my most fashionable friend, someone even Shari and Evan admit they can't compete with. Living in New York City does that to a person. I trust her taste unequivocally.

'Yes,' she gushes. 'You need to put this stool here—' she picks up the antique wooden stool I found in the attic and sets it down '—and move this hay bale to the red backdrop.' She hauls a large, shedding bay of hale to a different corner of the barn. She wipes her hands off afterward, surveying the space. 'This is perfect. In fact, can I use it?' She sits down on the hay bale she just moved and props her chin into her hands.

'Yes,' I say, 'but only if I get to use the photos.'

'Fine,' she laughs, while I take pictures of her. 'Tit for tat!'

For the next twenty minutes we cover every photo backdrop I bought from eBay. I found an old photography studio going out of business and snapped up their plain color sheets and their large softbox lights. Lily is a natural in front of the camera, something I also associate with New York, and before I know it, I have a picture of her in front of all four of the backdrops. I furnished each one with antique furniture languishing in the attic, and I do agree with Lily—they look pretty good.

'People will love this,' she says. 'Everyone's always looking for new content, and these are perfect and unique for influencers *and* for holiday-card photos. Especially when you combine it with the pictures they can take outside! I have to admit, Lou, this was a great idea for U-Pick.'

'Thanks.' I blush. I'm still riding the high of her approval when Lily goes inside to greet Mom, whose squeal of happiness sounds suspiciously like she just won another game on her phone.

The photo backdrops Lily liked were a ton of work. I had to get everything delivered to the garage, which was the fastest place they could dump it without Nick potentially spotting it and wanting to copy my idea, then I had to move all the props to the barn under the cover of night. It felt both silly and thrilling to keep everything so secretive. But now that Lily's seen it, I feel a seed of hope take root that U-Pick traffic this year could be higher than ever, that I could convince my parents not to walk away from the farm.

In a relentless continuation of our IOUs, I have to go to karaoke in exchange for Lily helping me. She's picked out her song, 'Redneck Woman,' which she sings *every* karaoke. She's also picked out my song, 'Sweet Caroline,' which, given my low mood, I will butcher with almost one hundred percent certainty. We speed to Tractor Tavern, leaving later than we wanted to because Lily made me change into her clothes—mine looked 'a little too comfortable,' which is how I ended up in a sheer black top that exceptionally showcases the goosebumps dotting my arms in the September cold.

We arrive to a packed, dusty, converted barn that's owned by Bennett, a kid we used to go to high school with. He's clearly still smitten with Lily. She can't get two steps through the door without him coming up to say hello, gushing about how successful his business is. I have to admit there's more people here than I thought. Maybe about sixty or so people, who look to be around my age, half of whom I recognize and the other half I'm scrutinizing, wondering where the heck they came from. I haven't gone out at home since before graduate school. I'm usually exhausted every night. There's also usually never new people here, one of the reasons there's so much buzz about Nick (Mom's reported he was the main topic at her book club again). But maybe I've been away from home for too long because the crowd seems to have changed. I heard buzz around town that more young people had started moving to the country after COVID, wanting some fresh air, but I didn't know it was actually true. *Maybe there's something to capitalize on here*, I think, staring at the pulsing crowd. Maybe some of these people would actually want to learn about the land they live on.

'Want a beer?' I ask Lily, who is flashing eyes at me as Bennett continues his third-degree.

'Yes,' she says, gripping my forearm and waving Bennett goodbye, cutting him off mid-sentence.

'Be right back!' she trills. We duck around the crowd pulsating in front of the makeshift karaoke stage, singing along to a man belting out 'Save a Horse (Ride a Cowboy)'. She gushes about the price of beer—'so affordable!'—before launching into a litany of complaints for how she had to come home for her grandmother's ninetieth birthday even though her younger sister, Maude, was allowed to stay in London.

'New York is practically just as far!' she whines. I open my mouth to remind her that it is not, in fact, just as far, but before I can her song starts playing.

'Already!' she whoops, pausing to give Bennett a wink. She chugs the remainder of her beer saying, 'Damn, it feels good to be home,' before sauntering up to the stage to hoots and hollers.

I start recording her, knowing the beginning of the song is her favorite. Sure enough, she warms up the whole crowd to a scream before she belts the end of the first chorus and is answered with a deafening call and response. Lily winks at me, launching into the next verse, and without thinking, I press post, adding her vocal talents to my Instagram story.

An hour later, we are sweaty and breathless when we collapse at a high-top table. I know by the look in Lily's eyes that she's seen someone attractive before she even opens her mouth.

'Who's with Amie?' she asks, catching me off guard as I was preparing for something along the lines of 'Who's the hottie?' Or, 'Now that's an ass I could grab.'

'What?' I turn, following her gaze. The grating sounds of a person belting a very off-key 'Mr. Brightside' fades away.

Realization dawns on Lily. 'Ohmigosh, that's—'

'Nick,' I finish for her. Anger rises in my chest.

'Damn. Amie pulls.'

Lily's right. Nick looks good. He's in a long-sleeve flannel that's rolled up to his elbows, exposing strong forearms tanned from weeks working in the sun. His hair is gelled back just like the first time I saw him in the grocery store. He's even in new shoes—vintage cowboy boots from the looks of it. He looks like he . . . belongs. God, he's hot.

I have a visceral flashback to his lips on mine, the heat of his hips between my legs, the groan that rumbled out of him. I swear under my breath.

'What?' Lily turns her focus back on me. 'Lou!' she exclaims. I know that look. 'Spill.'

I press my lips together and train my eyes on my beer. I've managed to avoid the topic with Lily so far—at first it was because I didn't want her to get excited about someone who wouldn't stick around, but then . . . well . . . everything went to shit and I didn't want to talk about it then either.

'I should have known.' Lily shakes her head. 'He's been right next to you this whole time and he looks like *that*! And you're, well . . . *you*!'

'What's *that* supposed to mean?'

'Um, that you're hot, dummy. Now spill.' Lily leans so far out of her stool she almost topples over. We're seated at a high-top strategically placed at the back of the room so we can monitor everything that's happening, and make sure that Bennett doesn't ambush Lily again. He already cornered her once more when she was leaving the bathroom trying to ask her on a date. She furrows her eyes at me. 'Did you . . . ?'

'No! We barely know each other.' I squirm under her gaze. 'OK, we made out once.'

'Ah!' Lily squeals. 'You dog.' She looks over at Nick and Amie again. They've made their way fully inside only to be bombarded by Amie's friends, a group of women our age who have lived here their whole lives. They're really nice, usually inviting me to hang out when I'm home for the summer, but I always felt like the odd one out around them because I wasn't living at home. 'He's looking over here,' Lily whispers under her breath. 'He's staring at you! How did you go from making out to this? You could cut the sexual tension with a knife.'

I can feel heat rising to my cheeks. 'Stop staring at him!' I whisper-yell at her.

'Only if you tell me what happened.'

'We got in an argument.'

'I mean, yeah, obviously something happened between you guys if he's here with Amie.'

Another round and two bad karaoke renditions of 'Dancing Queen' later and Lily is fully caught up. She knows about our mornings together, how good of a kisser Nick is, and how when I first told him Amie wanted to ask him out he didn't care. I don't have to tell her how much the situation, the fact that it's a ticking clock until

Nick goes to San Francisco, reminds me of Linden, of her, in a way, of all the people I love who have left.

'Damn, Lou. You fell for a guy who is effectively trying to ruin your big hero plan to save your parents. I can't believe it.'

'It's not that big of a deal,' I demur, although secretly I love Lily for this quality, her ability to always make other people feel like they are the star of her show. 'I was not in love with him. Also, it's not a big hero plan, it's my only plan. What else am I supposed to do?'

'Well, you could try what I did and let your parents fend for themselves. They'll be fine and they'll still love you.'

'That's not an option,' I say, but my voice wavers a little. 'What about the farm? And JJ?'

When Lily's eyes meet mine they are full of sympathy. 'Hey,' she says softly. 'I get it, OK. I know what that place means to you, and I know how much you love JJ. And I know you want to show your love to Cal and Hazel, I know they've always been a little softer to Linden. But they love you even if you don't take care of them, you know that, right?'

I blink hard, concentrating with all my might not to cry. I nod. 'I just . . .'

'I know,' Lily says. 'And I think it's how we were raised and it sucks. My guy friends in New York, most of them don't remember their mother's birthdays until the day of, half of them see their family every other year and even then it's for two days. But *every* girl I know is organizing the family reunion and buying a Father's Day card two months in advance. I know you feel responsible for your parents, but it's not fair. And I don't think they even know how much you feel this way. Do they?'

I shake my head. 'No, they don't. I know they don't. But I can't help it.'

Lily squeezes my hand. 'It makes it even more frustrating that the men get to jet off to wherever they want with seemingly no guilt about it.'

'Exactly,' I agree glumly.

'Not that I'm one to defend Nick,' Lily says, squinting in his direction, 'especially seeing as he's here with Amie, but he also isn't your brother. He has none of the Carnation baggage the rest of us do. He is making choices the best he can, for his mom and for himself, just like you are.'

'The way he talks about his mom *is* really cute,' I admit. 'I know at the end of the day he's trying to succeed for her.'

'See—' Lily nudges me with her elbow '—maybe there is a chance for a fall romance after all.'

'He just doesn't understand this,' I sweep my hand out towards the bar. I glower towards Nick and Amie. 'And he's here with *her*.'

'It's hard when you're not from here,' Lily agrees. 'There's just a way we like to do things.' She pauses to give Nick the side-eye. 'And I agree, they do *not* involve going out with other girls to make somebody jealous.'

Both of us look out onto the crowd, watching people mingle, everyone in dusty jeans and worn T-shirts. My eyes can't seem to stop returning to Nick and Amie who are chatting at the bar, their heads bent towards each other. Just then, I hear the microphone screech. 'Lou!' The emcee calls out. 'We're ready for you.' My stomach sinks.

'I can't,' I say to Lily, 'you have to go up for me.'

'No way.' She crosses her arms in front of her chest. 'I have way too high of a register for "Sweet Caroline."'

'I can't do this in front of Nick!' I plead.

'You can and you will,' she says firmly, steering me towards the stage. 'He doesn't matter anyways. He's moving. He's here with Amie. And he's a hack. Fixing farming with marketing? As if.'

Even though I don't know if she's right, her words make me feel a little better. Even so, I stall at the foot of the stage.

'Lou!' Bennett shouts from the back. 'Get up there!'

'I hate you,' I say to Lily.

She doesn't say anything in response, she simply pushes me up to the stage. It's too embarrassing to turn around now, not to mention I would have to physically fight Lily to get out of it, so I climb onstage on shaky feet and grab the mic with a sweaty palm.

'Just start it,' I say to the emcee. The music starts low and slow. I squeeze my eyes closed and take a deep breath. Three minutes and it will be over. And if I'm lucky, someone else will start to sing along. If I'm *really* lucky, Nick will have left already. Although thinking about him leaving with Amie makes my stomach clench.

'Lou!' Lily yells. I've missed my first cue. I hurry to catch up to the music, singing along to the first verse as fast as I can, my voice full of trepidation as I mumble the words. Lily stays right next to the stage, her head bopping in time with the beat. I keep my eyes on either Lily or the lyrics, knowing full well that if I make eye contact with Nick, I'll lose all concentration. I pray he isn't listening to me sing, that he's too busy talking to Amie.

'Louder!' Bennett yells from the back of the crowd. I have to fight not to roll my eyes. I shift my weight from one foot to the other.

I shout about the changing of the seasons a little louder, all too aware of my abysmal singing voice. *I'm gonna kill Lily after this.*

As I get to the chorus, my anxiety rises with the music. I am horrible at hitting the high notes. Just as I sing the final words before the titular phrase kicks in, I hear a strong low voice from the back of the crowd join in. A voice I've heard humming pop songs next to me in the mornings, asking Dad if he needs any help, telling Mom she looks beautiful in her sun hat. I would know that voice anywhere. I'm too overwhelmed to be anything but thankful for the show of support. Nick sings the chorus so loudly he inspires a swell in the crowd, so almost everyone is singing now. I start to belt too. I lift my gaze up, seeing him in the back, his eyes pinned on me, his mouth open in song. My knees feel weak. Thankfully the crowd continues to sing for the rest of the song, so no one can tell how much Nick took my breath away.

Chapter Twenty-Six

Nick

Lesson learned. Big time. Do *not*, under any circumstances, use a very nice girl to piss someone else off. Do not take said girl to town karaoke only because you know the girl you actually want to see is there. Don't sing so loudly when the girl you like is up for karaoke that the girl you're with gives you a confused look and says, 'Are you obsessed with this song or something?'

Amie won't stop texting me. Which is a problem for two reasons. The first being, I am not interested in Amie. The second being, she is painfully nice and I have no reason to not be interested in her apart from the fact that she isn't Eloise. After Anna visiting the farm didn't elicit any sort of emotion from Eloise at all, I figured whatever we had was gone. I agreed to meet Amie for a beer, but before I knew it I had seen Eloise's Instagram story and Amie had been thrilled at the prospect of going to karaoke and . . . well . . . that's where we ended up.

At least the guilt I'm feeling over Amie is overshadowing the guilt I feel for reaching out to Scott's Orchards. A text from her startles me from my train of thought, which was barreling towards imaginary scenarios of

Eloise finding out about my trying to sell the Parkers' farm to a conglomerate.

An email pings in as I'm drafting a response to Amie about how glad I am to have a new *friend* in town. It's Scott's Orchards, confirming the meeting we set up for next week. It took a lot of convincing for them to give me the time of day. To them, we're a small fish in a big pond. It's up to me to prove to them that the Parkers are worth the investment.

But the meeting comes at a good time, a little more than halfway through my stay here, and next week gives me plenty of time to give the Parkers a heads up. Lord knows Betsy will be stressed and want to get a new outfit. Joe will protest, claiming he can't take any time off work. Then he'll get to the real reason, the reason I'm here in the first place. Betsy and Joe don't want to sell. But once they see the how much Scott's Orchards made last season, they'll be changing their tune.

I'm packing the farmers' market supplies into the truck with Betsy when a rusty red pickup pulls into the drive behind the Parkers' blue one, effectively boxing us in. A young man hops out with a huge grin. It's a little after seven in the morning and we're rushing to get ready to go. The spots at the market are doled out on a first come, first served basis, and you have to time your arrival right when the coordinator arrives to make sure you get a visible lot. I think I've arrived on the perfect time after the last two weeks of trial and error. The Anderson farm got the better spot twice after the Fall Festival, something Eloise wouldn't stop smirking at me about. Not that it mattered, we still had longer lines. But I want the best spot and the longest line today and I am determined to get it. I've been eyeing the middle lot facing the street for weeks.

This is our last farmers' market before our meeting with Scott's Orchards. I've designed my whole pitch around how much this will diversify their current offering. They are in need of a rebrand, nobody likes a conglomerate anymore, and they could make the Parkers the new face of their brand. A 'cultural revitalization' is what I'm calling it. A way to bring their consumers back to the things that make farming special—nutrients and people. Strong farmers' market sales will boost our pitch, giving Scott's Orchards yet another reason to invest in the farm. If things go according to plan, Betsy and Joe would still live here and manage it, but they would get an influx of cash to keep them afloat and a larger company to fall back on in case things go wrong. In return, Scott's Orchards gets a cultural revitalization. A win-win.

But in order for me to get the win, we have to do well at the farmer's market. I do not have time for any distractions.

I eye the young man in the driveway warily. 'We're kind of busy,' I say.

'Thanks for getting that outside for me,' he says at the same time, clearly not hearing me. He nods at the tent.

'That makes this a whole lot easier. Two hundred, right?' He starts to peel off bills from his wallet.

'What?' I ask. I glance at Betsy, but she looks just as confused.

'Two hundred,' he repeats, looking at me then back at Betsy. 'Which one of you is Nick?'

'Me,' I offer, 'but I don't know what you're talking about.'

'The Craigslist ad!' he says brightly. 'I'm coming to buy the tent. It says first come first se—' He stops talking as a large van pulls in right behind him, spraying up dust and gravel. 'Oh hell naw,' he says, looking at us, 'I was here first.'

'I'll give two-fifty!' hollers a woman as she climbs out of her van and jogs towards us. 'I really need it.'

'Wait a minute,' I say, throwing my hands up, 'I don't know what you're talking about.'

A third car pulls in behind the van.

'The Craigslist ad,' the strangers in the driveway say in unison. The woman takes out her phone and extends it towards me. Sure enough, there's a photo of our farmers' market tent. It's clearly been taken in the dark, with flash. I think back to the time a couple weeks ago when I swore I saw flashlights in the back barn and Mrs. Parker told me she thought it was fireflies.

'We're not selling,' I explain. 'I'm so sorry. There's been a mistake.'

The woman looks absolutely crestfallen and the man just looks pissed. When the third person gets out of his car, the first man turns around and yells, 'Trevor, I knew I'd see you here. Scram!' And much to my surprise and relief, Trevor does, in fact, scram.

'I'll handle this, Betsy. Can you finish getting ready to go?' Betsy nods, scurrying into the house. I check the time. We were already cutting it close and now we'll be late.

'Look,' I say to the folks waiting in the driveway. 'I am so sorry, but we're also in a hurry. We aren't selling, so you can go.'

The woman rolls her eyes at me and mutters under her breath, 'Fucking internet,' before reversing her car down the drive. The man, however, lingers. 'Look,' he says, leaning against his car door, 'I'll give you three hundred.'

'We're really not selling,' I plead, 'and you really need to go.'

'Three-fifty.'

'This isn't a negotiation!' I shout. Betsy is back outside now, waiting for me.

'Four hundred, last and final offer.'

'Just go,' I plead, turning to climb into our car.

We race to the farmers' market, passing the Anderson farm on the way. It's quiet, which means only one thing. Eloise is already at the farmers' market waiting for an assignment. 'God damnit,' I mutter the entire way there.

At last, we pull into the parking lot for the farmers' market. I sprint to the stand that assigns permits even though I don't see anyone else in the parking lot. *Please,*

I think. I arrive breathless. The coordinator looks up, surprised.

'Here,' he says, passing me a permit. 'Same as last week.'

My shoulders sag. 'I was really hoping I could get the another spot this week, you know maybe one closer to the front?'

'It's first come, first served.' He shrugs.

'I know, I just . . .' I trail off. 'Got it,' I say finally. I trudge back to the car. We'll just have to make do. It isn't the end of the world.

But when I walk onto Main Street to find Eloise in the best spot again, laughing with Hazel like she doesn't have a care in the world, it feels a lot more like the end of the world. Eloise clocks my arrival and turns towards me. 'Hey.' She waves. 'Looks like you're stuck at the back again today, huh.'

My fists ball at my sides.

So, this is how she's going to play it? Affecting my class is one thing, but messing with the Parkers' business is another.

'Looks like you'll be stuck with just your farm,' I retort.

'What does that mean?' Betsy asks. I forgot she was trailing me.

'Nothing,' I say quickly. 'It's not important.'

But when I glance behind me one more time, Eloise is glaring in my direction.

Two can play at this game, I think to myself as I unpack our supplies. My phone starts pinging with notifications. I scheduled another reel to go out this morning. Three of the pigs are here today. Eloise doesn't know what she's gotten herself into.

Chapter Twenty-Seven

Eloise

Reasons Fall Is the Perfect Time to Get Your Wisdom Teeth Removed (Technically There Is No Perfect Time, But Fall Is As Good As It Gets)

- Soup season
- Perfect timing to rewatch *Gilmore Girls*
- Furry blankets, cozy cardigans, and thick sweaters are already unpacked
- Darker mornings make sleeping in easier
- Applesauce is fresh

After seeing our stand-off at the farmers' market, Mom sends me up to the Parkers' to borrow some eggs. I have to hand it to her, she's strategic. She sends me early in the morning, claiming our hens didn't lay enough and she had promised her friend Peggy she would bake her muffins after her knee surgery. Dad rolls his eyes at me across the table—Emily Chickenson always lays more than enough eggs. When I suggest that Dad go Mom stares daggers at me for so long that I simply slink upstairs to change. Arguing with her isn't worth it. She is insistent on Nick and I 'patching things up.'

I knock on their door, fidgeting on the doorstep. Mrs. Parker lets me in, ushering me into the kitchen. Only Joe at the table. I try not to look too hard at the steaming cup of coffee and half a piece of toast at the abandoned third place setting.

I find my anger is quite an effective way for me to stop missing him. I can't seem to stop being mad he went to karaoke with Amie. I don't care how loud he sang. I don't care if I told her to ask him out. He went out with her in public and I know it was to get to me, which is completely inappropriate on a lot of levels.

The sun is high in the afternoon sky as I stare in the Parkers' direction, squinting to see if I can make out who is in the small group of people thinning the apples at the western edge of their farm. Dad shuffles up behind me. He's been checking on me more often lately.

'How you doing, champ?' He claps me on the shoulder.

I blink. 'Fine,' I lie. I look back towards the Parkers' before I return to work. Screw that guy. If only I could forget that he exists.

My plan to bring a baby goat to our next farmers' market is derailed by emergency surgery to remove one of my wisdom teeth. My jaw had been getting increasingly sore for the past week, something I attributed to grinding my teeth at night, a habit I've had in the past when stressed. But I woke up in the middle of the night on Wednesday to worse pain and reluctantly called the dentist, who was able to squeeze me in the next day. The surgery was seamless except for the fact that I kept asking the nurse to remember to take a video of me for Evan and Shari, who let me know very sternly that while they wished for my speedy recovery, they also wished for a video of me on pain medication.

Fortunately, I completely blacked out on the way home (during which I recorded said video) and slept on and off, in a complete haze, for an entire day.

My memory returns the next day just in time for me to be roused from bed by the smell of Mom's cooking, which wafts upstairs and pleasantly tickles my nostrils. Thankfully it's cold enough for soup.

I'm rounding the corner into the kitchen when I almost run smack into my dad, who grumbles a panicked hello on his way out the door.

'Cal!' my mother shouts from her seat at the kitchen table. She rises from her seat, bustling towards me with both hands outstretched. 'Are you OK? You're really supposed to be protecting your mouth you know.'

I roll my eyes. 'I know, Mom. I wasn't *trying* to run into Dad.' I pause mid-step, freezing in place before I can reach the table. My voice sounds garbled and slow, almost like I've been drinking but I know I haven't. And a weird dream keeps tugging at the sides of my brain. I sink into a kitchen chair and squeeze my eyes shut, trying to remember what I was dreaming about. Bits and pieces of it flash behind my eyelids, being at the Parkers', seeing Nick, watching a movie . . .

My mom places a glass of salt water in front of me. 'Drink up,' she says gently.

I groan. 'I had the weirdest dream,' I say.

'Medication will do that to you,' Mom soothes, patting my back. 'Are you feeling up for some soup?'

I try to smile gratefully at her and end up wincing with pain. She tuts at me, ladling soup into a bowl.

'Want to play a round of cards when your dad gets home?' she asks as soon as I've finished.

I stretch my arms over my head, nodding. 'That sounds really nice, Mom. I'll walk and see JJ for a bit before dinner then.'

Mom nods with approval and I make my way out into the cold sunshine, a heavy sweater on and a cup of applesauce for JJ—he loves it as much as he loves unripe apples.

'Hey, boy,' I greet him. I take extra care brushing his coat today, moving slowly as I let him out. I watch him prance around the paddock, so full of energy now that his leg has healed. 'I need to be out here with you more, huh?' I ask him. He nickers in reply.

'I'll find you a good home,' I say to him, soft enough that he can't hear. I leave the rest of my sentence unsaid—*I'm not ready to part with you yet.*

Four hours later and we're gathered around the kitchen table, hunched over a card game. Linden calls while we're playing. 'Honey, you're on speaker,' Mom announces. 'I've got Dad and Lou here with me.'

Dad and I both laugh, Mom always answers the phone like she's a newscaster. 'Lou,' Linden says, 'I was calling to see how you were doing.'

'Oh, um, I'm good,' I say. Linden and I haven't talked in a while, he must have heard about the surgery from Mom. My heart squeezes a bit that he took the time to call. He chatters on with Mom and Dad about what they're excited for about U-Pick.

'Lou, will you hand out any more of those seedling kits?'

'How do you know about—?' I stop myself short, of course Mom told him. 'I have my hands full with some other plans,' I admit.

'Other plans,' Linden laughs, 'sounds like I'll have to call you myself to find out about those.'

'I'd like that,' I reply, avoiding Mom's gaze. I can't bear to see her so happy that Linden and I have made plans to call each other—all she wants us to do is stop arguing about the farm. Sometimes I feel like it's all I have to hold on to, that I'm the better daughter, and some days, like today, I miss my older brother and I'm tired of holding a grudge. Linden tells us about his new girlfriend, during which Mom mutes the phone and admits she thinks that's the reason he's been better about calling. 'Not that I'm complaining,' she's quick to add.

By the time we hang up, our enthusiasm for the game has waned. We all miss our fourth player.

Chapter Twenty-Eight

Nick

WEEK SEVEN

The day has arrived—two executives from Scott's Orchards are coming by this afternoon to meet Joe and Betsy. Based on the email they sent over prior, we won't be discussing too much business. They want to get a feel for what we're doing. I have all the confidence in the world that Joe and Betsy can deliver.

Joe and I spend the morning putting up signs for U-Pick. I thought the blue truck was hard to drive, but the tractor is something else. As it rolls and teeters over the dirt beneath me, I realize it's as close as I've ever come to riding a wild animal. I think about JJ, wonder if Eloise has been spending more time with him now that she's not with me.

'I think we need a sign here.' Joe interrupts my train of thought, pointing to a small mound in the dirt.

'Are you sure?' I ask. Joe's been carting me around on his tractor instructing me as to where to stake directional signs in the ground for U-pickers for the better part of three hours. We've already put down close to thirty, and we need to head back soon to prepare for the meeting.

Joe turns slowly from his vantage point in the driver's seat, giving me ample time to regret opening my mouth. Clearly I had gotten too used to talking to Eloise, who tolerated my curiosity a little bit more. Joe didn't say another word.

'Thought you would need some nutrition before the big meeting!' Betsy trills as Joe and I enter the kitchen for lunch. I'm ravenous and she's made her famous chicken salad. I'm salivating before she even hands me a plate. I was never this hungry in the city, but farming works up an appetite. I can tell I've put on muscle even though I haven't been to the gym once.

Even my mamma chastised me last time we were on the phone, saying I looked different.

'I'm the exact same.' I squinted at her over FaceTime, doing my best Blue Steel impression which always makes her laugh. 'I'm just in better shape, Mamma. I promise. I'll be home in three weeks.'

She raised her eyebrows but didn't dwell on the subject. There was too much church drama she needed to fill me in on. One of the members of her congregation had won the lottery (a *local* lottery, she made sure to tell me, *not* the state lottery. And do *not* try this at home. Gambling is a sin.) and it was the talk of the town.

In between bites, Betsy and Joe filled me in on what we had left to do before U-Pick was upon us.

'Clear the debris, double-check the signage, do another round of insecticide—'

'What is it, honey?' Betsy asks me, interrupting Joe, who grunts his displeasure.

'Oh, nothing,' I say, quickly taking another bite. I guess I had made a face without realizing it when Joe mentioned insecticides. Eloise *hates* the type the Parkers use. She claims it leaches down the hill and affects their crop. She also says it's not safe to eat and the Parkers shouldn't be getting anywhere near it. 'I was just thinking about the meeting,' I lie.

Betsy fans her face with her hands. 'I'm nervous about it,' she whispers.

'Betsy,' I say, with all the sincerity I can muster. 'You'll be great.'

Two hours later she comes downstairs in a freshly pressed dress. 'We got this.' I high-five her. Her chin wobbles, but she nods and sets her shoulders back defiantly. 'If I can handle owning four pigs, I can handle a couple bigwigs.'

'That's the spirit!'

Scott's Orchards sends a woman and a man, Sarah and Harvey, and we've barely ushered them in before I hear a knock on the door. Mrs. P. startles, looking up from the pitcher of sweet tea she's carrying.

'I'll get it,' I offer. 'You four enjoy the tea. I'll be right back.'

I ease myself out onto the front steps only to be met with a completely and utterly loopy Eloise. She flops into my arms, more excited than I've ever seen her. Her cheeks are bright pink and swollen, puffy like a chipmunk.

There's a piece of gauze pressed to the inside of her cheek. Tendrils of her hair are escaping, framing her face in a beautiful blonde halo. *God, I missed her.*

'It's you!' she exclaims, her whole face brightening.

'It's me,' I reply, feeling my heart swell in my chest. 'Are you OK? What's going on?'

She points at her mouth. 'Teeth,' she says, rolling her eyes. 'You have my movie.' She points at my chest, flailing her arm in a circle to do so.

'Your movie? I'm pretty sure it's Betsy—'

'Yes!' She pushes her way inside. 'I texted you! The DVD.' She pauses in the doorway, holding up an empty hand and pointing at it, clearly thinking she was pointing at her phone.

I think back to the texts she sent me an hour ago, ones I was so excited to receive and then so dismayed to read. Ones I dismissed as some kind of distracting gibberish, realizing they were totally serious.

Eloise: Got ur number from Mrs Parker. She says u r home? I am on my way to get a movie.

Me: Eloise? Is this another one of your stupid pranks? We kind of have something important going on today.

Eloise: I'll be there in five.

Me: What? We don't even have movies.

'These kitchen towels are something else,' I hear Sarah say to Betsy, and I breathe a sigh of relief. I strain to hear the rest of their conversation, wondering what the more standoffish businessman, Harvey, will add. He seems cutthroat and sharkish, and I'm worried leaving the Parkers alone with them will turn them off to the whole deal.

'I'll go get your DVD if you tell me which one you need,' I whisper, hoping she'll keep her voice down. I glance back down the hallway but I can only see Harvey's back.

'*Bring It On!* All day long! Bri—'

'Eloise,' I hiss, cutting her cheer short, 'can you be a little quieter?'

Admonished, she nods meekly before smiling again. 'You want to take me somewhere secret?' she asked, trailing a fingertip up my chest.

It was all I could do not to kiss her forehead again. 'Not right now,' I whisper. *Where are Cal and Hazel?* I think. 'You stay here, I'll be right back.'

I manage to find the DVD in my room, thankfully I had spent enough time in there that I knew there was a DVD collection in one of the baskets underneath the desk, and I scurry downstairs, depositing it in Eloise's waiting arms and shooing her out the door in just enough time for the executives to hardly notice I'd been gone.

I breathe a sigh of relief when Eloise left with her movie, assuming the crisis was averted.

Thirty minutes later . . .

Eloise: I told u there were movies.

Me: Technically, you picked up a DVD.

Eloise: Blah blah bring it on!

Eloise: Do u like them because I am going to surprise visit again.

Me: Twice in one day? Are you sure you should be doing that? I feel like the hike up here isn't great for someone in your condition . . .

Eloise: Need *Bring It On: All or Nothing*.

Me: I can bring it to you! I just need to finish something.

Each time she stops by, Eloise looked a little less swollen and a little more like herself. And each time she acts like she's madly in love with me, smiling up at me adoringly, prattling off sexual innuendos. She doesn't seem embarrassed in the least to be throwing herself all over me, and I can't hide that I love the attention. It's entirely impossible for me to continue to be mad at her when she's so loopy. As Mrs. Parker would say, I felt my anger towards her disappearing faster than dew under a hot sun.

When I catch up to the group during the farm tour after staying behind to give Eloise another movie, Mrs. Parker winks at me and I feel like my cheeks are on fire. *Eloise likes me again* is blaring through my head so loudly I can hardly focus on the rest of the pitch. Harvey intimidates me into concentration, though. He appears to be exactly how Eloise would characterize someone who works for a conglomerate. He reminds me of my future boss, someone who values ambition over all else, something I used to value. But now it seems a little sinister, lacking in empathy. I wonder what Harvey would be willing to sacrifice to move further up the corporate ladder. I sure hope it isn't the Parkers' welfare.

Just as the Scott's Orchards reps are about to leave, my phone vibrates again.

Eloise: I need a hug.

Me: Don't come up here again, OK? Just ask, and I'll come bring you what you need.

Me: I can come give you a hug.

Eloise: Now? Where's my hug?

Nick: I'm wrapping up something but I can come in twenty minutes. I'm in a meeting for school.

Eloise: Schmool. Mouth hurts.

Me: You can't meet me halfway again if I say I'm coming to you, OK? You really shouldn't be walking around. I'll text your mom.

I race down to Eloise's place as fast as I can, only to see her blonde head bobbing through the fields. I jog to catch up to her and she smiles at me so hard she winces, bringing her hands to her mouth in pain.

'Hey,' I said, gently resting my palms on top of hers, 'how are you?'

'Better now,' she says, and she presses her forehead to mine, breathing deeply before wrapping me in a hug, her arms tight around my torso, her cheek softly resting against my chest. I stand there, dumbfounded, wondering what on earth I had been doing these past two weeks when the best feeling in the whole world, the feeling of holding Eloise, has been right next to me all along.

Me: How are you feeling? It was good to see you yesterday. *Laughing-crying emoji* You were pretty cute.

Eloise: I am so sorry. Please blame the drugs. And honestly also my mom, she shouldn't have let me outside. It won't happen again.

Me: Eloise, it's fine. I meant it. It was good to see you.

Eloise: I'm sure you loved seeing me at my worst.

Me: That isn't what I meant.

Eloise: Look I'm sorry about coming over. I clearly didn't know what I was doing. We're busy getting ready for U-Pick so I'll talk to you later.

In the following two days, I get nothing but radio silence from Eloise. I haven't heard from Scott's Orchards either. Even the Parkers have been quiet, saying they would 'think about how they wanted to move forward.' I didn't bother telling them that they didn't need to think about their options before they had any—we opened the conversation with a tentative offer, and Scott's Orchards hadn't gotten back to us formally yet.

'You guys think any more about Scott's?' I ask the Parkers as we sit on their front porch. We're down to the last dregs of our apple cider.

Joe shakes his head.

'We don't know how we feel about it,' volunteers Betsy. 'It would be a big change for the community . . . Scott's coming in here like that. Everyone would think we were sellouts.'

'It's better than being a land grabber,' I said under my breath.

'What was that, sweetie?'

'Nothing, Mrs. P. Just that I didn't think anyone would think you were a sellout. You'd still be here, at least if they take what we offered.'

Joe grunts. 'It's not the same,' he says.

'Because you'd have more money?' I ask. Even though I know that's not what he's referring to, I can't help but point it out.

'Because someone else would be making the decisions.'

'You would *all* be making the decisions. And I'm not saying you have to say yes. We don't even know if they'll say yes. But part of my internship is to leave here having given you some options.'

'We know.' Betsy softens, fixing her gaze on me. 'He's not meaning to be hard on you, are you, Joe?'

Joe mumbles an affirmative.

'Nick, I've been meaning to tell you,' Betsy says, her expression is one I can't read, one I haven't seen before. She looks . . . disappointed.

'Amie asked about you the last time I was in Hal's.'

My face falls. 'Oh,' I squirm, 'we're just friends.'

Betsy arches an eyebrow at me. 'You sure seem to be just friends with a lot of people these days.'

I gulp.

'Best to get that straightened out before next week. She'll be at the County Fair, I'm sure. And so will you. I need help presenting my applesauce. Now that I think of it . . .' she pauses and looks at me '. . . I need your help prepping too. There's an applesauce contest every year. I never win. But you could help me this time. I want to taste test something new.'

Thankful that Mrs. P. seems to have put aside harassing my relationship choices, I smile at her. 'Sure thing, Mrs. P. I got your back.'

'Wonderful. I'm sure you know who we're competing against.'

I had a hunch, but now, I'm positive.

'The Andersons,' Betsy and I say together.

Well, I think, I may not be thrilled at helping Betsy make adult baby food, but it wouldn't be so bad to see Eloise again. Just to check and see if she's recovered. As a friend, of course. Even though Betsy thinks I have too many of those.

Chapter Twenty-Nine

Eloise

My Favorite Fruit Trees

- Pear
- Peach
- Lemon
- Apple
- Mango
- Lime
- Pomegranate
- Plum

It's been a week and even though I can't remember it, I still haven't recovered from the most embarrassing day of my life. I showed up at the Parkers' to pick up *Bring It On*? Out of all the movies, I couldn't have requested something cooler like *The Shawshank Redemption*? I've been trying not to cave to the magnetic pull that is this disaster, but I can't help it. I reread the texts at least once a day, cringing so hard I think I'm giving myself a wrinkle. I really up and went to the Parker's *three* times.

I take a bite of a pear Mom picked this morning.

'So good, right?' Mom asks.

I narrow my eyes at her. 'I still haven't forgiven you, you know.'

'What!' She throws up her hands. 'For letting you walk to the Parkers'? A walk you've done a thousand times?' She walks over to me and wraps me in a hug. 'I love you, sweetheart.'

I groan, but I wrap my arms tightly around hers. As U-Pick approaches, so does a fork in the road for our future. I still have no idea if our loan will be approved. I have no idea what my parents will want to do. I have no idea if we'll keep the farm.

Ironically, my favorite part about the lead-up to U-Pick has nothing to do with apples and everything to do with pears. At the very south-west corner of our farm there are two rows of Asian pear trees, Mom's pride and joy. Every year in early September they ripen with the most beautiful green fruit, dappled with freckles and spots of blush. Each bite is fleshy and powerful in flavor. Mom bakes pear tarts and pear bread and slow cooks pears with ginger, and she doesn't tell anyone, she's never even told me, but I know she puts pears in her famous applesauce. It's what makes it unbeatable. She can't always win the apple pie contest, but she's pretty consistent about keeping her applesauce crown.

I've helped her out this year, she claims, because all I could eat for the past week was applesauce. After I fully recovered we settled into a rhythm, a better one than we had at the start of summer. I didn't realize how much

Nick had thrown off my mornings, which I now get to spend waking up slowly and alone with my own thoughts as U-Pick days loom on the horizon. Even though U-Pick is where we make a bulk of our revenue, the pickers only cover about a quarter of the orchard, focusing on specific varietals that we grow and prune especially for that purpose—Honeycrisp, Gala, Granny Smith.

We've never done U-Pick big like some of the other growers do, instead we pride ourselves on our small and intimate setting, we make sure there's always one of us in the area to answer questions and we make everyone feel at home. But this year, things have to change. I came out of my drug-induced haze with renewed energy about the Parker situation. Nick can social media his way to the top all he wants, but he can't stop me from doing the exact same thing. If he wants to drive all these sales to the Parkers', fine by me, I'll direct them to our farm instead. City Council responded about my request for a permit to hold weddings, so I've started calculating possible profits in case the loan falls through. I've had large signs made that advertise Anderson Apple Orchards as the only non-insecticide farm in the nearby area *and* the only one with photo backdrops perfect for family photos in any weather.

DID YOU GET DRESSED UP TO TAKE PICTURES AT OUR APPLE ORCHARD? Reads one sign, THEN YOU'LL LOVE OUR UPDATED BARN! FEATURING FOUR DIFFERENT BACKDROPS AND ADJUSTABLE LIGHTING, YOU CAN MAKE SURE YOUR HOLIDAY-CARD PHOTOS ARE EXACTLY WHAT YOU WERE DREAMING OF.

Mom does her part too, preparing for the bake stand at U-Pick by baking apple pies, cookies, cakes, and muffins, anything that she can freeze after partially baking it. The outdoor freezer is so full, I've had to drive pastries to Lily's parents' place to store them.

'Eloise?' Mom asks, taking a slice of pear off my plate. 'Are you doing OK?'

'Me? Yeah. My mouth is almost completely back to normal.'

She sighs. 'That's not exactly what I was referring to.'

'Oh. Yeah, I mean, I'm fine I guess . . .'

'I'm just checking in. You seem . . . different than you were at the start of the summer . . . not as happy. And before you reply, I don't think it has anything to do with the surgery.'

Her words hit me like a punch to the gut. 'Hmm,' I mutter in response.

'I hate to say it,' she says.

'Then maybe don't say it,' I mumble.

'I think it was Nick.'

We both stare out the kitchen window. Ever since the surgery debacle, I haven't talked to him at all except when I texted him to apologize. Business is business, something I feel like I should have known all along.

Shari: GUYYYYSSSSS

Evan: Just when I was beginning to wonder if you were dead.

Shari: SORRY I WAS TOO BUSY LITERALLY RECREATING THE LIZZIE MCGUIRE MOVIE.

Evan: Do I even want to know

Me: Did you ride with an Italian man on a Vespa . . .

Shari: YES.

Me: Did he hold your hand and walk you through the city?

Shari: YES.

Me: DID YOU SHARE A PLATE OF PASTA?

Shari: WE DID MORE THAN THAT.

Me: OH MY GOD I'M SO JEALOUS.

Evan: You're jealous?! I'm the one who has resorted to dating someone named Kevin. Is there a bigger ick than their name rhyming with yours? You're the one living next to a HUNK.

Evan: Happy for you, Shari, mean it.

Me: Evan, shut up.

Me: Shari, send pics. Tell us everything. Actually, can you voice memo it. I want to know ALL the details. Do not spare a thing.

God, I'm jealous. Reading Shari's texts gives me a nagging feeling in the pit of my stomach. Maybe if I had her confidence, then I would be in a different position—instead of resenting Nick I could be making out with him behind the barn *and* secretly plotting his downfall without any complicated feelings. I could have forgone the drama and instead be having a summer fling that even my mother thinks I desperately need.

The Carnation County Fair takes place right outside of the town hall, which is right off of Main Street where the farmers' market happens every weekend. The town hall is a looming old building made out of wood, with high ceilings and exposed beams. When there's events in the town hall building, the cavernous room is filled with folding chairs. I'm in charge of setting up the folding chairs today and I'm on my last row when I feel the air in the room go still. I don't need to turn around to know who just walked in.

Because I don't remember seeing him when I went to get those godforsaken movies, I feel like I haven't seen Nick in weeks. It's the longest we've gone without seeing each other since we met. I stiffen, my back to the door. I hear Betsy's voice echoing off the wood floor and I cringe. 'Lou!' she trills excitedly, forcing me to turn around.

Nick falls into a quieter step behind Betsy, slowing down so he doesn't get as close to me. He lingers behind her as she fusses over my outfit, which is a variation of what I always wear—jeans and a white T-shirt.

'You're just so beautiful,' Betsy says.

I redden. I've got to get out of here. It's one thing to daydream about Nick when he isn't around, but seeing him in person makes the lies, the rejections, the way I've humiliated myself feel ten times worse. 'I've actually got to go help my mom.' I turn to go but Betsy sticks out her hand, grasping me on the forearm with unexpected strength.

'Just wait one minute,' she says, her voice laced with a 'don't-mess-with-me' tone. 'Won't you try my applesauce? I think it might rival your mother's this year.'

My gaze flutters to Nick, I can't help it. His face is unreadable, stoic . . . handsome. I love Betsy. I've known her my whole life and she's always been nothing but kind. But being this close to Nick without being able to touch him, to talk to him, is torture. I take a deep breath. 'Sure, Mrs. Parker.'

'Nick.' She beckons him forward. 'Give our Lou a taste of that.' Then she walks away faster than I've ever seen her walk, leaving Nick and me alone in a sea of folding chairs, under the bright fluorescent lights of the town hall.

Nick shrugs awkwardly, holding up a giant container of applesauce. 'I don't know how she wanted me to give you a taste,' he says finally, after a minute or two of us avoiding eye contact.

I'm finding it hard to breathe standing so close to him.

'It's OK.' I wave him away. 'I'm busy anyways.'

'I know. I've been on the receiving end of your busyness once or twice, remember?'

I look up, embarrassed, wondering what he's talking about, but he starts to laugh, setting me at ease. 'The Craigslist ad was good, I'll give you that.'

I blush. 'I'm so sorry about that,' I say. 'It was a low blow.'

'You should have seen the confusion on Mrs. P.'s face.'

I hide my face in my hands. 'I can't believe I let Evan talk me into that.'

'All is fair in love and war.'

I hesitate. 'Love and war' hangs in the air. The ache I feel for him, the way I miss him, is palpable, but I can't think of anything to say. *Don't move back to San Francisco. Can we start over? I want to walk by your side again.*

'You look like you're almost done,' he points out. There's only three chairs left to unfold.

'Right. I better finish,' I say lamely.

Nick takes a hesitant step towards me. I gaze up at him, letting myself take in his big brown eyes and thick frame of lashes. He still smells like himself—mint and cinnamon. He's tanner now and more muscular. I didn't think it was possible for him to get hotter. I feel like I'm being drawn closer to him by a magnet. I blink and we're only inches apart.

He leans in closer. 'It's not that good,' he whispers, his voice sending a shiver down my spine.

I stay rooted to the floor. 'What?' I whisper back.

'The applesauce. Hazel's is much better. She'll win.'

'Yeah,' is all I can think to say in reply. 'Maybe.'

'Eloise,' Nick whispers. His voice is filled with something I can't place. 'I've missed you.'

'You haven't filled my absence with Amie?'

'God. That was really dumb of me. No. We're just friends, Amie and I. I promise.'

I knew that was the case—I would have heard in the town gossip mill if they did start to date, but even so I feel the coil of anxiety around my heart start to ease.

'I haven't seen Amie since karaoke. And I've missed *you* every day.'

I wring out my hands. 'That's not fair,' I whisper.

'What's not fair?'

'You saying you'll miss me when you're the one leaving.' The words hang heavy in the air between us. Nick opens his mouth and closes it like he's unsure of what to say. I feel deflated, like someone let all the wind out of my sails. 'That's what you don't get,' I say softly. 'You get to walk away. This doesn't really matter to you.'

A crease forms between his eyes, an expression I've only seen on him one time, that afternoon we were trapped in the barn during a rainstorm. Nick stills, pausing, thinking. 'No,' he says softly. Reaching up to cup my cheek in his palm, he tilts my chin ever so gently until our eyes meet. 'You're right about a lot of things. You know everything about soil and bees and apples and pears and, hell, even applesauce. But you're wrong about this. It *does* matter to me. The Parkers matter to me. I want to take care of them. I want to graduate and take care of my mom. But *you* matter to me, too.'

Rationally, I know I shouldn't take his words so much to heart but I do. Hearing him say I matter makes me feel like my heart is full of helium, it could lift me right up off the floor. 'Even after I showed up three times at the Parkers' unannounced?' I ask in a small voice.

'Even *more* after you showed up three times at the Parkers' unannounced.'

He's still holding my cheek as he leans forward, moving his hand to the small of my back, his forearm grazing my waist. He pulls me in slowly and I feel my eyes start to close. I can't control my own body anymore. My rational thoughts are sounding the alarm, screaming THIS IS COMPLICATED. YOU CAN'T AFFORD DISTRACTIONS, while my physical body is melting into Nick.

'Nick?' Mrs. Parker calls out, her voice bouncing across the wooden floor.

Nick pulls back abruptly, almost dropping the bowl of applesauce.

'There you are.' She rounds the corner, coming into view. 'The judges need the applesauce.' She beckons for him to follow her before giving me an apologetic look. 'He'll be right back,' she says.

Nick gives me a wide-eyed look as he follows her, mouthing, 'Wait for me.'

Long after he's gone my lips are still buzzing with energy from grazing his. Tension is pooling in my low abdomen and my thoughts are spinning. I think about Shari's texts. I think about how nice it would be to just say *fuck it* and get some.

Chapter Thirty

Nick

WEEK EIGHT

I walk the path to Eloise's house as fast as I can. Ever since I saw her at the Carnation County Fair, I've been anxiously awaiting the moment when I get to see her again, hopefully when we're alone. As soon as our eyes met in the town hall, it felt like everything else melted away. And even though Mrs. P. couldn't have interrupted us at a worse time, I still got to show Eloise how I felt *and* I got to see how she responded, her upturned chin, her gently parted lips, the desire in her eyes . . . I haven't been able to stop thinking about her.

It didn't end up bothering me at all that Hazel won the applesauce contest. She deserved it. And Eloise looked so happy. The only bad part of the day was that Betsy insisted on taking me to every other contest—bobbing for apples, churning butter, yodeling. Every time I tried to find Eloise, Betsy was introducing me to someone else or trying to wriggle her way to a front-row seat. Just when I thought the festivities were over Betsy insisted on tracking down the second-place yodeler to tell him that he should have won first.

I texted Eloise when I got home.

Me: I'm so sorry I couldn't find you again—I swear Betsy was trying to set us up when I got there but then she developed a thing for the yodeler.

I watched as her typing bubbles appeared and disappeared. Once, twice, then a third time before text appeared.

Eloise: *eyes emoji* The second place one?

Me: Not you too!!

Eloise: What can I say, Betsy's got good taste. Come over Monday morning?

Her groggy visits weren't just a fluke. I could have jumped in the air for joy. Now, as I half-walk, half-run my way to her place, I couldn't be happier. I've borrowed one of Joe's thick Carhart jackets to beat the chill in the air. I wear my farm boots so often they feel like a second skin. I take a deep breath of the crisp morning air as I round the corner and the Andersons' fields come into view. It's taken some time, but I finally feel like I earned my place here.

Eloise is leaning forward, picking apples off some lower tree branches.

'Morning,' I call out to her, my spirits lifting as I watch her straighten up, one hand holding her beanie into place, the other giving me a happy wave.

Uncharacteristically, she pulls me in for a hug, her expression cheery. I'm not ready to stop wrapping my arms around her when she pulls away. My shoulders tingle where's she's touched them, like her energy has lit them on fire.

'It's good to be back,' I admit.

Eloise smiles at the ground, wrapping a wayward strand of hair around her finger. 'About that,' she laughs, 'Mom got on my case for not having you over anymore.'

'Did she now?'

Eloise nods. 'She did. She said I was unhappy without you around.'

'Hmm,' I say, trying and failing to stop my smile. 'Were you?'

Eloise punches me on the arm softly. 'Yes,' she whispers.

'Come on, I can't have made you *that* happy.'

'Well—' suddenly she's squirmy '—there is something else.'

'What is it?' I ask, feeling my suspicions rise. For a moment I wonder if the Andersons have been contacted by Scott's Orchards. Scott's had finally gotten back to us, wanting control over the whole farm. Betsy and Joe would retain ownership of the land and the house, though, which is what I fought the hardest for.

Joe *hated* it. He insisted he would think about nothing less than equal shares. I countered with fifty-fifty ownership, but I wondered if Scott's would decide at some point in our back and forths that we weren't worth the trouble. With bated breath, I wait for Eloise to continue.

'We're just selling out of our U-Pick tickets way earlier than we usually do,' she says, looking sheepish.

I sigh with relief. 'That's great!' I respond enthusiastically. 'More business for you is more for the Parkers,' I say without thinking.

Her face falls again. 'Right,' she mutters.

Damnit, I think. I've only been with her for five minutes and I'm already ruining it. 'Hey,' I say, placing a hand on her forearm. 'Why don't we not talk about business.'

She looks up at me, her cornflower-blue eyes impossibly beautiful. 'We only talk about that.'

'That's not true,' I argue. 'I've told you my whole family history by now. I think if you were asked to be my mom's primary caretaker you would know her medical history as well as I do.'

Eloise softens. 'You're right. I forgot how much ground you can cover when you're working the ground.'

'Horrible pun.' I shake my head at her in mock disappointment.

'Nick!' I hear Cal shout. 'Glad to see you back!'

'Glad to see you too!' I call out. He's riding a tractor parallel to our row.

'Of course he's nice to you,' Eloise grumbles. 'Wait until you hear what he says to me.'

As if on cue, Cal yells, 'Eloise, those trees won't pick themselves,' and laughs so loudly I can't help but laugh too.

'Dad!' She rolls her eyes and we get to work, picking the trees together one by one. I stay close to her, taking every chance I get for our shoulders to brush.

'Julian and Isaac are visiting for U-Pick,' I remind her. 'They want to meet you.'

'You told them about me?' she asks. Her gaze is focused on the apple she's just picked, but by the way her head is cocked towards mine I know she's pleasantly surprised they know who she is.

'Of course I did.'

'Linden might be coming that weekend too. He usually surprises us, but he hasn't visited this year. I keep wondering if this will be the first year he doesn't come home at all . . .'

'Would that upset you?'

Eloise sighs. 'The million-dollar question.'

Birdsong floats through the air as I wait for her response. 'The truth is,' she says, 'I've been trying to let go of some of my resentment towards him lately.'

'You filled your resentment quota with me, huh?'

She chuckles. 'You could say that . . . or you could say I'm growing tired of resenting people for moving . . .' She pauses, turning to face me. 'It's an effort to dislike people when they're not really doing anything wrong.'

My mouth feels dry. 'Yeah,' I croak out. *If she knew about Scott's Orchards . . .*

Easily, we fall back into side-by-side rhythm, our conversation waxing and waning with the breeze. She tells me something about apple blossoms, how they used to be a symbol of love, and right after she says it she asks nonchalantly, 'Will you put that in a TikTok?'

'So you've seen them?'

'Maybe.'

'And?'

'And ... my words look better on a screen than I thought they would.'

'Ah. About that—'

'It's OK,' she interrupts me. 'I was really annoyed at first,' she admits, 'but the videos are good.'

'I knew I'd win you over.'

Eloise toys with her bottom lip. 'Speaking of winning me over . . .' She hesitates, before her eyes light up with an idea. 'You're leaving in, like, two weeks,' she says.

'Yeah,' I acknowledge, even though the words make my heart sink.

'So, what if we call it a truce until then?'

'You? Eloise? The girl who told me I was threatening her entire future with my schemes, wants to declare a truce with me?'

Chapter Thirty-One

Eloise

Things I Would Usually NEVER Write Down, But I Can't Seem to Focus on Anything Else

- Sliding a finger under the waistline of Nick's jeans
- Nick's breath in my ear
- The pads of Nick's fingers
- The stubble on Nick's chin scraping against my inner thigh
- The feel of Nick's lips pressed to my forehead
- The way his eyes light up with gold when he smiles

'Yep. I, Eloise Anderson, want to declare a truce with you.' I fidget where I'm standing, the two of us pinned up against an apple tree. He's stooped ever so slightly to avoid hitting the branch above his head and to lean a little closer to me. Shari's voice memo runs through my brain again and all I'm thinking about is how good it would feel to have some of her energy. I would explain it to Nick, but smelling his signature combination of cinnamon and mint is stealing all my concentration.

His eyebrows pull together. 'This feels fishy.'

'It's not,' I protest, hoping he doesn't press. How am I supposed to explain that this is all I've thought about since the County Fair? I like him too much to ignore him completely. And I'm rationalizing it by needing to know how the Parkers are doing in U-Pick season. I would rather know sooner than later if my plan will be blown to smithereens. The anxiety of it is killing me.

'OK.' He looks at me, grinning. 'I would really like that, then.' He leans in slowly and I relax into the tree, letting my weight shift ever so slightly forward until our lips just barely touch. Just like before, the slightest graze of his lips sends electricity buzzing through me, but now there's no one to interrupt us. Nick kisses me deeply, so deeply I feel it in my toes as they curl into my work boots. *Has he somehow gotten better since the laundry room? God, how have I been living without this?* My lips part of their own accord, inviting his tongue in. He's greedy all of a sudden, one of his hands is on my lower back and the other is on the nape of my neck and God, he feels amazing. My back is scratching against the tree but I don't even care, I can hardly even think about anything other than *this kiss*.

I reach around for his lower back, snaking one hand up the back of his shirt and sliding two fingers in between his pants and his skin, skimming the ridge of his underwear. He presses his hips into mine and I feel him getting hard. I gasp into his mouth and he sucks on my tongue, wetness gathering between my legs.

'God, Eloise,' Nick pants in between kisses.

My body feels so much like a live wire I can't even form words.

Suddenly, Nick pulls away. 'Maisy!' he screams, sending us careening apart, my head slamming into the branch above me. Confused, I squint at Nick, who has already taken off running, so quickly that he's almost run right into a tree across the way.

'Nick!' I yell, chasing after him. He thuds to a stop at the end of the row of trees and I crash into his back, sending us both skittering forward, finally coming to a stop right in front of a giant pink pig, who is nosing around in the roots of a tree.

'We have to corner her,' Nick whispers, 'sometimes she gets out, but she's too heavy to pick up, we have to corral her back into her pen.'

'All the way into her pen?' I exclaim.

Nick's eyes widen, sheepish. 'I don't know how she got out.'

Working together, slowly, we stay on either side of Maisy, gently nudging her all the way back up over the hill, towards the Parkers' barn. Every time she starts to stall, nosing at a tree or snorting at Nick, he talks to her softly, like she can understand him, asking her to please keep going. His earnest tone sends me into a fit of giggles every time. Halfway up the hill Nick reaches for my hand, intertwines his fingers with mine, and squeezes.

Clink.

I look up from the book I'm reading, confused. I cock my head at the door. Mom and Dad went to bed not long after me, I heard the usual rhythms of the house shutting down, their door closing, the creak of their footsteps across the floor.

Clink.

It's coming from the window. My stained-glass window. My favorite window. I take a step towards it and pause, listening for the wind. Is it breaking? I take another step so I'm right up in front of it, just in time for a pebble to sail straight towards my face.

'Shit!' I exclaim, ducking as fast as I can. *Clink.*

Trying to stay as quiet as I can, I take the stairs two at a time until I'm easing the front door closed behind me.

'Nick!' I hiss into the darkness. 'That better be you.'

'Who else would it be?' Nick appears, a shadow morphing into his strong stature as he gets closer.

'What are you doing here?'

'We didn't get to finish what we started earlier. So . . .' He thrusts his hands in his pockets and shrugs sheepishly.

'So you thought I wanted more?' I tease.

'Well, you did declare a truce.'

'Oh, come on.' I reach for his hand and thread my fingers through his, pulling him towards me. 'Be quiet. And no more throwing pebbles at my window. It's stained glass! It's fragile!'

'Promise,' he whispers. He follows me diligently, even stepping over the third stair like I do, which is a small miracle because that's the one that creaks the loudest.

'So, this is your room?'

I nod, suddenly embarrassed at the state of things. There's laundry covering a threadbare armchair and my vintage purple lampshade is tilted. I shift my weight from foot to foot.

'I love it,' he says. He takes a turn around the room, picking up the book I had left on the bed. 'What's this?' he asks.

'No.' I go to grab it but I'm too late, his eyes are already widening.

'Wow,' he says, 'I didn't peg you for . . .'

'It's really popular,' I whisper defiantly, fully aware that my cheeks are bright red. I was just reading a scene about a sexy warrior's first tryst with a cursed prince and based on Nick's face I'm confident he skimmed straight to the part where the warrior suggested they take things even further and explained what she was looking for in great detail.

'It's . . .' He gulps. '. . . it sure is something . . .' He places the book down gently and sits down on the bed.

I remain standing, feeling vulnerable being in such close quarters with him with no warning, suddenly wondering if I left moisturizer on my face accidentally or if my hair is a mess from getting ready for bed.

'Do you want to sit?' he asks. 'Or I can stand?' He gets up, his body rippling as he pulls himself to his full height. I forget how tall he is when we're standing in the fields, not hemmed in by anything. But in my room he looks so large. 'I'm so sorry for just coming over here.'

'No, don't be,' I tell him. 'I'm happy you did. Sit back down.' I climb onto the bed next to him, so we're facing each other but we're not touching. The air between us is filled with tension.

'Have you found out if your brother's coming this weekend?'

'No.' I shake my head. 'No idea.'

'I hope he does. I'd like to meet him.'

'I'm excited to meet Julian and Isaac.'

Nick rolls his eyes. 'They'll love you.'

I pick at a loose thread on my bedspread. 'Are you excited to see them?'

He nods. 'They're my best friends . . . I don't know if I told you this but right before I started graduate school I hit a rough patch. Just not really sure why I was going back to school, what my purpose was.' He shrugs. 'They helped me through it. Didn't even need to ask them, they just picked up on something being off and started coming over. Isaac even called my mom at one point.'

I reach over and grab his hand, anything to help the sad expression that overtook his face go away.

'They seem great.' I rub a thumb over the top of his hand. 'I can't wait to meet them.'

'Yeah,' Nick sighs. 'They're different than what you're used to around here, but they're good people.'

We talk about everything and nothing for what feels like hours, our conversation evolving from Nick telling me about his college shenanigans with Julian and Isaac to me telling Nick more about Evan (although I don't tell him how big Evan's crush on him is). Before I know it, we're lying side by side, staring up at the ceiling in the dark, one of my legs underneath one of his and my head on his chest. I can hear his heart beating, and by how fast it sounds I know he isn't ready to go to sleep either.

I turn to face him, our noses brushing in the pitch-black night.

'Eloise,' he says softly, 'I can't believe how much I like you.'

I lean forward and kiss him, *finally*, and he wraps his arms around me, pulling me closer. Our bodies press together, his mouth all over mine, and I feel his heart beat even faster. Somehow his lips get sexier every time we kiss, hungrier, softer, he bites my lower lip and I pin my hips to his. All I want to be is closer. All I've wanted, all day, all month, is to be closer to him. His hand slides towards the base of my neck and he gently teases his fingers into my hair, leaning my head back and pressing kisses to my throat, trailing them down towards my chest as I writhe with pleasure.

'Nick,' I murmur. As his mouth presses delicate kisses in a trail towards my breast, his other palm slides from my hips to the swell of my breast and his thumb circles around my nipple. His hand is calloused, rough from weeks of work, and feels desperately good against my skin. I arch into him and when he kisses my nipple, his tongue flickering the sensitive tip, I moan so loudly that we both freeze.

A barn owl hoots outside.

'Eloise!' he admonishes, but I don't have to see his face to know he's pleased.

'I'll be quieter,' I promise, 'just don't—'

Before I can finish, he presses his mouth to mine, murmuring his words straight into my lips, 'I wouldn't be able to stop even if I wanted to.'

I sigh with pleasure as his mouth works his way back down my throat, past my breasts, towards my belly button. His other thumb resumes circling my nipple, building pleasure so white hot through my body that I start to feel like I could explode just from his touch. A deep murmur of appreciation escapes his lips as he kisses my stomach. But when his kisses get even further away from my head I still, anxiety interrupting my pleasure.

Nick picks his head up right away. 'Are you OK?' he asks.

'I just . . .' I trail off, not sure how to explain this to him. Every other guy I've been with has gone straight to penetrative sex the first time. There's been no slowness, no reverence, no appreciation. I don't know how to handle it.

'You can talk to me,' Nick says, settling his head besides mine on the pillow. His hands are still at my sides now.

'We're in the dark, but it feels like we're under a bright light . . . That probably makes no sense . . .'

'It does,' he says, patient, reassuring. He strokes my hair with his hand and pulls me closer to him.

'I'm sorry,' I murmur, embarrassed.

'Eloise, all I've wanted since the very first day I met you was to hold you in my arms. If you think you have anything to be sorry for then you're crazier than a hound dog with a flea in his ear.'

A laugh escapes my lips. 'A hound dog with a flea in his ear?'

'I got it from Betsy,' Nick explains, he's started laughing too. 'I'm trying it out.' He kisses me on the cheek. 'Let's get some sleep, beautiful,' he says, pulling me closer.

I startle awake in the middle of the night, only to be immediately calmed by Nick's steady breathing next to me. Tentatively, I curl up closer towards him and he stirs gently, a small whimper of satisfaction escaping from his lips. His arms tighten around me and I melt back into a dreamless sleep.

My alarm blares. I move to get up like I usually do, but something is pinning me to the bed. *What the . . . Nick*. I peel his heavy forearm off me and blearily shut off my alarm. *Damnit*. My parents will already be up. I *cannot* handle hearing what Mom will have to say. We already have enough going on this week

'Nick,' I whisper, 'time to—' the words die on my lips. He looks so peaceful sleeping. He stirs so gently, his hand reaching towards my body.

'Eloise?' he murmurs, his voice thick with sleep.

'We gotta get up.'

Nick shakes his head vigorously, like he could shake the sleep right out of his body.

'Damn,' he says, sitting up and running a hand through his hair. 'I haven't slept that deeply in . . . ages.'

I can't help the shy smile that curls up my lips. 'Really?' I ask. 'I thought you were sleeping better out here.'

'Really.' He cups my cheek with his hand. 'I am sleeping better out here but being next you takes it to a whole other level.'

I hear the stirrings of my parents' downstairs and my gaze snags on the door.

'Damn.' His expression changes, worry snagging at the corners of his mouth and pulling them down. 'I better get back.'

'We have to sneak you out,' I tell him. 'We can do it when I go downstairs for breakfast. We wouldn't want Mrs. Parker speculating as to where you've been.'

'Are you sure?' he asks, with a glint in his eye. He glances at the book I had tossed to the floor, the one where very dirty things were explicitly described, and he wiggles his eyebrows. 'I could just give her your book, tell her that's what we were doing.'

I squeal, covering my eyes. 'You wouldn't dare.'

Nick stands, wrapping one arm around me and pulling me closer to him, tilting my chin up towards his face. 'The things I want to do to you, Eloise,' he breathes, 'they don't even have words for in that book of yours.'

I let out a little moan before I can help myself. Nick smirks, kissing me chastely on the lips, before heading out the door. He pauses in the doorway and whispers, 'Don't worry, I'll skip the third stair.'

I have never been more motivated to pick apples than I am this morning. Which is shocking considering prior to this I was motivated by the harvest determining my entire future, my loan application still hanging in the balance, my ability to make a living still undetermined. But today, apples are standing in the way of great sex. Ergo, I am picking apples more efficiently than a machine.

Nick is meeting me in East Barn later, and if our impromptu make-out sessions in the fields have been any indication, we're going to have a mind-bending afternoon. But the unsexy thing about being a farmer is that if I don't get enough done before then, I can't get my to-do list out of my head. It's like my body slams on the brakes when all I want to do is press on the gas. After the night we spent together Nick has been slowly eroding my lapse in self-confidence and with every stolen kiss, every brush of his fingertips, my body has become more and more alive. I'm thrumming with so much desire I feel like a tuning fork.

Nick meets me with a giddy smile plastered over his face. We pass by North Barn on our way, and I sneak JJ one of the unripe apples I plucked earlier. He nibbles at Nick's hand too and cocks his head at him as if asking, *Why didn't you bring me a treat?* We laugh at JJ's antics until we approach the door to East Barn and we both still. Nick pushes the heavy wooden door with a soft touch. It creaks open, letting slanted shafts of light spill onto the floor. As soon as we step inside, our bodies smash together, hands everywhere, Nick's mouth on mine. I feel like I've been overtaken by an ocean wave, everything else melting away. I wrap my arms around his neck as he presses me against the barn door and kisses me even deeper. His hands clutch my ass and he lifts me up, pressing his hips to mine as I wrap my legs around his waist. I feel him harden against me and my breath catches in my mouth. 'Eloise,' he breathes. I unravel my legs from his waist as he wordlessly tugs my hand towards the side of the room and we make our way up the ladder to the small loft that overlooks the cavernous space.

He lays me down in the soft hay, trailing a slow, calloused finger across my belly button and curves his hand up over the side of my ribcage, letting his thumb bump over every bone. My body sinks into his touch.

'We shouldn't,' I say, as the top of his thumb grazes my nipple.

'Why? Because we're in your childhood hangout?'

I nod, but I can't speak, it's too hard to find the words when Nick is touching me like this.

'But you want to,' he breathes, feeling my nipple peaking at the slightest brush of his touch.

'I want to.' I'm half moaning, breathless.

Under his touch I'm completely blissed out, my head on a cushion of straw, both of our feet dangling off the small ledge of the loft that overlooks the concrete floor below. Light drips in from the single window, illuminating the dust motes floating in the afternoon air.

Nick slides my shirt off, his eyes dark with hunger as they rake down my exposed body. As he releases my breasts from my bra, I arch towards him, moaning softly. He presses a finger to my lips and smiles coyly. 'Can I finish what I started?' he asks, trailing kisses down my neck.

I nod.

He looks up.

'Yes,' I pant.

He makes a sound in the base of his throat, a cross between a growl and a moan, and kisses me again, this time gently taking my nipple between his teeth.

'Yes please,' I breathe.

Nick wrenches off his T-shirt, his abs rippling as he positions his mouth over my thighs and presses his lips to my hip bone. I feel my body start to turn to liquid, to melt underneath his touch, my knees falling sideways, opening up for him. He works slow kisses until he arrives right where I need him before he hesitates, kissing me swiftly on the lips while teasing a finger inside me. I writhe with pleasure and he practically purrs, 'You're so wet for me.' I nod, completely breathless, as he works my clit with his fingers. I feel need building inside of me, I want him inside me more than I've ever wanted anything.

Until he sucks on my clit and thinking about anything else is completely obliterated. 'Nick,' I moan, 'Oh, my God.' I must have more nerve endings than I ever thought possible. He teases his fingers around me and slips them in, filling me completely as his tongue continues to circle slowly, methodically, and my breaths get more and more rhythmic, faster and faster his hands move and before I know it, I'm crying out loudly, my entire world exploding. Nick continues, lapping me up like he'll never get enough, reverently consuming me until I stop shuddering and my body goes limp in his arms.

'That was incredible,' I murmur.

'I was going for the gold star.' He winks at me, before pulling his body up to rest atop mine, his forearms on either side of my head. He kisses me slow and deep.

'I think it's my turn to go for the gold star,' I sigh, my lips pressed to his, my insides hot with desire.

'You already got one,' he says. His breath hitches when I tug at the hemline of his pants. 'God, you're sexy.'

Another gold star, this time for both of us, later, and we return to the fields, hair messy, limbs liquified, blissfully exhausted.

It's Friday and U-Pick officially kicks off tomorrow. The Parkers and my parents are so busy planning they have hardly kept tabs on where we've been. Which is lucky considering we can't keep our hands off each other. We've earned more gold stars than I can count. Even though Nick and I declared a truce, I allow myself to ask one time how the Parkers are doing. The uncertainty is killing me.

'Let's just say I held up my end of the bargain,' Nick says. He has my back pinned to the wooden fence that separates our property from the Parkers. 'I thought we weren't going to talk about that anymore,' he murmurs into my neck, sending chills up my spine.

'I know,' I breathe. 'I told myself I could ask one time though.'

'Honestly.' Nick pulls away from me, looking at me intently with his big brown eyes. 'I don't know what will happen. I did what I came here to do. The rest is in their hands.'

'My dream is in their hands,' I correct him.

He runs a hand up my forearm. 'I know,' he mutters. 'I would never have accepted this job if I knew what succeeding meant to you.'

'But you can't just not succeed, for once?'

He shakes his head before he looks towards the Parkers' home. 'I can't do that to them . . .'

'I know,' I say glumly. That's one of the things I like so much about Nick, his devotion to the Parkers, his sense of loyalty. I kick at the dirt under my shoes.

'Let's enjoy the time we do have,' he says, before hoisting me up to sit on the fence, the perfect angle for me to wrap my legs around him.

Fuck it, I think, before I do exactly that.

Evan: Lou, I'm coming to help U-Pick.

Me: What?

Shari: What??? I can't leave the strawberry farm, I just got back!!

Me: Shari, relax. I don't know what Evan is talking about.

Evan: I texted Hazel already *Sent with invisible ink*

Me: You did what?

Evan: I NEEDED some apple pie. Like STAT.

Evan: Plus I have nothing going on.

Evan: Also I was supposed to go away with Kevin this weekend. And before you say it, I know, Kevin and Evan would have never worked anyways, but he bailed. So . . . I'll see you Saturday morning, Eloise!

Me: Oh I'm sorry about Kevin, Evan. LOL it's hard to even type that out with a straight face. I would love to see you. Did Mom say anything about Linden?

Evan: Linden? No. She just said I could have the guest room.

Me: Weird. He always surprises us during early harvest.

Shari: Thank God. Honestly. If your hot brother would also be there I would have had to come. I MISS FABIO.

Me: Shari, I think you need to be grateful for your Lizzie McGuire moment for a little longer before coming on to my brother. Also, yuck. Also, you know he has a girlfriend.

Evan: Speaking of hot, how's the hot intern?

Me: You're making him sound like a glorified secretary.

Evan: Coming to his defense? Unlike you.

Shari: OMG WHAT IS GOING ON. Something *fish emoji*

Shari: My radar has been ON ever since my LMMM (Lizzie McGuire Movie Moment). I'm a new person when it comes to love.

Evan: Come to think of it, Lou hasn't complained about him at all this week. For weeks it's been Nick is ruining my life and Nick came to karaoke with Amie and Nick this and Nick that and Nick and the stupid pigs.

Shari: And this week . . . crickets.

Shari: I bet she finally caved. He is so hot.

Evan: DID YOU.

Me: Maybe? *Sent with invisible ink*

Evan: SCREAMS.

Shari: You two better call me when you're together.

Evan: OMG ELOISE. YOU TEMPTRESS. THIS WEEK OF ALL WEEKS. THE WEEK BEFORE U-PICK. YOU SEDUCE?

Me: Can you stop texting in all caps. It is so hard to read.

Me: And no. Or at least, I didn't mean to. It just . . . happened.

Evan: That's what they all say.

Shari: Drool. He's so dreamy.

Me: It's not important. He's leaving like the week after next anyways.

Shari: Acting like you don't have the date written in sharpie in your calendar.

Evan: I can't WAIT to debrief.

Me: Evan. No time to debrief. It will be crazy here! Be prepared to work.

Evan: As long as I'm paid in apple pie.

We're going all out this year. We've never done anything like it before. I'm not sure whether to staff Evan at the JJ meet and greet, the photo backdrops, or at the bake stand. Although given his love for apple pie, I'm thinking the latter. We've never invited visitors to meet JJ, but with his renewed strength I think he's up for it and I know it's time to see how he interacts with new people, the first step of many to potentially finding him a new home.

'God, you're sexy,' Nick breathes into my neck, pulling me out of my train of thought just in time. I bury my nose into his hair and inhale the minty smell of his hair gel.

'I don't know what you're doing to me, Nick Russo.' I sigh.

He runs his hands through my hair and I squeal with happiness. Suddenly his hands are everywhere. For the past three days we've alternated between exhaustion and overdrive—all hands, urgent, panting, sweaty and fast. We've spent every night together since the first night Nick slept over, but usually by the time we collapse in bed next to each other all we do is snuggle and sleep. Nick wraps his arms around me or a leg on top of me and I feel luxuriously cozy under his muscular limbs.

Yesterday morning he came back over to our farm like he usually would, after he had breakfast with Betsy. We had just started taking soil samples, doing our best to act normal, when Dad asked if I could grab something from the basement storage room.

'Sure,' I said, 'wanna come?'

Nick nodded and I saw the glint in his eye. I saw what was going to happen in that basement storage room a mile away.

It was damp and dusty, so unsexy that it *was* sexy. Nick lifted me on top of a work table before I could even question what was going on, his tongue in my mouth, my hands greedily pulling his T-shirt off.

He nibbled the top of my bum and pulled my pants down with his teeth, grazing my skin while he did it. I writhed with pleasure. 'Nick,' I warned, 'ten minutes.'

'Ten minutes, Scout's honor,' he said, pulling my pants down with his hands. He slid a finger between my thighs, his other hand reaching up my shirt and thumbing my nipple. My breath hitched in my chest. I whimpered.

'You're so wet for me already,' he breathed into my ear, nibbling on the bottom of my earlobe. My toes curled. I arched my back up into him. Felt his hardness against my backside.

'I'm not the only one who's ready,' I replied.

'It's not about me today.' His thumb pressed on my clit right as he said it and I gasped. He flipped me over again. 'It's about you,' He said, before he kissed each of my nipples, flicking his tongue around them so expertly that I moaned. He trailed kisses down my belly button until he reached his hand, his thumb never hesitating, still circling my clit with expert rhythm.

When his lips reached me, I felt like I could dissolve with pleasure. 'Nick,' I moaned, thrusting my fingers into his hair and pulling gently, guiding his tongue to exactly where I needed it. 'Just like that.'

He obeyed, one hand palming my breast, the other working in tandem with his tongue. He swirled and licked and sucked in a perfect rhythm, building me closer and closer to the edge.

'Keep going,' I moaned, and he sucked harder, my vision clouding with stars as I completely let go.

He raised his head from between my legs and licked his lips.

'You are,' he said, with more sincerity than I've ever heard from him lips, 'perfect.'

I felt like the heroine in my book. And it felt *so* good. It felt so good *twice*.

Chapter Thirty-Two

Nick

WEEK NINE

The earth is damp this morning, soil packed tightly underneath my boots. Not like yesterday when everything felt dusty. It was the perfect rain before U-Pick, Joe told me this morning—enough to bind the soil together, to stop everything from being coated in silt, but not too much that it turned everything to mud. We officially open our doors to folks this weekend, who will come in from across the state to pick apples with their families, their friends, and their partners.

I'm exhausted, it's the first night I've spent without Eloise all week and I didn't sleep well. I tell myself it's because I like her mattress better than Betsy's, trying to pretend that I don't already know insomnia will plague me again when I return to San Francisco. I tried to bring up visiting the last time we were together, asking if she would go see Linden if he didn't end up making the trip during the summer, knowing the answer was probably no.

'I don't know,' was all she said before she quickly changed the topic. I took it as a no. Not that I expected anything else. Eloise makes her disdain of San Francisco clear. Although I can't help but wonder if that's because her dream is there waiting for her. Or in Seattle. Or anywhere but a farm, anywhere with a lab, with research and young people and so much potential.

I take a deep breath of the crisp morning air to clear my thoughts. I can't afford any distractions today. There's a buzz of nervous energy about the place, we've had a handful of additional workers arrive to help with the anticipated swell of guests, and it feels like there's a lot of responsibility on my shoulders. Whatever happens here will determine what Joe and Betsy decide to do, I can feel it. If they have a great weekend they might think twice about Scott's. If they have a great weekend and Scott's knows then they might give the Parkers something more to think about. And if they have a bad weekend . . . Well, I try not to think about that.

I head to check on the pigs. Maisy squeals as soon as she sees me, trotting over to nuzzle at my palm, undoubtedly looking for treats.

'Hey, sweet girl.' I greet each one. 'My princess,' I say to Peach. I give Buttercup a belly rub. 'You'll be the stars of our show today,' I tell them.

Walking away from their pen, I'm overwhelmed by a wave of nostalgia. I'll miss them. I love their distinct personalities and their noises. I love the way their snouts are wet with dew in the morning. I love the way the air feels in my lungs, so pure. I love how little I have to check my phone or my email.

I think about how hard I've worked to set myself up for success. It's not like I'm going to abandon it now, I just wish it looked a little different. But struggling to make ends meet my whole adult life will not be success. I know that much.

I glance down towards the Anderson's farm as I walk back towards the kitchen. We open in a little under two hours. Julian and Isaac should arrive about that time too.

Seeing them will be nice. A good reminder of what I'm missing out on in San Francisco—the reasons I need to go back.

I spot Julian's unmistakable head of curly black hair towering over the other customers, weaving closer and closer to me. We're only an hour into U-Pick and it's crazier than I thought. Vans are rolling up by the dozen, muddying up the fields around the house we designated for parking. Families are piling out in color-coordinated flannels, matching red beanies, and plaid scarves. We hired a couple teenagers from the local high school to man the ticket stand and the pig pen and their mops of unruly hair are unmistakable.

My lips are already splitting into a grin, I'm picking up my pace. I've been waiting all morning for them to arrive, and based on the relief I feel was more worried about them getting here in one piece than I let on. Those country roads are no joke.

'If I had known you'd be so happy to see me I would have come earlier.'

I turn to my right, where the voice came from, to find myself face to face with Harvey, one of the executives from Scott's Orchards. I almost don't recognize him. He's in jeans and a button-down, infinitely more casual than the last time we met when he was wearing dark slacks and a suit jacket.

'Millie, can you say hello?' he asks a little girl at his feet, her strawberry-blonde head barely reaching past his knees. She nods and looks up at me with huge eyes. 'Hi,' she says quietly.

I kneel down so we're at the same height before pretending to pull an apple out of thin air from behind her head. She's delighted.

Harvey gives me a quizzical but amused look. 'Magic camp one summer.' I shrug.

'Between you and me—' Harvey looks around '—everyone else wanted to give up on this place.'

I resist the urge to roll my eyes. I don't know who I'm more annoyed at—Harvey, for showing up out of nowhere playing the hero or Joe and Betsy, for dragging their feet so much to respond to the offer in the first place.

'I don't mean to be a bother,' he says, 'I just came to check things out, see how you're getting along.'

'Don't be silly,' I say, ignoring the sinking feeling in my chest that it will be even longer before I can spend time with my friends. That little sacrifice is worth it if I can give the Parkers a little bit more time to make one of the biggest decisions of their life. 'I'll take you on the grand tour.'

I straighten up in time to see Julian materialize from the crowd. He starts jumping up and down with excitement. I point at Harvey and his daughter Millie, who thankfully needed her shoe retied so both of them are looking down and make a slashing motion across my neck. If it was only Julian who'd arrived, I would have taken him on the tour with us. But Isaac is a wild card, and I can't have him blowing up the Parkers' chances with a stupid comment that would fly in the city but not here.

Isaac slams into Julian from behind and Julian turns to whisper something to him that seems to be along the lines of play it cool, because Isaac's expression neutralizes and he stands still, shifting his weight from one foot to the other, grinning at me all the same.

'This place is sick!' Isaac mouths to me.

'Business,' I mouth, pointing at Harvey. 'Sorry. See you later.'

Julian flashes me an OK sign. One thing I can count on with my friends is that they can have fun doing anything. With or without me, when I catch up with them later, they'll have had a grand old time.

I lead Harvey and Millie into the fields, promising Millie the best apple she's ever had. I turn around to glance at Julian and Isaac, hoping they'll make their way inside or Mrs. Parker will notice the strays when I see Eloise appear next to them with a smile on her face.

Stunned, I watch as she beckons them towards the trail that goes to the Andersons' farm. They haven't even bought tickets to our U-Pick yet! Eloise is going to take them on their first apple farm visit? Our eyes meet and she waves happily. 'We'll miss you,' she mouths to me.

I can't help but smile. As much as I wanted to be the one to do it, if there's anyone else I want to take Isaac and Julian on their first farm tour, it's Eloise.

I just hope Isaac and Julian don't do anything stupid.

Chapter Thirty-Three

Eloise

Things I hate

- Liars
- Liars
- Liars

'Oh, Nick *loves* that team.' Isaac looks up at me as we pass a family in matching red jerseys emblazoned with an SF logo. 'You didn't know?'

The only scene that even remotely relates to sports replays in my mind. *I actually hate football*, Nick confessed, his voice dropping to a whisper. *That's my secret.* I gulp. 'Right! I think he did mention that once or twice.' I smile at them, hoping they can't detect the change in my voice, but they both carry on chattering and laughing while they pick apples, oblivious.

'That's actually why he's out here,' Julian says. 'Woah, look at that one!' He spots a perfectly circular bright red apple on one of the top branches and jumps for it.

'What's why who's out here?' I ask, half paying attention to him and half squinting at the front of the barn where families are standing in line to have their picture taken. We hired the community college's amateur photography class to do the portraits and so far it's been a big hit. Even Evan congratulated me on that one. Although I doubt he'll be as happy with me after his workday today.

He talked up Mom's apple pie so much that I assigned him to the bake stand. He's been swamped all morning.

'I haven't even been able to eat a sample,' he whined when he saw me grabbing Isaac and Julian to take them out for the tour. 'Can't I come with you?'

'You said you were coming to help,' I said sternly. 'Plus, I'm just dropping them at the fields.' At least that's what I intended to do until I started talking to them and realized how much dirt they had on Nick.

'That's why Nick's out here.' Julian snorts. 'He lost a stupid fantasy football bet. That stubborn motherf—'

'What?' I wheel around. I must have misheard. 'Nick is out here for a school project.'

'Right,' Julian says happily, like he's relieved we're all on the same page. 'A project he only took because he lost a fantasy football bet.'

'What, did you think he was here out of the goodness of his heart?' Isaac laughs. 'Unfortunately, that is *not* something we learn in school.'

My mouth opens and closes while I try to think of what to say. I *did* think Nick was here out of the goodness of his heart. He kept telling me how important it was to him to help the Parkers. How he had to succeed to make his mom proud. Why would I have thought otherwise?

Julian and Isaac's chatter sounds like a faint buzzing in my ear as I keep processing what they just said. 'I thought he *had* to be here for school?' I ask finally, interrupting them.

Isaac doesn't seem the least bit concerned. 'Yeah, I mean, I guess. He's got his job after school anyways.'

'You're telling me he's done all this work for some stupid sports league?' I ask, trying to decide just how angry to be with Nick.

Isaac shrugs. 'I wouldn't exactly say stupid, but . . .'

Nick was ready to ruin my life, my business plan, my shot at providing a secure future for my parents, over a fantasy football bet. My decision is easy, I don't even need to think about it. I am as angry with Nick as physically possible. I am seething.

Chapter Thirty-Four

Nick

'So, what did you think?' I ask Isaac and Julian, finally getting to spend time with them for the first time all day. We're sitting on the Parkers' porch, staring at the fields now streaked through with boot prints and tire tracks. I tried to find them after Harvey's tour, but they were with Eloise and by the time they got back I got pulled into an issue at the pigsty. Buttercup had peed on a little boy. Refunded tickets and some free apples later and it was like it never happened.

Thankfully Mrs. Parker had swept in to take care of Isaac and Julian, getting them settled in the guest room and ushering them out to the front porch with fresh beers.

'It's pretty sweet out here,' Isaac says. 'I gotta admit, I thought you were really gassing it up at the beginning, but I see why you like it.'

'Oh,' I confess, 'I was. It was really hard work at first. But now, yeah, I guess you're right. I do like it.'

'Eloise is cool,' Julian says.

Isaac nods enthusiastically.

'Yeah, she is.'

'Look at you grinning!' Isaac teases.

Ignoring him, I pull out my phone to text Eloise:

Do I even want to know what you said to Julian and Isaac to make them like you so much?

Then I slide it back into my pocket.

We sit on the porch again after dinner, watching the fireflies blip in and out. I check my phone. Still no text from Eloise. Earlier this week we had talked about potentially getting together, how fun it would be to hang out with Isaac, Julian, and Evan. I gaze at the Anderson house and watch as the front porch light clicks on.

'Want to walk to the Andersons'?' I ask them. 'You can meet Evan, one of Eloise's best friends. He's great.'

'Works for me.' Julian gets up from his seat.

'The stars are so bright out here,' Isaac says as we're walking down the hill, his head craned back to look at the sky.

'Watch out, it's bumpy,' I call out, just as Issac fumbles, careening forward and spilling some beer on his shirt before righting himself.

We're laughing when we arrive at the porch to find Eloise and Evan talking in hushed tones.

'Hi,' I call out. 'First U-Pick day is done. How are we feeling?' My smile falls as soon as I see Eloise's face.

'What are you doing here?' she asks. She seems exhausted. I'm overwhelmed by the impulse to gather her in my arms.

Evan looks at Eloise questioningly.

'I just thought we'd say hi . . .'

Eloise glances at Evan with a mixture of panic and anger.

'I'm Evan,' Evan introduces himself to Isaac and Julian, smoothing out some of the awkwardness while I try desperately to meet Eloise's eyes, and she keeps her gaze firmly fixed on the ground.

'Really nice to meet you guys,' he continues, the picture of charm. 'But we're pretty tired. I think we might head in.'

'OK.' I feign indifference, even though my heart plummets. I look at Eloise one more time but she's still looking at her feet.

'Goodnight,' she says quietly. Evan shepherds her inside.

'What was that about?' Julian asks as soon as we're out of earshot.

'I have no idea,' I say, firing off a text to Eloise asking if she's OK.

'Did she seem normal today?' I ask them.

'Yeah.' Isaac shrugs. 'I think.'

I glance at Julian, the more introspective of the two.

'She was kind of weird about the fantasy football thing,' Julian offers, 'but girls are always weird about that.'

Shit. I stop walking, going completely still. My hands feel clammy. 'You told her about the fantasy football bet?' I gulp.

'Well . . . yeah? Was it a secret?'

'I mean . . . I guess not, but . . .' *Fuck. Fuck. Fuck.*

'What?' Isaac asks. He hates being out of the loop.

'It's just . . .' I sigh. 'Eloise wanted to buy the Parkers' farm. We didn't exactly see eye to eye at the beginning because if I turn it around, she can't buy it anymore.'

'Damn,' Julian breathes. 'What changed?'

'I don't know, we just both agreed to ignore it, but if she thinks I'm putting her future in jeopardy of for a stupid bet . . .'

'Well, you are,' Isaac points out. 'Aren't you?'

'I mean, no . . .' But I have to pause to think about it. Am I? I thought all this time I was doing it for the Parkers. Or I was doing it for school. I *had* to do a good job. What kind of a person would I be if I slacked off? But the more I think about it the more uncertain I feel. Why was I so sure that what I was doing was right? But I am right . . . aren't I? The Parkers deserve a chance to succeed.

Thoughts swirl in my head all night long. I text her again, telling her I can explain if she'll just let me. No response.

I toss and turn, wondering if I did the right thing, wondering if Eloise will forgive me, wondering when exactly I started to care so much about what she thinks . . .

At least Isaac and Julian don't know about Scott's Orchards. If Eloise found out about that from them it would be beyond forgiveness. I'll have to tell her. The thought alone fills me with so much dread I spend the rest of the night staring at the ceiling.

When the rooster crows in the morning, I've already been up for hours.

Chapter Thirty-Five

Eloise

A Few of My Favorite Things When I'm Feeling Bad (à la Julie Andrews)

- Sweatshirts so worn in they have holes (preferably Dad's)
- A hug from Mom
- *The Notebook* or *Dead Poets Society* (different vibes, same tear-jerk quality)
- Quilts
- Bright copper kettles (with chamomile tea)
- Drawn blackout shades

Evan sent me to bed promising that a night of sleep would help diminish my anger. It didn't. I'm so angry at breakfast that I'm seeing red. I can't believe I took my eye off the ball. This was supposed to be the most important harvest of my life, my chance to give my parents a feasible option to keep the farm, and I've been distractedly hiding away in barns and basements instead of working hard.

'What do you want to do?' he asks between bites of cereal.

'Hit him with your car,' I reply truthfully. 'I wish I hadn't lied for him to his friends,' I mutter. 'I should have just told them he hates football. All this, for a bet? I can't believe it.'

'Can you repeat that?' Evan asks. 'I'm so sorry. I can't hear you over my chewing.'

'Let's talk about it later,' I mumble, hearing Mom's footsteps echoing in the hall.

'Another busy day today,' Mom trills as she walks into the kitchen.

I groan. The last thing I want to do is put on a fake smile and welcome people to the farm, but I'll have to grin and bear it.

'I got you.' Evan squeezes my hand. 'We're in this together.'

'Thank you,' I mouth. I don't feel like explaining what happened to my mom—especially seeing as she's the kind of person who would want me to forgive Nick, which is the last thing I want to be told to do.

'Remember that time you stayed up with me all night while I learned the names of fancy wines so I could work at that restaurant?' Evan asks. 'Think of it as payback for that.'

'Except you'll still owe me,' I say, a hint of a smile playing at my lips, 'because you never even took that job. So, the all-nighter was a complete waste.'

'So true. 'Evan smiles. 'Hindsight's twenty-twenty.'

'It sure fucking is.'

*

Evan's beat-up Camry stirs up clouds as he pulls out of the driveway. I stand on the front porch, waving goodbye until he disappears from view. My heart feels heavy as I sit down on a rocking chair on the front porch. I let out a huge sigh. This fall didn't turn out anything like I thought it would.

I hear heavy steps plod up the front porch. 'Ahem.' I don't need to turn around to know Nick just cleared his throat behind me. I stare straight ahead. Isaac and Julian probably just left as well. 'What do you want?' I ask.

'To talk.'

'I'm not in the mood.'

'Look, I know they said something to you about the fantasy football bet. But it's not like this wasn't for school—it *was*. It *is*. For school, I mean.'

'I don't really care,' I say sharply, still staring off into the rolling hills in the distance. There's a storm cloud forming to the west.

'Eloise.' Nick's tone takes on a pleading note. 'Please, I'm sorry.'

'You should really get home before it starts to rain.'

I feel Nick's hand gently on my shoulder, his fingertips barely brushing the fabric of my shirt. My body betrays me, radiating heat towards Nick. But my mind still feels cold. 'Eloise,' he says again. His voice breaks a little bit on the last syllable and I feel my heart soften. 'This was for school, I swear. I would never ruin something so important to you for a stupid bet.'

Something about the way he says it, with so much finality, makes my spine stiffen. I brush his hand off my shoulder. 'You what?' I say in a low voice.

'I wouldn't ruin something so important to you.' Nick is earnest.

'You're acting like it's already happened.' The edge in my voice could break skin.

'I-I—' Nick stutters out.

I turn round to face him. His face is wan, his expression full of remorse, of emotion. His bottom lip is trembling ever so slightly, his eyes wide.

'You can't take away what I've worked my whole life to keep. I won't let you.'

'I don't want to,' he says. He reaches for me, and I stare at his hand. I'm torn between the desperate, almost primal need to grab it, and the betrayal I feel roiling through my body.

'Then don't.' I cross my arms across my chest, keeping my hands away from his, worried they'll grab onto him on their own accord. 'You don't even have to change plans for me. Do it for my parents. I'm doing it to ensure they have a future too.' I open my mouth to remind him how much he likes my parents, how much they like him, but then I close it. He doesn't deserve the satisfaction of knowing how much they adore him.

I watch as his expression transforms from remorseful to exasperated. There's a glint in his eye as he says, 'They didn't ask you to do that for them.'

I snort. 'They didn't have to. Nobody else will. Did you see Linden come up to check on them this summer?'

'Eloise, you're acting like they're eighty years old! They can take care of themselves. What about your dream to do research? You don't think they would think that's more important?'

'Than their wellbeing? They can take care of themselves now, but what about in five years' time? In ten?'

Nick scoffs. 'You act like they're not taking care of themselves just fine.'

'They're not, Nick. You don't know anything about the finances of the farm.'

'And you don't know anything about being a parent if you really think they'd want you to give up on your dream.'

'You clearly don't know my parents if you think that's important to them. They love me *because* I help them. That's who I am to them. A devoted daughter. You would know what that felt like if you didn't run off to the country for the summer and leave your mom behind.'

Nick's mouth forms a tight line. It was a low blow to say that; I know Nick really misses his mom, but something about his comment that my parents don't need me really hit home. Nick takes a deep breath and his face relaxes. 'Your parents love you no matter what. I've seen them with you. They don't love you because you take care of them.'

'That isn't true.'

'Yes, it is.' Nick takes a small step towards me. We're inches apart now, squaring off on the porch as the rainclouds gather on the horizon. 'You're lovable, Eloise. I know it because—'

'That's not true,' I interrupt him, feeling panic rise in my chest. 'You don't know what it's like to be me, to hear your whole life that what you're good at is showing up, is being there for other people. You know what they cared about for Linden? His grades, his sports performance, his internships. They only cared if I was polite, if I put on appropriate clothes for the school outing, if I respected the adults around me. It's didn't matter if I excelled in a lab, it didn't matter if my future had promise, it mattered that I was a good girl, *then* I would be loved.' I pause to take a breath. Nick staring at me, stunned by my outburst. 'You know what the worst part is? I grew up my whole life thinking everything was different for women now, that we could have the world too, that we could dream just as big. But look who's stuck at home taking care of her family? Me. Look who takes on the burden of caring that our farm does something actually good for the planet? Me. While Linden is off doing whatever he wants.' I'm breathing hard, my body temperature rising. I can feel anger radiating out of my pores.

'Eloise.' Nick steps even closer towards me, putting a hand on my arm. 'I'm so sorry. You *are* lovable. You're just as lovable as your brother. You deserve to chase your dreams too. You can always come back here if they're not what you thought, but you should at least try to do what *you* want . . .' He trails off.

I swallow, trying my best to maintain composure even though I feel like I'm about to cry.

'You are so worthy of love.' Nick shakes his head, like he can't bear to imagine a world where I didn't agree with him. 'You love everything.' He throws his hands up. 'You even love dirt! You care about every animal and you talk to every tree. You basically exist to make your father proud and you would do anything for Evan and Shari and Lily . . . You're incredibly smart, you're creative, you have this tireless work ethic. Eloise, I've never met anyone like you. You have no idea how special you are. If you were just honest with your parents, I know they'd understand. You don't need to carry all these burdens alone.'

I blink back tears. I remind myself that Nick is about to leave. *He doesn't care that much about you if he's still planning to abandon you*, says the little voice in my head. I remind myself that he lied to me, that he never told me he was ruining my dream for fantasy football. Then I take a deep breath.

'That advice is rich coming from you,' I say. 'You couldn't even be honest with me about why you were really here. You said you were here because you believed in a job well done, but you don't even have a shred of a good reason to be doing the job in the first place. You talk such a big game about succeeding. For what? To prove your friends right? To feel like *you* deserve your mother's love, that you don't deserve your father's absence?' My voice breaks as I finish the sentence. I went too far. I can see it in Nick's eyes. But it's too late. I'm too angry. I'm too hurt.

Nick's face falls just as raindrops start to hit the driveway. 'If that's how you really feel.' He takes a step backwards.

'I think you should leave.' I can feel tears threatening to spill down my cheeks and the last thing I want to do is cry in front of him. 'Just go.'

His face darkens and he opens his mouth like he's about to say something but then he turns to go, shoulders slumped.

I head inside, desperately craving a soft blanket, a warm cup of tea, and a good cry.

Chapter Thirty-Six

Nick

Isaac: Yo, bro, when you coming back into town?

Julian: Kara's having a party this weekend. Try and make it?

Me: As much as I want to meet your new girl, I don't leave until Sunday.

Julian: Don't be lame, change your flight! Our last party before class starts.

I stare at my phone. I type out *I'm trying to find a way to say goodbye to Eloise before I go*, then I delete it.

Me: I'll try.

Technically, my capstone was supposed to be eight weeks. But I dragged my feet booking flights, not quite ready to leave everything behind. And before I knew it, I was staying an extra week. The Parkers didn't mind, of course. But my mamma sure did. And so did Isaac. He was *not* happy that I missed another pickup game.

I went over to the Andersons' again yesterday afternoon. Hazel was home but she said Eloise and Cal were out in the fields. She invited me in, we had a glass of iced tea. I really like Hazel. In some ways, she reminds me of my mom. She's stubborn and a little intimidating, but she has such a warm heart.

'Do you think Eloise will stay here forever?' I found myself asking her, a little nervously, wondering if she would admonish me for being intrusive. But her face just softened.

'I hope not,' she said.

I must have looked as surprised as I felt because she laughed. 'It's not that I don't want her to!' she said, 'but I don't think *she* wants to. Does that make sense?'

I nodded. 'It sure does.'

Our conversation moved on. We talked about the unseasonably cold weather and whether or not we should be caving and turning on the heat. Hazel joked about her relief that the butcher is almost back from maternity leave. Eventually, I stopped going through the motions just hoping Eloise would show up at the back door.

'I'll tell her you stopped by,' Hazel said as she gave me a hug.

I waited all night for a text from Eloise, anything to acknowledge I had been there, but heard nothing but crickets.

I started to look at flight options to leave earlier. There was no point in staying anymore.

Me: I came over yesterday to say goodbye but you weren't home. I leave Friday. Can we talk?

Twelve hours later . . .

Me: Eloise. Come on. I know you're getting these. Can you stop ignoring me?

Eloise: I don't want to stop ignoring you.

Me: Can't we act like adults?

Eloise: Adults are honest with each other.

Me: Are you still mad about the bet? It didn't even impact anything!

Eloise: No.

I stare at my phone, a sinking feeling in my stomach. The realization hits me like a ton of bricks. Eloise knows about Scott's Orchards. I start to pace the outline of my bedroom.

Me: What's this about?

Eloise: You know.

Me: Is this about the offer the Parkers got?

Eloise: The offer you orchestrated for them? The offer that you negotiated? The offer that bails them out and screws me over? That you conveniently didn't tell me about? That AMIE told me?

Frustration rises in my chest that Betsy told Amie who told Eloise. I should have been the one to tell her. We both know it.

Me: It's not what it looks like. I was just doing what I could for them.

Ten minutes later . . .

Me: They're nice people! They deserve it.

Eloise: And our town deserves more than another conglomerate buying up family-owned land. Our planet deserves more than another conglomerate treating soil like it's replaceable. Our families deserve more than apples filled with insecticides!

Me: Look, I get why you're angry.

Eloise: That's why you didn't tell me, isn't it. You knew how mad I'd be. What were you trying to do? Get in another week of whatever the fuck we were doing before this before you skipped town and left this bomb behind you?

Me: No! That's not it at all. Eloise, if you would just let me explain.

Eloise: I never want to see you again.

Eloise: I know you don't have a great relationship with the truth but believe me when I say that I am one hundred percent serious. Don't come near me again.

I wake up earlier than usual on my last full day. I'm not sure if it's because I was tossing and turning from my last message exchange with Eloise or because my body knows how much I'll miss the farm and is determined to soak up every second. I lay in my bed thinking about how I've grown accustomed to this room, the pink walls, the NSYNC posters, the way the clutter feels cozy and homey. I walk downstairs to the smell of coffee and step onto the front porch where Joe is already reading the newspaper. I take a deep breath of chilly fresh air, gazing out at the rolling hills that are glazed with dew. There's something so serene about an early morning on the farm, before the workers start arriving and congregating in the field, when the animals are still quiet, barely rustling as they wake up too, the sun just beginning to break over the hills.

Joe clears his throat. He doesn't usually talk in the morning. 'I've been meaning to say thank you,' he says gruffly, clearly having not spoken since he woke up.

'It's nothing,' I say. 'I've been really happy to help.'

Joe grunts again.

'You, darling,' Betsy says as she steps out on the porch, 'we'll miss you so much!' She walks over to squeeze my cheeks. 'I can't believe you're leaving after today.'

'I'll miss you too, Mrs. P.'

She smiles as she sits down but it doesn't reach her eyes. 'It'll be so quiet when you're gone, won't it, Joe?'

He grunts in affirmation.

That's another reason why I think the Parkers should accept Scott's Orchards's deal. They're lonely out here now that their girls are gone. The farm is a big place, and they don't fill it.

I try to do my normal chores but even the pigs can tell I'm down. Buttercup gives me extra snuggles, digging hard into my palm with her snout. I'm surprised at my own reluctance to leave. I've known this was coming. I have a life to get back to. I miss my mom. But . . . I feel unsettled, like I haven't tied up all the loose strings, like I can't count my time on the farm as a success. I don't even know what success means to me anymore. I curse Eloise for putting all these thoughts in my head.

'Nick?' Betsy asks me when I come in to shower for dinner. 'Do you want to invite Eloise over for dinner? I know you two have grown close.'

My heart sinks. 'It's OK.' I wave it off.

'I'm making my roast chicken.'

'I think she's busy tonight,' I lie, barely able to choke the words out of my throat. *She never wants to see me again*, I think.

'OK.' Betsy tsks before getting back to the salad she's making.

We sit out on the porch after dinner and watch the fireflies light up the sky. Betsy asks me what I'm most looking forward to in the city and I tell her I really miss driving my own car. That gets a chuckle out of Joe, who asks why his old blue pickup isn't good enough.

'We'll be fine without you,' Betsy whispers to me when Joe goes inside to refill his drink.

'I know,' I tell her. I mean it.

'Then what's got you so down?' she asks, her eyes wide with concern.

I open and close my mouth. It's not my place to gossip about Eloise, especially to Betsy who notoriously can't keep her mouth shut. 'Is it Eloise?' she prattles on, almost talking to herself. 'I thought it was curious you didn't want to invite her. Lord knows you've spent enough time over there.'

I pinch the bridge of my nose long enough to gain composure. 'Yes,' I say quietly.

'Because you're leaving?' she asks.

Lying is easier than the truth, so I nod.

'Hmmm . . .'

'What?'

'That girl wasn't meant to stay here.'

'Betsy,' I say, turning to face her profile, which is illuminated in the early moonlight, 'I don't think anyone bothered to tell her that.'

Chapter Thirty-Seven

Eloise

Things I'm Grateful For

- I found a new home for JJ (mixed feelings about this, trying to be grateful)
- Living in a place where I can hear the birds sing.
- Gas is cheap here
- U-Pick is busy
- ~~The air isn't polluted~~. The air isn't *as* polluted as other places
- I've finally won a round of gin rummy
- I don't have to cook (even though I have to clean)
- Shari, for making me start this. I guess

Nick: If you ever come visit Linden, you know where to find me.

Nick: That is, if you change your mind.

'I'm beginning to think doing all the social media marketing for the farm has made you addicted to that thing,' Dad grunts as he fills up his coffee.

I click out of my messages in a hurry and stow my phone in my pocket. 'It worked, though.'

'Sure did. Our busiest season yet.'

'Not that it matters,' I sigh.

'Eloise,' Dad says sternly, his reading glasses perched on the bridge of his nose like they are every morning when he reads the paper, 'it does matter.'

I shrug and pick up my coffee. Suddenly the room feels too small for my thoughts. I head to the front porch. Mom isn't far behind me, settling onto the front stoop next to me without saying a word. We both watch the morning fog baking off the grass as the sun rises.

'It's not like you to be so short with your father,' she says.

Tears sting my eyes. 'I'm just tired.'

Mom sighs. 'Is this about Nick, JJ, or that offer from Scott's Orchards?'

'There's so much going on.'

Mom nods. 'I know, sweetheart.'

I pick the simplest topic first. 'I'm happy. And relieved. And I know JJ will be so happy,' I sniffle, my sadness at the prospect of losing JJ hitting me like a ton of bricks, 'but he's one of my best friends.'

'Oh, honey.' Mom rubs a gentle hand on my back. 'The family that met him last weekend at U-Pick, I think they'll be a really good fit. Their daughter is the age you were when you got JJ. And they live on a big farm too. It's not so far, you can visit.'

'I know,' I say glumly.

She stares out at the fields. 'I know it's hard to say goodbye.'

'I don't want him to think I don't love him anymore.'

'Sometimes doing the uncomfortable thing, the scary thing, sometimes that is how to love somebody best.'

I pinch the bridge of my nose. We both know she's right. 'How did you know about Scott's?' I ask her.

Mom harrumphs. 'You think you heard about it from Amie and nobody else did? That girl never hushes up.'

'Yeah, you're right,' I mumble. 'I just can't believe it.'

'We don't know if they actually signed it.'

I fix my gaze on her. 'Mom,' I say, 'there's no way they didn't. If they haven't already, there's no way they won't. Scott's? Come on. They probably offered them more than was fair.'

'Did you hear *any* of the details from Amie?'

'No.'

Mom sips her coffee and sighs. The sun is creeping past the horizon now, a soft orange and yellow cascading over the hills. 'Scott's put in only a half offer. The Parkers would still manage it, Scott's would just bring in some folks to help.'

I'm stunned into silence. That isn't what I expected. 'Oh.'

'I was surprised too. I thought they would want to get all out.'

My response comes flying out of my mouth before I can stop it. 'You mean like you guys did? Like you guys do?'

'That isn't fair,' Mom says, but her shoulders slacken with resignation. 'Selling just might be our best option. You know that.'

I pick at a piece of wood peeling up from the deck, tearing it away from the front step.

'I still can't believe Nick went on a date with her.' Mom deftly changes the subject, jostling me with her shoulder. 'She never hushed up about that either.'

'I don't want to talk about him,' I grumble.

'Oh stop,' she hushes me. 'He had eyes for you. We all saw it. And you spent so much time with him. You must miss him a little.'

'I don't,' I retort. But my words are hollow. The morning swallows have started to sing, and their chirping fills the silence.

After a beat Mom says, 'You know the Scott's deal isn't Nick's fault.'

'But it is,' I protest.

'They were looking for a way out before he even got here.' She throws up her hands. 'Hell, that's *why* he was here in the first place.'

'That way out could have been me. It could have been us.'

'Honey.' Mom reaches a hand over to pat my knee. 'This might have been a blessing in disguise. We have to face it. It will be too much for us as we get older.'

'But that's why I'm here.' My voice breaks. 'Isn't it?'

'Eloise.' Mom turns to me, her brows knitted together. 'What you're doing here is up to you to decide.' And with that, she gets up and walks inside, leaving me in stunned silence on the front porch.

Shari: How cute are these baby strawberry plants?? *Heart-eyes emoji*

Evan: love them. Could not be cuter. They deserve more.

Shari: I'm not enough?

Evan: OK hold up. Let's not cue the immediate post-grad crisis we all knew was on the horizon. I meant they deserve their own Instagram page.

Shari: OH. LOL. That they do.

Me: Not to be the bearer of bad news but I think I may have started my immediate post-grad crisis that I, in fact, did not see coming.

Evan: Babes. Nooooo.

Shari: Tell us more

Me: That's the problem. There is no more?? What am I doing here? I have spent the last week getting permits to host weddings. I put in an offer for a large-scale donut fryer. For what? So I can play my part to increase capitalism and obesity?

Evan: WOAH.

Evan: This may be bigger than the after-school crisis I was referring to.

Evan: I meant more like I thought one of you would get bangs. *Sent with invisible ink*

Shari: Weddings???

Me: AHHHHH.

Shari: Girl, you need to be starting a gratitude journal before this goes really off the rails.

U-Pick is still busier than ever, all the way through September. We're officially picked out of apples by October 1st, which is a first for us. Dad celebrates by breaking out his favorite whiskey. I try to muster up happiness but end up going to bed early. All the days feel the same now, even the ones when we celebrate.

Mom and Dad exchange a worried glance when I excuse myself for bed. I wasn't meant to see it, so I don't acknowledge it. I don't have the energy. JJ got officially rehomed last week to the family that met him during U-Pick. They have one other horse, so he won't be alone. Their daughter was the happiest ten-year-old I've ever seen when we dropped him off. I could tell he was happy, nickering and prancing around in the field they fenced in for him. I tried to muster up cheerful gratitude, I *am* happy that JJ has someone to ride him now, that he has a horse-friend to be with, but the farm feels empty without him. It's like the last dregs of my childhood are gone.

When I'm not missing JJ, I'm busy spending all my time trying to figure out how to raise the money myself, without a loan from the bank, to start regenerative agriculture on our farm. Maybe if I restructure how I was planning to do things, maybe if I build hydroponic gardens to increase our potential yields instead of buying the land next door, I can still figure this out.

The only unfortunate thing is that weddings are still looking like our best option.

And thinking about other people finding their soulmate, falling in love, makes my own heart hurt more than I care to admit.

Mom reminds me every now and then that we have no idea if Betsy officially signed, that my plan might still work. It speaks to how depressed I must seem that Mom is now the one reminding me that I could still buy their property when at the beginning of this summer she was staunchly against it. I return the favor by reminding her that the bank hasn't even told me if my loan was approved. It's a vicious cycle. One that Dad stays out of by quickly ducking into another room when it comes up.

The day after we 'celebrate' U-Pick being over, Mom asks me if I've considered going back to the city.

'San Francisco?' I ask, confused.

'No,' she returns an equally confused expression. 'Seattle.'

I cringe at my Freudian slip. I've thought about San Francisco a lot since Nick left, my thoughts often a swirling mass of confusion over the siren call of a big city. The more I think about it the more I feel myself softening towards Linden, towards Nick . . . if I'm thinking about leaving the farm too, how can I fault them for it? But as soon as the thought completes another one replaces it, *Who will I be if I leave the farm? What will anchor me to this world, what will be my purpose?*

Mom is staring at me intently. I try to brush past it. 'I guess I could visit Evan,' I wonder aloud. I feel tears sting my eyes. It takes almost nothing for me to cry these days.

'Honey, I just think you might need a break. Now that you say it, San Francisco could be good for you. You could go see your brother.'

'So that's it, you've had enough of me moping around and want to pawn me off to someone else?' I ask, anger edging into my voice.

Mom sighs. 'That isn't it exactly—'

I bristle. Whatever I was expecting her to say, it was *not* to acknowledge that she was in fact trying to get rid of me moping around.

'We are worried about you,' she says. 'We think maybe you need some space to think about what you want to do next.'

'So, you and Dad have been talking about me.'

'You say that like that isn't in our job description.'

I stare glumly at the kitchen table. 'What is *my* job description?' I say in a small voice. *It can't be licensing out the barn for weddings. It can't be.*

'Only you know that.' She squeezes my hand before heading out the door, reminding me that she agreed to volunteer at the soup kitchen that morning.

I thought my job description was to take care of you, I think, as I watch her retreat into the mudroom.

Lily: Excuse me, since when did the girl who basically swore off men forever get into wedding planning?

Lily: Is there something you need to tell me? What alien exchanged places with you?

Me: Ugh. Who told you?

Lily: My mom said you reached out to her for catering.

Me: Right. Duh. Sorry, I should have texted. The whole thing kind of bums me out.

Lily: What is the 'whole thing'?

Me: Hmm. Do I start with the fact that I literally spent the past five years of my life getting a degree

in agriculture only to come to a farm my parents don't even know if they want? Here I was thinking I could use my degree to offer classes or tours or something but no. Now, in order to save us from financial ruin, I need to start hosting weddings in the back barn?

Lily: Uh-oh.

Me: Or that I actually had a good plan to revamp the farm with regenerative ag but now the Parkers have this crazy offer from a conglomerate so we can't buy their farm? So now we're totally stuck? So now I've bought an industrial fryer so we can make more donuts? Because that's what the people want?

Lily: OMG.

Me: I'm sorry I'm dumping. I miss you. When are you coming home again?

Lily: I feel like I should be asking you when you're leaving home. Because it seems like a little space could do you good. Especially now that JJ isn't around.

Me: I don't have anywhere to go.

Lily: Linden has space in his fancy new apartment.

Me: What fancy new apartment?

Lily: He just moved into a new place? What is the point of you having an Instagram for the farm if you aren't using it to keep tabs on your own family. He has a spare bedroom. I mean, it's ugly because he's a boy, but it exists.

Me: I can't go to San Francisco. *Sent with invisible ink*

Lily: Right, because of the minuscule chances you'll run into Nick?

Me: Only 800,000 people live in SF. Those chances aren't miniscule.

Lily: Did you seriously just google how many people live there? I bet you did the stupid thing where you only cared about the actual San Francisco zip code.

Lily: EIGHT MILLION people live in the Bay Area.

Lily: I've won.

Lily: Tell me when you've texted Linden. He owes you. Cash in that favor.

Chapter Thirty-Eight

Nick

I hesitate at the door to the coffee shop wondering if this is the creepiest thing I've ever done.

It isn't *my* fault that Linden decides to put his whole life on a very public Instagram page where he's found a niche doing fit checks for tech bros. It isn't my fault that he does his bi-weekly outfit rundowns at one of the most well-known coffee shops in Cow Hollow. It isn't completely unlikely that I would also want to grab a latte here. Never mind that I live in Haight-Ashbury, which isn't exactly close.

I take a deep breath and push open the door, surveying the small space as quickly as I can. Just as I expected, Linden is sitting at a corner table, headphones on, starting intently at a computer screen. He looks incredible, tailored pants, a perfectly fitted short-sleeve collared shirt, a sweater slung over the back of his chair.

I didn't know until I found his page that so many other men cared about how to dress well for the office. But they do. And Linden has capitalized.

I would have been able to find him even if I hadn't stalked him on Instagram—he looks just like Eloise. They have the same colored hair, but hers is lighter, probably because she spends more time in the sun. The same sloped nose. Linden glances up at the door as if the bell startled him, and even though I knew it from the pictures, I'm still shocked when I see Eloise's piercing light blue eyes looking back at me.

I look down as soon as I get my composure, not wanting to be caught staring. I fumble through ordering my coffee and take a seat at the table next to Linden, pulling out a textbook. School feels like a joke now. I'm one of the only ones in my friend group that still studies. But it's our last semester. And I still feel like I need to earn the perk of graduating early. Even if I already have my full-time job lined up. It crosses my mind that Eloise would have a field day at this line of thinking, my questioning my own need for success even when it's completely worthless. I think about her so often still. Picturing her thinking about me working in an office, a corporate sellout, puts a pit in my stomach. I'm so focused on my anxiety that I don't notice the shadow looming over me until Linden clears his throat. I look up, surprised at his height.

'Is this seat taken?' he asks.

I shake my head dumbly.

'This might seem crazy,' Linden says, with a genuine smile, 'but you look really familiar. Were you working on a farm this summer?'

Of course, Linden would have seen my videos. Eloise probably sent them to everyone with clear instruction to kill me upon sight.

But Linden doesn't look like he wants to kill me . . . 'Yeah, the Parkers'.'

'Right on,' Linden says, making himself completely at home at my table. 'I'm—'

'Linden,' I supply. 'Ah, that might have seemed creepy, but you look just like your sister. I'm Nick,' I say, extending a hand.

Linden's grin widens. 'We both look like our dad. I saw your videos. Really cool stuff. I bet that helped the Parkers out a lot.'

Right, I remember. Eloise barely talks to Linden. He doesn't know she hates me. I shrug. 'I did my best.' I glance at Linden's open, friendly face, my feelings spiraling out of my head before I can get a handle on them. 'I actually really miss the farm,' I admit.

'It sucks to come back to the city after all that fresh air,' Linden agrees.

'Why did you leave?'

A shadow crosses Linden's face, and I immediately walk my question back. 'Sorry, man, that was intrusive.'

'No, no, it's OK.' He sighs. 'I think it always felt like Eloise's space, you know. I'm sure you could tell when you met her—she's meant to be there. It means everything to her.'

'Yeah,' I hesitate, not knowing how much to reveal about my relationship with his little sister and deciding to air on the side of caution. I twiddle my thumbs. 'So, what do you do when you really miss it? Hike?'

Linden laughs. 'Hiking doesn't really cut it for me.' He gives me a shrewd look and I still underneath his calculating stare. Eloise told me he was smart, but not that he was so intimidating. I set my shoulders, not wanting to seem cowed. 'I volunteer,' he says after a beat.

'That was not the answer I was expecting,' I admit. 'But I'm intrigued.'

'With the Sausalito farming community,' Linden explains. 'I work in finance, and I help a lot of them apply for loans.'

'That's really cool.'

He nods. 'I've gotta get back to work, but you seem business savvy—' he glances at my backpack, which has a Stanford MBA logo emblazoned across the top '—so if it's something you're interested in, you should come to our next meeting.'

'Yeah, definitely . . . that'd be great, man. I really appreciate that.'

Linden nods once before heading towards the door. 'DM me. I'll send you the details.'

'Will do. Nice to meet you,' I call after him.

Maybe creepily stalking my ex-girlfriend's (*am I allowed to call her that?*) brother wasn't such a bad idea after all.

I'm rebuffing Linden's laughter when Harvey skirts around me, narrowly missing running straight into my chest and spilling the cocktails he's carrying.

It's a little after 9 p.m. and Linden and I are out at a bar after the Sausalito Farming Committee's weekly meeting.

Linden is in the middle of roasting me alive for buying a carbon copy of the outfit he was wearing last week.

'But that's the *reason* you have an Instagram,' I remind him, 'so that people will buy the clothes you wear!'

He's still laughing at me when I clock Harvey.

'Harvey—' I tap his shoulder '—good to see you, man.'

'Nick Russo,' he returns, ever the businessman, grasping my hand in a firm shake. 'What a surprise.'

'What brings you to town?'

'Oh, you know—' Harvey shrugs '—this and that.'

'This is Linden. Linden, meet Harvey. He's one of the brokers for that Scott's Orchards deal I told you about.'

Harvey and Linden greet each other with the practiced warmth of people who make deals for a living, but before Linden can explain he's an Anderson, I ask Harvey if he's heard from the Parkers. I've followed up with Betsy about once a week since I left, wondering what she decided to do, but as far as I know they're still undecided.

Harvey shakes his head. 'Still nothing. I don't know what I expect from those hicks. They don't know what's good for them.'

Linden stiffens beside me. He's not one for confrontation, but I wouldn't be surprised if he let a punch loose and caught Harvey square in the jaw.

I steady the anger roiling within me with a deep breath. 'The Parkers are smart, Harv,' I say, my voice low.

Harvey's eyes widen almost imperceptibly, but he takes a step back. 'Of course,' he says, 'I was just joking. I didn't mean anything by it.'

The three of us are silent for a beat before Harvey mutters an excuse and leaves with his drinks.

'Man.' Linden runs a hand through his hair.

'Look, I'm really sorry about that,' I say quickly, 'I didn't know he was such a dick. I thought he made the Parkers a good offer.'

Linden sighs, his shoulders drooping. 'He may have offered them money, but I can guarantee that isn't the only reason they do what they do. Farmers are a hell of a lot smarter than assholes like him give them credit for. They could do something else if they wanted to make more money. But they care more about their communities, about doing something tangible and gratifying . . .' He trails off. 'Sometimes I wonder if I care more about that too,' he admits. 'But I can't give up my eight-dollar morning lattes to save the world. At least not yet.' He forces a chuckle. 'Not that I've gotten Eloise to understand that.'

'Yeah,' I agree. But it's hard for me to focus on what Linden's saying when all I'm thinking is, *Oh shit*. If Harvey's character is any indication, Eloise was right about Scott's Orchards. Was I too blinded by my own ambition to see it?

Chapter Thirty-Nine

Eloise

Things I Like About San Francisco

- Fresh croissants at the corner bakery
- Hiking the headlands
- Bagel shops (they're everywhere!)
- Beating Linden at gin rummy
- Espresso martinis
- When the morning fog breaks

I never believed in Mercury being in retrograde until today, which has been the weirdest day of my entire life.

> **Linden: Hey, do you want to come visit? And no, Mercury isn't in retrograde or whatever you call it. I was thinking of you the other day. Thought maybe you could use a change of scenery.**

I assume Mom texted him letting him know that I was moping around the house, at a loss as to what to do with myself now that the season had wound down and I still hadn't heard back on my loan application or on the state of the Parkers' place. I roll my eyes at the picture I make of her in my head, texting Linden: *Please help her. Our darling son, please. We're counting on you.*

But I push out my negative thoughts. I swallow my pride and think of Lily instead. I reply that yes, I would in fact like to come visit.

Linden: Great. Let me know when you buy your flights.

Linden: And you can stay as long as you want. We have an extra bedroom.

Me: OK. Thanks for being so cool about it.

I want to type out, *Thanks for being so cool about it even though I've held the world's longest grudge against you moving*, but I delete the second half, worried the sentiment is too heavy to be sending over text.

Linden: No need to thank me.

I spend an inordinate amount of time looking at flights before I scamper downstairs feeling marginally better now that I have a plan to do something other than work on the farm and stare at my parents during mealtimes. I even pull up a job board and scroll aimlessly through research jobs in San Francisco. Sure, there's a world in which I start research that doesn't have anything to do with agriculture but maybe some off-the-farm experience wouldn't be the worst thing.

An email pops up in my inbox as I'm just about to shut my computer. My loan application. It's approved. I stare at my computer, slack-jawed. Not that it matters much anymore—if the Parkers aren't bankrupt, then they're not going to sell. But it does mean that I wrote a proposal convincing enough that a bank approved me for money. I let myself bask in pride, staring happily at the email. The email means my dreams weren't stupid. They weren't silly. What was I thinking almost giving them up?

'Honey?' Mom calls, having arrived back from the grocery store.

'In the kitchen!' I shout gleefully, excited to share the news.

'You'll never believe what I just heard,' she says, as she unloads bags from the counter. 'Betsy and Joe refused the offer.'

'What?' I breathe. Hope a pounding, tangible thing in my chest.

'Yep. Apparently Nick told them he was wrong, that they shouldn't take it.' She stops unpacking groceries to lean in closer to me. 'He told them to put it on the market. Let someone else be the steward.'

'Mom,' I say, my voice shaky. 'My loan just got approved. Today.'

'Oh, Eloise,' she says, pulling me in for a tight hug. 'You must be so excited.'

I pull back from her embrace. 'Aren't you?' I ask, even though I know the answer isn't what I want to hear.

She shifts her weight from one foot to the other, a habit I also do when I'm nervous. 'Well . . . your dad and I have been talking.' She pauses. 'Cal!' she yells to the office.

Dad sticks his head out and seeing the hesitant expression on my face, he wanders into the kitchen slowly.

'Your dad and I . . .' She twists her hands. 'Well, we've been talking about our future here . . . and . . .'

Dad's eyes drop. 'We do want to sell the farm,' Dad says.

My heart falls into my stomach.

'And if Betsy and Joe don't want to sell to Scott's . . . well . . . we might want to.'

My jaw drops. 'You can't be serious.'

'It's too much for us. We're not the spry young kids we used to be.'

'So, you're just giving up on your dream?'

They look at each other. 'It isn't our dream anymore.'

I feel tears welling up in my eyes. 'OK,' I breathe. 'So, the loan doesn't matter because I won't even have anything to start from.'

'Well, we've been talking about this too, but you could take over the farm if you wanted. You know, use the loan to buy it from us.'

'But where would you go?'

Mom shrugs. 'I don't know. I've been dreaming of living in the city.'

'Then what would be the point of being here?!' I practically scream. 'I hate Mercury!'

In the week after the Parkers officially put their farm up for sale, formally rejecting the Scott's Orchards offer, I run the numbers over and over. They still work with my original plan, but they do *not* work if I want to buy my parents out of their stake in the farm too. Dad, in classic fashion, offers to stay on, to keep owning the farm while I get things up and running. But I can't do that to them. I don't want to force them to keep living in a place they don't want to be anymore. It's already too much to reconcile that I may have misread their expectations from me in the first place.

I'm staring at a crummy hand of gin rummy when Dad gets a call from an unknown number.

'Hello?' He runs a hand through his thinning hair. 'Oh, I wasn't excepting to hear back from you so soon.' His eyes crinkle at the corners.

Mom peeks her head out from the kitchen.

'OK.' Dad's grinning now. 'That's great.'

I try to catch Mom's eyes, confused as to who Dad could be talking to that's making him so happy.

After a few more minutes, he gets off the phone and turns to me, still smiling. 'Lou, a family from Seattle wants to lease the farm.'

'What?' I put my cards down face up on the table, there's no going back to the game after this.

'We don't have to sell. We have time.' He grins at Mom, who's dabbing her eyes with the corner of her apron. 'We got you some more time.'

I let the realization sink in. I have a few years, however long the lease lasts, before our farm could go on the market. We'll still own it, someone else will temporarily manage it. I have *time*. That night I start packing a bag for San Francisco. With JJ in a new home, with my parents' new income stream from the lease of the farm . . . I'm starting to feel like a week in the city might do me some good, maybe help me see if I could envision a life for myself outside of Carnation.

On the fourth morning I'm in San Francisco, I decide I don't want to go back to Carnation at the end of the week like I'm supposed to. I like the energy here. I've gone hiking with Shari's cousin, who I felt instantly connected to (although I have yet to determine if that's simply because she reminds me of Shari). Linden and I are learning to live together again and it's shockingly easy, like driving a car after you haven't driven one in a while. Although I'm not sure if this is entirely due to his girlfriend, who is *awesome*. Mom was right about her being the influence that makes Linden call home more. She's thoughtful and patient and is giving Linden and me space to reconnect while also folding me into her group of friends.

I make us breakfast most mornings, fresh eggs (he buys them from a nearby farming community that he loves) and toast. He's a surprisingly good cook and usually makes us dinner. I even have a lead on a few jobs.

Linden's sitting at the kitchen table, thumbing through his phone, when I get up the courage to ask if I can stay longer.

'Linden—' I set down my coffee cup next to his '—I've been meaning to say I'm sorry. I misjudged you when you left the farm. I felt alone and scared. I didn't want to be left behind. But I see why this is so great.' I gesture to the window, where the sun is peeking through the fog. 'I like it here.' I squirm in my seat. 'I kind of want to stay a little longer . . . if that's OK? I mean, ask Julia first, of course, but . . .'

Linden's shoulders slacken. 'I never meant to leave you behind, Lou.' He gets up and walks around the table, arms outstretched for a hug. 'I'm sorry too. You vocalized that you were worried about Mom and Dad, and I felt guilty for leaving so I didn't want to engage. It's a two-way street. I'm happy you're here.'

'So, you'll ask Julia if I can stay?'

Linden laughs. 'Only if you keep making breakfast.'

I find a job researching the genetic potential of hybrid radishes. I pay Linden less than I should for rent. I hike on the weekends with Shari's cousin and her friends. I talk to Mom and Dad with Linden (Mom is *thrilled* at this development). And three weeks in, I decide to date again.

There's just one problem—I can't quite stop thinking about Nick. During my first date in San Francisco all I can think about is how much more handsome Nick is. How I love the way his haircut brings out his cheekbones. How I love the way the sunlight sparkles in his eyes. How I yearn for his touch again, for our chemistry.

I'm on another date tonight, with someone who looks vaguely like Nick, and all I can think about is how much I miss Nick's brain. I miss the way he approaches problems; I miss the way he asks me questions. I miss how interested he is in everyone around him, how he is always thinking, calculating, wanting to know more, to do better. I miss his ambition, even when it aggravates me. I miss how well he knew me after such a short time, how he makes me feel like I'm worth knowing.

I get home, missing him so badly that I look him up, the first time I'd let myself do it in ages.

I'm expecting to find a grid filled with pictures of him with his friends, of restaurants, of hikes. Instead, I find nothing. Not a single new post since he stopped posting about the Parkers. I hover outside of Linden's room, wondering if I should confide in him, tell him what's on my mind. It would be nice to have a fresh perspective on the situation. Maybe I should call Nick, maybe I should be the one apologizing. But Nick was the one that lied. I don't need Linden to tell me that makes him bad news.

Just as I'm turning to go to bed, his door opens.

'Lou!' he says, surprised. 'I was just going to find you. Hey—' he stops short '—how was your date?'

'Ugh,' I say. 'A colossal waste of time.'

'I'm sorry,' he says, looking genuinely disappointed. 'I was wondering, do you want to come with me to the Sausalito Farming Convention tomorrow?'

Linden's been trying to get me to go with him for ages. But something about farming, about Linden farming . . . I just haven't wanted to go. It's been easier to separate things fully for me, to not straddle the line between two worlds. But his expression is so hopeful . . . 'I guess I could make that work.'

'Great.' He beams. 'It's at seven. Don't be late.'

Me: Is it crazy that I think Linden and I are like . . . getting along?

Evan: Crazy? We've been telling you since we met you that Linden was cool.

Shari: Preach. I've been telling you I wanted to date him which is the highest compliment.

Me: I was going to say I can't wait until you guys come and visit . . .

Shari: Relax. He's taken! And I want to come visit. As soon as my berry babies are settled in.

Evan: So I take it your heart to heart with Linden went fine.

Me: He was like . . . so cool about it that it made me feel bad yk?

Shari: Ah, an emotionally adjusted man. The rarest of them all.

Evan: Hey, proud of you for admitting you were wrong.

Me: Not wrong, just changed my mind.

Me: Kidding, was a little bit wrong. And harsh. And mean.

Shari: Women bear an extra burden. Glad Linden didn't make yours heavier by adding guilt.

Evan: ^^^.

Chapter Forty

Nick

She's here. I know it before I see her. I can feel the energy in the room like an electric current. Pulsing, waiting, wanting. Eloise is *here*. I turn quickly, pivoting towards the double doors that mark the entrance to the dusty schoolroom we use to meet. Sure enough, tucked into a crowd of people, right next to Linden, is Eloise.

Just like the first time we met, her beauty takes my breath away. She looks so . . . at home . . . like she's met these people before, or she's been here. But that's impossible. I'm here every week. She hasn't been. But . . . I scan her body—her jeans are different and she's wearing a shirt I've never seen. She's dressed like everyone else. Not like a farmer. Questions are buzzing through my mind. Why is she here? What is she doing with Linden? Did they resolve their issues? Does she know I'll be here? Will she talk to me? Does she hate me still?

Just then Eloise looks up, straight at me, her eyes tunneling all the way into my soul. She smiles softly, one corner of her lips tugging upward. Just like that, my last question, the most important one, is answered. By some miracle, Eloise doesn't hate me. I may still have a chance.

I give her a small wave, trying to ignore that I see her frantically tug on Linden's sleeve. So, she didn't know I would be here. Oh well. I can't worry about that right now. I have a presentation to make.

I finish my speech to a smattering of applause. Quickly, folks get up to mingle and the room is filled with a low hum of conversation.

I stand my ground, hoping Linden will bring Eloise over. Ever since I quit my job to lead marketing for the Sausalito Farmer's Committee, including orchestrating the farmers' market every Sunday, Linden has been at every meeting. He's really had my back.

Sure enough, I feel a hand on my shoulder, breaking the conversation I was having with one of the vendors about the definition of organic. 'Sorry to steal this one,' Linden says with a charming smile. 'Nick, I brought my sister Eloise. I know you guys briefly met before, but figured it could be nice to reconnect.' He takes a step back as Eloise takes a step forward. *God, I missed her.*

'I actually think you two could really hit it off,' he says with a wink, making a beeline for the snack table. I turn to Eloise, about to ask her what exactly she told Linden, only to find her starting to laugh.

'You mean . . . you didn't . . . ?'

'Nope,' she says in between giggles, 'didn't say a thing.'

I grin at her, a smile bigger than I've felt on my face in ages. 'I missed you,' I whisper, pulling her in for a hug.

'I missed you too,' she says shyly.

'Would you want to maybe go on a date with me?' I ask. 'That is, before you head home?'

'Oh.' Her cheeks color a bright pink as she shifts from foot to foot. 'I—um—I live here now.'

'You're kidding.'

She shakes her head. 'I actually live with Linden.'

'But the Parkers didn't sell . . . you mean you didn't buy them out?'

There's a glint in her eye as she responds. 'Hmmm, I thought I might have you to thank for them not selling. But don't think that means I forgive you for lying to me about fantasy football—' she whacks me with her arm '—of all things!'

'Did your loan not go through?' I ask, still trying to understand what Eloise is doing here, still trying to balance the declaration of anger coming out of her mouth with the good nature of her delivery.

'It did. But I deferred it. I'm waiting until I'm there because I want to be there, and not because I think I'm needed.' She blushes. 'I think I have you to thank for that too.' She shifts her weight slightly. 'My expectations of myself were, you know . . . a little high.'

'We both have some thanks to give apparently. I have you to thank for giving me a sense of moral decency.'

'Am I also who you should thank for quitting that high-paying, uber-successful job of yours to do this?' She gestures at the room. 'Marketing for SFC?'

I pretend to think. 'No, that was all Linden.'

She swats me on my arm, laughing. 'Cut that out.'

'Seriously, you didn't buy the land?'

'No.' She shrugs her shoulders. 'Turns out, my parents didn't even want to be farming. And I think I want to live a little before I settle down to do it forever. They're leasing it out for a few years. Then I'll decide if I want to buy it.'

'I don't think that's a bad plan.'

'I thought about reaching out,' she admits. 'I had no idea you'd be here.'

'I've thought about you every day,' I confess. 'The closest thing I could get to you was . . . well . . . this.'

She smiles so big it breaks my heart. 'Really?'

'Really.'

'So, who's gonna tell Linden that it wasn't an original thought of his that we would hit if off?'

'Unfortunately, I think that has to be your parents.'

'Deal. But only if we last until we see them again.'

'If we last until then?' I ask with a theatrical gasp. 'Eloise Anderson, I plan on making this last a very long time. Maybe forever.'

'Forever with you,' Eloise muses, as she tilts her chin up to mine. 'I like the sound of that.'

Epilogue

I take a deep, steadying breath, filling my lungs with fresh air and the smell of apple blossoms. It's May on the farm, and the trees are just starting to bud in bursts of white and pink. Nick's on his way back to meet me at our favorite spot on the ridge, the one that overlooks the valley, the one that makes the surrounding hills look like the back of sleeping dragons.

We've come a long way since our second meet cute at the Sausalito Farming Committee, the one orchestrated by my brother, who was hilariously wrong about how well we knew each other and totally right about how good for each other we were. A first real date, a first hike, a first visit to his mom's, and a first fostered puppy. A first move, a first yard, and finally a first farm (even if it's an old farm to me). A first day breaking ground on a carriage house so his mom can come and stay whenever she wants, for as long as she wants to.

I pull a crumpled piece of paper out of my pocket to steady my beating heart.

Reasons Why I Want to Ask Nick to Marry Me

- He's my best friend
- There will always be a pack of cinnamon gum around

- He knows how to apologize
- I love the way he sticks his hand into his back jean pocket
- I will never have to pretend to be interested in football
- I knew I applied for the wedding permits for the farm for a reason
- My excitement makes him more excited than anything he's excited for on his own (even worms)
- I will never be able to live down not knowing that 'How do you like them apples' was a *Good Will Hunting* quote
- I know I love Nick Russo the same way I know the sun will rise and the apples will grow—like it was a foregone conclusion all along

Author's note

Turns out there's a limit as to how much griping one can do about the state of agriculture in the U.S. before a romance novel morphs from 'easy-read' to 'technical nightmare.' Anderson Farms may not be real, but the concerns Eloise shares throughout the book are. While I'm not an agricultural expert by any means, I know our soil, our farms, and our planet need our help.

If you want to learn more, *Biggest Little Farm*, *Kiss the Ground,* and *Common Ground* are fantastic, informative documentaries.

If you want to donate, Tilth Alliance (Washington) and Sky High Farm (New York) are great places to start.

If you want to have fun, try finding the ingredients to any of the recipes included in this book from your local farmers' market, butcher, or baker. All recipes are family recipes, collected by @bunsinthekitchenvia Instagram.

Acknowledgements

Tanera and Melissa, this book was a whirlwind. Thank you both for calmly steering me through the chaos. I hope I never have to stumble my way through this process without you by my side.

Laura, Mary, Georgia, Holly, Chelsea, Sandra—everyone at the Bonnier and Greenstone teams, thank you so very much for all you do. *Apple of My Eye* would not be out in the world without you. I am so grateful.

To those of you who listened to me prattle on about apples, sent me documentaries to watch, and visited apple farms with me, *thank you*. Rashell, thank you for welcoming me to your strawberry farm and graciously answering all of my questions, and yes, of course, Shari is loosely based off of you.

To the community of people who reached out to me after my first book was published, who bought it, shared it, and gifted it—your support means the world to me. Getting messages from people I haven't talked to in years saying they bought my book felt almost as good as publishing it to begin with. Every single one of you made my heart feel so full.

To my friends—every friendship dynamic I write has some of you in it. Laughter, unwavering support, levity, and love, through everything. If I listed you all out, my acknowledgements would be longer than the book itself. You know who you are. I love you so deeply. Thank you.

To my extensive family—every family dynamic I write has some of you in it too. My cousins, aunts and uncles, bonus family, and in-laws supply me with endless encouragement. Every time you reached out to me about my book I felt my heart soar. Every time my older family members let me know, respectfully, they would be skipping over my steamier scenes, I felt sweet, sweet relief. I love you all. Thank you.

To my grandparents, my parents and my sisters, thank you for shaping who I am today with (mostly) gentle persistence. Kasey, thank you for the recipes in this book. I am so excited to share your cooking with the world.

Whit—every time a character falls in love, I write it for you. Somehow, I find myself falling in love with you over and over again. Thank you.

Anderson Farm Family Recipes

Chicken Cacciatore

Total Time: 30 Minutes

Servings: 3–4

Ingredients

- 2 tbsp olive oil
- 6 chicken thighs, skin on (bone in or boneless)
- 1 medium yellow onion, diced
- ½ bulb of fennel, diced
- 2 large cloves garlic, diced
- 28 oz (792 mL) can crushed tomatoes
- 1 tsp dried oregano
- 1 tsp dried thyme
- 1 tsp salt
- 125 mL red wine
- 60g Castelvetrano olives, chopped
- 60g parsley, finely diced
- Polenta, optional

Instructions

Heat a very large pan over medium-high heat. Once pan is hot, add oil and add chicken, skin-side down. Let cook for about 6 minutes until the skin is crispy. You will know when it's done because the skin no longer sticks and it easily pulls away from the pan. Pull the chicken out and set aside.

Turn the heat down to medium and using the pan with the chicken fat, sauté the onion and fennel. Add more olive oil, if needed. After about 5 minutes, add the garlic for 1 minute. Then, pour in the can of crushed tomatoes. Gently stir in the dried herbs and salt.

Bring the heat back up to a simmer and stir in the red wine. Place the chicken gently in the tomato sauce skin-side up for 25 minutes to fully cook the chicken. Use a meat thermometer if possible; temperature should be 75°C. Add in olives a minute or two before serving.

Serve the chicken over polenta or mashed potatoes. Top with parsley.

Courtesy of @bunsinthekitchen

Easy Apple Pie

Total Time: One Hour

Servings: One Pie

Ingredients

- 9-inch pie crust/short crust (store-bought or your favorite recipe)
- 750g Anderson Farm apples, peeled and chopped
- 150g sugar
- 1 tsp cinnamon
- 125g flour
- 110g brown sugar
- 110g butter, chilled and cut into small cubes

Instructions

Preheat the oven to 175°C. Place the crust into the pie pan.

In a large bowl, mix together apples, white sugar, and cinnamon. In a separate bowl, mix together the remaining ingredients until you have a clumpy, sand-like texture. Dump the apple mixture into the pie pan and cover with the flour, sugar, and butter mixture.

Bake at 175°C for 45 minutes.

Courtesy of @bunsinthekitchen

London Fog Concentrate

Total Time: 30 Minutes

Servings: 8 London fogs (roughly)

Ingredients

- 1 quart of water (4 cups)
- 125g of Earl Grey loose leaf tea
- 32.5g sugar (~2.5 tablespoons)
- 7.5g vanilla paste (~2 teaspoons)

Instructions

Boil 1 quart of water. Turn down to a simmer, add the tea (I use a large tea infuser) and leave for 15 minutes. Then, remove from heat, stir in the sugar and vanilla paste, and let cool for at least 15 minutes. Pour into a large mason jar or other container and store in the fridge. It will stay good for a couple weeks. To make a London Fog, mix the concentrate with equal parts milk of your choice (I prefer oat). Serve over ice.

Courtesy of @bunsinthekitchen

Blackberry Cobbler

Total Time: 50 Minutes

Servings: 8–10

Ingredients

- 106g old fashioned oats
- 94g all purpose flour
- 110g brown sugar
- ½ tsp cinnamon
- ¼ tsp nutmeg
- 125g cold salted butter, or vegan butter, cubed
- 1 tbsp water
- ½ tsp salt
- 600g blackberries (or blueberries, or a mixture)
- 2 tsp fresh lemon juice
- 1 tsp lemon zest
- 2 tsp cornstarch
- 100g granulated white sugar

Instructions

Heat oven to 190°C. Grease an 8x8 pan.

Pulse all ingredients for the crumble in a food processor until combined. Gently press half of the crumble into the pan.

Cut blackberries in half. Toss the blueberries/blackberries with lemon juice, lemon zest, cornstarch, and sugar.

Put the berry mixture into the pan. Sprinkle with the rest of your crumble and bake for 30 minutes, or until lightly browned. Eat with a fork or serve with ice cream as a cobbler. To cut into bars, let cool for a few hours or overnight in the fridge in the pan.

If using a glass pan, bake it at 175°C.

Courtesy of @bunsinthekitchen

Banana Pumpkin Muffins

Total Time: 25 Minutes

Servings: 48 Mini Muffins

Ingredients

- 113g butter or vegan butter, softened
- 50g granulated sugar
- 110g brown sugar
- 310g flour
- 1 tsp allspice
- 1 ½ tsp cinnamon
- 1 tsp baking powder
- ¼ tsp baking soda
- 3 ripe bananas, mashed
- 1 can of pumpkin
- 1 tsp vanilla extract
- 170g chocolate chips
- 40g shredded coconut, optional

Instructions

Heat oven to 175°C and grease two mini-muffin tins.

Put butter, granulated sugar, and brown sugar in a bowl and beat with an electric mixer or stir until combined. Add the rest of the ingredients except for chocolate chips and beat until combined. Stir in chocolate chips.

Put a heaping tbsp of batter into each muffin cup, it should fill to the top of each muffin cup, and bake for 14 minutes.

Courtesy of @bunsinthekitchen

Carrot Cake

Total Time: 45 minutes prep + 30 minutes in the oven

Servings: 3 6-inch cakes, for layering

Ingredients

- **Date Base:**
- 120g chopped Medjool dates (packed)
- ¾ tsp baking soda
- 180mL boiling water
- **Dry Ingredients:**
- 280g all-purpose flour
- 1 ½ tsp baking powder
- ¾ tsp baking soda
- 1 ½ tsp ground cinnamon
- ¼ tsp ground nutmeg
- 1 tsp allspice
- ¾ tsp salt
- **Wet Ingredients:**
- 165g brown sugar
- 6 tbsp white sugar
- 3 large eggs
- 180mL neutral oil (canola, grapeseed, etc.)
- 1 ½ tsp vanilla extract
- **Add-ins:**
- 225g finely grated carrots (loosely packed)

Instructions

Preheat oven to 175°C. Grease and line a 6-inch round cake pan with parchment paper.

Soften dates: In a small bowl, combine chopped dates and baking soda. Pour boiling water over and stir. Let sit for 10 minutes, then mash with a fork or blend until mostly smooth. Set aside to cool slightly.

In a medium bowl, whisk together dry ingredients: flour, baking powder, baking soda, cinnamon, nutmeg, and salt.

In a separate bowl, whisk together brown sugar, white sugar, egg, oil, vanilla, and the mashed date mixture until smooth.

Fold in the grated carrots then gently fold in the dry ingredients until just combined.

Pour batter into prepared pan. Bake for 28–32 minutes, or until a toothpick inserted into the center comes out clean.

Cool in the pan for 10 minutes, then transfer to a wire rack to cool completely.

Maple Icing Recipe

Ingredients

- 450g butter, room temperature
- 157mL Maple syrup
- 1 tsp vanilla
- 840g powdered sugar, sifted
- 7 tablespoons milk, of any kind

Instructions

In a large mixing bowl, combine butter, maple syrup, and vanilla. Sift the powdered sugar over the mixing bowl, stirring and adding tablespoons of milk as you go until you reach a thick, spreadable consistency. Pipe on cupcakes or spread on cakes. Enjoy!

Courtesy of @bunsinthekitchen

Gnocchi Tomato Soup

Total Time: 30 Minutes

Servings: 4–6

Ingredients

- 3 tbsp olive oil
- 1 sweet yellow onion, diced
- 1 can white beans or cannellini beans
- Sun-dried tomatoes, 175 mL, diced
- 1 tbsp tomato paste
- 3 cloves garlic, diced
- 1 quart vegetable broth
- 1 tsp salt
- ¼ tsp black pepper
- 120g parmesan cheese, grated (this is best grated at home, not pre-shredded)
- 1 package of gnocchi

Instructions

Add olive oil to a medium-sized pot over medium heat. Sauté onion in the pot until translucent, about 8 minutes. Keeping the pot over medium heat, add sundried tomatoes with a little oil from the jar, tomato paste, and garlic and stir for about 2 minutes. Garlic should be fragrant and tomato paste darkened in color.

Add in vegetable broth, salt and black pepper. Add in drained cannellini beans and heat for 5 minutes. Add the soup to a blender or, using an immersion blender, blend until the beans are no longer whole and visible.

Return the pot to the stove and bring to a slow boil.

Add gnocchi and follow directions on the package. This should only take a few minutes for the gnocchi to be done.

While the gnocchi is cooking, add shredded parm. Serve with crusty bread, or not!

Courtesy of @bunsinthekitchen

Spritz Cookies*

*You need a spritz cookie press for this recipe.

Total Time: 1 hour (50 minutes prep + 10 minutes baking)

Servings: 36 cookies

Ingredients

- 227g butter, softened
- 134g sugar
- 3 egg yolks
- 1 tsp vanilla
- 315g flour

Instructions

Preheat oven to 175°C.

Cream butter and sugar together until fluffy.

In a separate bowl, beat egg yolks in a bowl until lighter colored. Add vanilla to the egg yolks. Then, add this mixture to the creamed butter and sugar. Add flour a couple tablespoons at a time.

Put into cookie press and make your design.

Bake until light brown, about 8–10 minutes.

Courtesy of @bunsinthekitchen

Sticky Toffee Pudding Cake

Total Time: 1 hour 20 minutes (30 min prep + 50 min baking)

Servings: 12–16

Ingredients

- 440g brown sugar, divided
- 1 can coconut cream or coconut milk
- 227g salted butter or vegan butter, room temperature, divided
- 350g pitted dates, chopped
- 1 tsp baking soda
- 2 tsp vanilla extract
- 2 eggs, or flax eggs
- 250g flour
- Ice cream, for topping

Instructions

Preheat the oven to 175°C and grease bundt pan.

Make the sauce by combining 293g brown sugar, coconut cream or coconut milk, and 4 tbsp butter in a saucepan. Heat slowly and stir until combined, about 4 minutes. Pour about 177mL of the sauce into the bundt pan and reserve the rest of the sauce. Put bundt pan in the freezer.

Then, bring one pint water to a boil in a saucepan. Turn off heat, add chopped dates and baking soda. Set aside, let cool for at least 10 minutes.

Using an electric mixer, beat 4 tbsp butter, 147g brown sugar, vanilla, and eggs in a large bowl (mixture will be grainy). Add flour and the date mixture and beat until just combined.

Take the pan out of the freezer and pour batter into the pan. Bake for 45–50 minutes, or until knife comes out clean.

To serve, drizzle with saved sauce and top with ice cream, if desired.

Courtesy of @bunsinthekitchen

Cheese Crackers

Total Time: 1 hour 30 minutes (15 minutes prep + 1 hour chilling + 15 minutes baking)

Servings: 50 crackers

Ingredients

- 115g butter chilled and chopped
- 80g cheddar cheese, shredded
- 55g parmesan cheese, shredded
- 150g all-purpose flour
- 1 tsp black pepper
- 1 tbsp everything bagel seasoning, optional

Instructions

Preheat the oven to 180°C.

Line a large baking sheet with parchment paper. Combine all the ingredients together in a food processor until you get a ball of dough. Wrap in plastic wrap or place in a bowl and pop in the fridge for an hour to firm up.

Roll out to about as thin as you can get it on a floured surface. Using a cookie cutter, cut into circles or cut into squares. Place all the pieces on two baking sheets, pierce with a fork, and bake for 12–14 minutes, or until barely golden. Let cool completely on the baking sheet out of the oven.

Courtesy of @bunsinthekitchen